"Are you scared of me, Maggie?"

"Stop calling me that! My name has never been Maggie."

John gave her a little shake. "Are you?"

"Yes," Margaret whispered.

"Why?" No answer. "Is it because I make you feel things? I hope I do." He kissed the tips of her fingers, and she began to tremble. "Your father wants me to marry you." Margaret tried to pull away, but he held fast to her wrists. "No, no, stay here," he said as she continued to struggle. "I didn't want a wife."

"I don't want a husband," she retorted.

John grinned. "Yeah, I know, but maybe I can change your mind."

Dear Reader,

Our titles for September include a new novel from June Lund Shiplett, *Boston Renegade*. When spinster Hanna Winters inherits a ranch from her long-lost brother, her quiet world is suddenly turned upside down.

In *Bodie Bride,* by Isabel Whitfield, Margaret Warren is furious when her father brings home a live-in guest, especially one who's so good-natured about disrupting her well-ordered life.

Knight Dreams is a wonderful story from first-time author Suzanne Barclay. Lord Ruarke Sommerville was drunk when he rescued French noblewoman Gabrielle de Lauren and impulsively wed her. Now he must learn to live with the consequences.

Mary Daheim's *Gypsy Baron* is the author's third book for Harlequin Historicals. Set in England and Bohemia during the early years of the seventeenth century, it is the story of an English noblewoman and a mysterious half Gypsy who draws her into a web of political intrigue.

Look for all four novels from Harlequin Historicals each and every month at your favorite bookstore.

Sincerely,

Tracy Farrell
Senior Editor

Bodie Bride

Isabel Whitfield

Harlequin Books

TORONTO • NEW YORK • LONDON
AMSTERDAM • PARIS • SYDNEY • HAMBURG
STOCKHOLM • ATHENS • TOKYO • MILAN
MADRID • WARSAW • BUDAPEST • AUCKLAND

Harlequin Historicals first edition September 1992

ISBN 0-373-28740-2

BODIE BRIDE

Books by Isabel Whitfield

Harlequin Historicals

Silver Fury #105
Bodie Bride #140

ISABEL WHITFIELD

Isabel Whitfield lives in a small town surrounded by mountains, with her husband and young daughter, one neurotic dog, two finches and two fat cats. Her favorite jobs of many tried are writing and working in bookstores. She dreams of having a garden, fruit trees and more time to read.

To my husband, Bob,
a great risk taker who always has a good idea.
To Angela, for her copious notes;
and Tootie, for making Helen happy;
and my dad, for his support.
And to my mom, a unique woman—
thanks for listening.

Chapter One

Margaret Ann Warren flung open the back door, stomped down the steps and upended the bottle of whiskey. The liquor chugged out, deluging the hardy leaves of a baby sagebrush and making aromatic mud out of the warm, dry Bodie dirt. Arm straight and fully extended, long brown skirts twitched out of the way, Margaret grimly waited for the last drop to drip.

Leaning out of the doorway to watch their elder sister, Victoria and Elizabeth met each other's brown eyes. Margaret gave the bottle one last shake and turned to the stairs.

"Oh, Mag," sighed nineteen-year-old Elizabeth.

Margaret's dark chestnut brows arched. She lifted her skirts in one hand and marched back up the steps, her sisters parting before her.

"Father will be furious with you."

Margaret looked down into Elizabeth's eyes. Her youngest sister was as short and prettily plump as their mother had been.

"But he won't be drinking," said Margaret.

"At least not here," added Victoria, sitting down in a kitchen chair. "Now what?" she asked patiently, her usually placid face amused.

Margaret examined the bottle she held by the neck with her thumb and forefinger. Her greenish blue eyes slowly lifted to Victoria's face. "Elizabeth, go cut some rabbit-brush."

The stage braked to a stop in a cloud of dust. On the plank sidewalk outside the saloon that was his pride and joy, The Fortune, Jeremy Warren squinted over his raised coffee cup. Boots rugged, filthy, flimsy, new and worn stepped out of the carriage. Happy exclamations sputtered from the descending passengers. Eight men and a lady were the newest citizens of Bodie, adding to a population of more than five thousand at the end of July in 1879. The recent arrivals retrieved their luggage and clattered up the plank walk.

Jeremy was turning away when he saw a hatless head emerge from the stage, followed by two large shoulders, then a denim-clad knee. The sun struck dark hair, stiff with the dirt and grease from what was a forty-hour trip, if the man had boarded the stage in San Francisco. The man planted laced boots in the dirt of Main Street and slowly stretched, relaxing.

Jeremy stared while the sleepy-faced newcomer reached back into the stage and pulled out a worn cap, which he flipped onto his head. If Jeremy had been blessed with a son instead of three daughters, or even a son plus his three daughters, this was the kind of man he would have wanted him to be. No foppish tendencies here. His wife would have been kept busy running after this boy to make him tuck in his red flannel shirt or some such nonsense, leaving Jeremy a small measure of peace. He watched the young man reach up and lift a large pack out of the driver's hand as though it were no heavier than a little tumbleweed.

Dumping his cooled coffee in the road, Jeremy kept his eyes on the man's face, a face darkened with dust, the eyes narrowed from tiredness or suspicion or maybe just from the sun. The nose was straight and the lips curved as pretty as a woman's, but his stubbled cheeks, his cleft chin and his muscled neck were all male. He slung his pack over one shoulder and stepped down the walk toward Jeremy, his gait rolling, his tongue licking dry lips. He stopped in front of the saloon doors, smiling at Jeremy without showing his teeth. "Mornin'."

Jeremy pulled out a cigar and bit off the end. Such a man's voice would have toned down the female shrills in his own home. "I've got just what you need."

"A dust chaser of beer?"

"Plenty." Jeremy led the way into his saloon wishing a man like this would be interested in his eldest daughter. She wasn't a bad-looking woman, even if she wasn't the most friendly. But as far as he knew, no man had ever taken a second look at his Margaret. And he'd brought home plenty the last couple of months to try to light a spark under her, though he'd never invited one who was this manly, this virile. The others had been dignified merchants, a barber who spent more time looking at his married daughter and a tailor who stayed late telling stories in the parlor. He had purposefully picked small, polite men who would not intimidate Margaret, but neither did they interest her.

Jeremy sighed as he watched his new customer drain his beer. There had to be someone who wanted a bossy, meticulous woman. It wouldn't hurt to ask this stranger a few questions.

"Elizabeth!"

The young woman jerked her lips from Danny's as her sister walked into the front room. Margaret's eyes were glacial as she looked down at Elizabeth sitting on Danny's lap. The blond man lounged against the chair back, his eyes half-shuttered, his lips almost grinning.

"He *is* my husband, Mag."

"And this is a common room. Save *that* for your own house. Will you set the table?"

Elizabeth slowly slid from her husband's lap. "Is that a question or an order?" She smiled, dying to tease but wary of her sister's humorless face. "Of course I'll set it." She tugged Danny up after her and whistled her way to the kitchen, patting her messed, curling golden hair, husband at her heels.

Margaret sighed inaudibly and stayed in the front room to pluck at her fern. This horrid, dry climate was hard on her plants. Her father had squawked when she'd insisted on bringing them from San Francisco. She would have brought her entire, beautiful, two-story home if she'd been able to stuff it in a wagon. Father had sold it when he sold his butcher shop. Margaret snapped off a brown, shriveled frond. She'd been told by ladies she'd met at church services in the Odd Fellows Hall—this uncivilized place didn't have a proper church!—that the flower garden she was accustomed to in San Francisco would never thrive here.

Raucous laughter rolled from the kitchen and footsteps pounded in what sounded like a game of chase. Margaret looked up to see Elizabeth sashay out of the kitchen, her cheeks flushed, her eyes bright, her hands full of silverware and her husband right behind her. Danny voiced some low-toned remark that set Elizabeth to giggling, and Margaret shook her head.

She had hoped marriage would calm her sister, that the responsibilities of a home would mature her. But three weeks of marital life had made Elizabeth worse, more exuberant and irresponsible. Her house was in dreadful disorder, downright dirty, and since she and Danny ate most meals here, Margaret guessed her sister's cooking skills were as horrific as her housekeeping. Elizabeth had copied only the candy apple, fudge and peanut brittle recipes from Margaret's box when she moved to her own home. And now Elizabeth suspected she was pregnant. She'd told only her sisters and would not tell Danny until she was certain. Margaret felt both Danny and her sister were too immature to have a child so soon, but how could she prevent such a thing? She could not understand why she was the only one worried by the news, when their mother had suffered through six miscarriages, the last of which killed her. Margaret had been in attendance at every one.

That Elizabeth would suffer scared Margaret more than she let her sisters know. Elizabeth was delighted by her upcoming motherhood, though concerned about Danny's reaction, and Victoria actually seemed a little jealous. But neither of them had been included in the bedroom while their mother had labored. By her mother's third miscarriage, thirteen-year-old Margaret had sworn she would never put herself through such heartrending sadness. Holding her mother's hand five months ago while the woman bled to death had hardened twenty-four-year-old Margaret's resolve. Marriage and children were part of God's, and definitely the body's, plan, but not hers.

Margaret's hands were trembling as she plucked and picked at her fern. She closed her eyes for a moment and stilled the tumultuous thoughts in her mind. She promised to pray extra long tonight for Elizabeth's well-being. When she opened her eyes she looked around the house that she now had to call home. She made a mental inventory of everything she hated about it. The list kept her mind off her fears. The house was small, built of rough, creaky boards, impossible to keep the dust out of, and had no locks on any of the interior doors and no private bathing room. She probably should be grateful it was so cramped, since she and Victoria had to do all the cleaning. Domestic help was not readily available in Bodie. The woman she'd hired had quit after a few days, explaining that Margaret tired her out too much for her evening dancing partners, who paid much more generously. Margaret had been appalled, but noticed her father and brother-in-law seemed amused. She didn't doubt they had known all along that she'd been working alongside a strumpet.

Thinking of her father, she looked to the window of the front room. It was the only large window in the house, due, she was told, to the severe winters, when she would be glad for few drafty windows. Her father and a stranger were walking toward the house.

"Set another place," she instructed over her shoulder. Her father had become a very social man since her mother's death. Or maybe she'd just never known how friendly he was. In San Francisco he'd gone to the saloon after supper instead of bringing men home. Almost every evening since they'd been in Bodie there had been a new acquaintance at the dinner table or on the parlor sofa, some true and untried friend to puff cigars and imbibe spirits with— or so they tried. Her father had been angered and embarrassed the last time she had shown his guest, a barber, the front porch when he pulled out a stinking cigar.

She glanced at the man her father was bringing to eat at her table. His honey-colored hair shone under a cap perched far back on his head and he nodded at something her father was saying. The contrast between the two men was marked. Her fifty-nine-year-old father was very thin, spindly legged, wielded an ivory-handled cane but walked just slightly bent. His black-and-white streaked hair was combed back from his high forehead, his mustache and beard were neatly trimmed, and his eyes were a piercing greenish blue. The stranger beside him was taller, broad and big and straight. He walked with an easy, springing step that reminded Margaret of Elizabeth's lighthearted bounce.

The vibration of their feet on the front steps shook the idleness out of her. Remembering the biscuits, she turned back to the kitchen.

The front door squeaked open and Jeremy Warren tossed his hat toward the hat rack and missed. "Rescued another good man from the saloon floor, Lizzy-beth! He found out every hotel and lodging house in town is busting open with folks. Least I could do was offer him a meal and a bed for the night."

"Of course!" Elizabeth smiled, looking up from placing the silverware. Victoria came out of the kitchen at her father's voice.

"My good friend here is Mr. John Banning." Jeremy gestured to the man by his side and introduced his daughters and Danny. "Where's Margaret?"

"The kitchen," answered Danny, stealing a hot biscuit from the basket Victoria had brought out.

"Follow me and I'll show you to your first-class accommodations." Jeremy led John across the parlor, with its lace curtains at the windows, embroidered pillows in the chairs, new pink cabbage rose wallpaper and a leather-bound Bible on a small table. They went through Jeremy's sparsely furnished bedroom to the door of his office, as he referred to the small room with the desk, even though the desk drawers were empty except for the one in which he had put that bottle of imported whiskey.

"Damn! That girl must have filched it."

"Pardon?" John stood just inside the door, holding his pack.

Jeremy straightened and pulled out his handkerchief and dabbed his face. "Blast!" He glanced at John and then back at his empty drawer. "Wait until you meet my eldest. You might decide the spit-soaked sawdust floor at some saloon is preferable over this cot with clean linen." He pointed to the narrow canvas bed.

"I doubt that, Mr. Warren."

"Jeremy! The name's Jeremy. I'm only a few years older than you."

John kept the grin off his face. "Thank you, Jeremy. I appreciate the hospitality."

The old man waved John's gratitude away. "Drop your things. I smell dinner. One thing my eldest can do is cook."

John set his pack on the cot and followed Jeremy. They walked through the kitchen, almost making a circle back to the front room, but stopped in the dining room. He felt good. He ran his fingers through his clean hair and rubbed his smooth chin. Finding a place to wash and get shaved had felt like a major accomplishment. Now he had a hot meal coming and a bed for the night—for free. His decision to visit Bodie looked like a good one. The people he had met were friendly; the hills were devoid of trees and giant buildings, leaving room for his mind to roam; the pounding of the stamp mills were like the beating of God's heart, constant, loud; the sky was clear, the fog of San Francisco not a possibility here; and the sun was big, capable of burning the grief out of his heart and soul.

A woman he hadn't met yet was facing the table, her straight back to him. She adjusted a fork under a slender white hand, her chestnut hair coiled so tightly on her head it looked like carved, colored wax. Jeremy stood behind her, irritably tapping his cane against the wooden floor.

"Margaret Ann, where is my new bottle of whiskey?"

The narrow back turned and John saw the same stunning green blue eyes as the old man's, only hers were frosty. Her complexion was smooth and pale, unmarred by even a freckle. Her lips were pale pink, full, especially the bottom. Her form was slim, her arms slender, waist tiny, hips slightly flaring. He looked back to her face and was arrested again by her clear, hard eyes. She was coolness in a hot Bodie summer. She was a pillar of civilization in a town pitted with saloons and swarming with single men. Her gaze turned to the table and settled on the whiskey bottle centerpiece filled with the brilliant yellow-flowered weeds that he'd noticed through the stage window since dawn. John heard the old man choking beside him and turned to see his host's red face.

"Daughter, it's not like I can't get more. I own a saloon, you know!"

Margaret faced her father in the silent room. "As if I could forget." She inclined her head toward John. "I haven't met your guest." The stranger's eyes surprised her. With his honey hair she had expected them to be blue but found brown—polished, dark, piñon-nut brown. His skin was golden brown, similar to Danny's but without the gray around the eyes and mouth that her brother-in-law had from the mine, the drinking, the late nights and, probably, life with Elizabeth. His nose was straight and thin, his cheekbones high and wide and his mouth perfectly sculpted. For one indecorous moment she actually stared.

"John Banning. My eldest." Jeremy flapped his hand at John, then Margaret.

"I'm pleased to meet you," said Margaret.

John had never heard a voice so perfect in pronunciation, so cool yet so polite. How could she be pleased without smiling? He wanted to touch her and see if her skin was warm.

"Dinner is ready."

"Of course it is," snapped her father. "I will fall over dead the first time you're late."

Once they were seated at the table, Jeremy turned to John. "Planning on purchasing any stock?"

John held his fork poised for his first bite of medium rare steak. "I haven't thought much about it."

"I have stock in the Standard myself. That's the strongest mine. Danny probably has a little in them all." Danny gave a quick nod and Elizabeth put down her fork. Jeremy turned to his son-in-law. "Or do you have much stock in them all?" Danny grinned and avoided his wife's confused gaze.

John had three helpings of mashed potatoes and gravy. The second time Margaret passed him the biscuit basket she set it and the crock of honey by his plate. Her father picked at his boiled cabbage and ate half his steak. John inhaled his share.

"You have a prodigious appetite, Mr. Banning," said Margaret.

John popped his last bite of biscuit, wet with gravy and cabbage juice, into his mouth, chewed and met Miss Warren's sea-colored eyes.

Victoria, who had finished eating, rested her hands in her lap and studied her older sister's face. Elizabeth's foot slipped off Danny's and she looked from Margaret to John and back again. Jeremy winced. He had realized his oldest daughter was out to embarrass all his guests the night she'd asked Roger Meeks to take his cigar on the front steps—in a one hundred mile-per-hour wind.

"*Prodigious,* Miss Warren?"

Margaret blinked. Why had she said such a thing? She had lectured Elizabeth years ago on never commenting on a guest's manners at table. She'd been paying an unpardonable amount of attention to what this man ate and *how* he ate. Her face remained expressionless. "Yes, prodigious—large, very big. Healthy."

"Enormous," added Elizabeth with a giggle, earning a wrathful look from Margaret.

John slowly smiled, his beautiful lips parting, showing Margaret white teeth. Every nerve squirmed inside her body under the assault of his amusement, yet she sat like stone at the head of the table.

"Big word for a little lady."

Little lady, repeated Margaret to herself with distaste. "I just meant you seemed very hungry. I intended no offense."

"None taken," he assured her in his slow, easy voice.

Margaret nodded and lifted her water glass. Jeremy breathed a sigh of relief and scratched his thigh.

"Thank you for the meal, Miss Warren. I'll give the dishes a lavation for you."

All faces turned to him. Margaret's cheeks burned with embarrassment she was sure the stranger intended her to feel. "That's entirely unnecessary. We don't expect guests to wash dishes."

"It's the least I can do for such a good meal."

Margaret's fingers clenched her glass. "Mr. Banning, you're our guest. I won't hear any more about it." She stood up and pushed her chair in. "The pie and coffee will be out momentarily." She stacked the plates and her sisters helped her clear the table. Jeremy and Danny exchanged looks filled with repressed hilarity then turned in unison to look at John as Margaret left the room.

"You fluttered her nerves," congratulated Jeremy. "Not an easy thing to do."

"Is that a real word?" asked Danny.

"Yeah," answered John, surprised they didn't mind that he'd teased and embarrassed a woman in their family, even more surprised that they found her difficult to agitate. "My mother was a schoolteacher before she had my brother and me. She made our vocabulary one of her duties."

"You poor man," commiserated Danny.

John grinned.

"You'll have to join Danny and me for a brandy and a cigar after dinner." Margaret returned with a peach pie and her father flinched under her eyes. "In the saloon," he added loudly. Margaret set the pie on the table, while her father stared at her. Obviously she didn't like John Banning, and Banning couldn't possibly like her, but at least he'd made *her* uncomfortable for a change.

"I'd like to join you, but first I've got some dishes to wash." John had eyes only for the pie as he spoke. Margaret stiffened on her way out to get the coffee. For once, her father voiced her thoughts.

"You can't be serious!"

"Jeremy," Danny said, then paused to make sure that Margaret was out of the room. "Think how riled Margaret will be with a man, an unfamiliar man, in her kitchen."

Jeremy studied his son-in-law's face and a grin quirked his lips. "Meet us after your woman's work."

Dessert was eaten without conversation. Margaret worried over how to keep Mr. Banning out of her kitchen. Jeremy and Danny kept smiling. Victoria watched Danny and her father suspiciously. Elizabeth studied John Banning, who ate two pieces of pie, one of them Margaret's, which she had no appetite for. When the pie was gone and the coffee cold, Jeremy stood up and glanced at Margaret.

"Good dinner, daughter. Elizabeth, get your things. Danny and I will walk you home."

The water was heating for dish cleaning when John stepped behind Margaret, who was scraping fat and gristle from plates.

"Got a rag?"

Margaret flinched at the soft gravelly voice so near her. Her hands tightened around the knife she held and she sought Victoria's eyes across the room, where her sister was covering the butter.

Victoria, her face calm, looked at how close Mr. Banning stood to her sister, his eyes angled down her neck. Never had a man dared to intrude so on Margaret. She didn't think one had ever wanted to.

Margaret set down the plate she held, took three steps to the left and turned to face the man, her chin high, her eyes glittering.

John grinned and hooked his thumbs in his pockets. "I'll wash."

Margaret's nostrils flared. She was always the one to wash. On rare occasions she let her sisters, but Margaret was the quickest. Even her mother had been impressed.

"Mr. Banning, I appreciate your offer. However, I wash and Victoria—" Margaret looked at her sister, but the plump brunette was gone. "Victoria."

"That settles it." He snatched up a towel and wrapped it around the hot handle of the pot of water. He poured it into the basin, scraped some soap from the bar into the water and grabbed up a rag from the counter. "Ready?"

Margaret ground her teeth together. "Very well." Standing two feet away, she watched him roll his red flannel sleeves above his elbows and expose golden brown skin barely touched with blond hairs. She jerked her eyes away and pulled another towel from a drawer.

"How long have you lived in Bodie, Miss Warren?" John soaped a glass inside and out, wiped the bottom, dunked it in the rinse water and then peered inside it.

Waiting for that glass, Margaret replied, "Three months." He set the glass on the edge of the towel nearest him and she grabbed it up.

"Your father bought the saloon when you moved here?"

"Yes."

"You don't approve of the business?" He set another sparkling glass down.

Margaret's itchy fingers closed around the glass. "Not at all." She had the glass dried and on the shelf and still she had to wait for the next one. John's large, long-fingered hands revolved the glass around the rag, his skin glistening with soap and water. With a step to the left he set the third glass down, then rested his weight on his left foot, his hip swinging closer to Margaret. She automatically stepped away and had to stretch to reach the glass. John grinned at the soapy water.

"What about Bodie? You like the place?"

"I prefer San Francisco."

"Live there long?"

"My entire life."

"Me, too. Bodie's a nice change."

Silence reigned for a few minutes while the slow washing continued. Margaret's tense neck muscles burned from turning to reach for the next dish, always placed on the edge of the towel.

"Aren't you curious about me, Miss Warren?"

Margaret glanced up in surprise and met his dark brown eyes. "You're my father's guest. That is all I need to know."

"He bring many men home?"

She nodded, wishing he would stop looking at her and get to the pans. He set down the plate he held and Margaret hurriedly reached for it, but John did not let go. She pulled and he held, his eyes on her face, hers on his dark hand against the white plate. He gently bounced the plate in her hand. "I see one little spot of gravy on here," he said and looked up at the green blue iris of her eyes veiled through dark chestnut lashes.

Margaret let him tug the pristine plate out of her hand and released the breath she had been holding. Was the man deranged? Insisting on washing dishes, inventing spots where there were none? Should her father have left her with him in the house? And they still had all the pans to do. She would be drying until dawn and she had wanted to bake an apple pie for breakfast, mend her petticoat and respond to Aunt Matilda's letter.

"Mr. Banning, you've been an enormous help, but I don't want to impose on you further. I will do the rest," she said, trying to smile graciously.

"It's no imposition. I'm enjoying our pleasant conversation." John leisurely scrubbed a frying pan. When he turned to her, Margaret gave him a hard look, trying to stab the lighthearted amusement out of him, but she was the first to look away.

John laughed to himself and pondered why her father thought she was so hard to unnerve. Yes, she was controlled and stiff and unfriendly, but she practically vibrated with strong emotion. He wondered what she'd look like if it all spilled out of her. He'd like to see that.

Margaret hung up her towel when the last pan was dried and shelved and went to fetch bedding out of the trunk in her father's bedroom. Her head was pounding and she would have loved a cup of herbal tea, but this strange man would probably insist on sitting with her. She marched through the open door of her father's office with her arms full of sheets, a red-and-black quilt and a plump pillow. The man sat on the cot, shoes off, shirt off, and pushing his long underwear off his shoulders. Margaret dropped her gaze to his feet and noticed his toes wriggled. Turning her back to him, she walked to the desk.

"Your bedding, Mr. Banning." She set her armful down on the desk chair.

"Many thanks, Miss Warren."

She turned around, careful to keep her gaze above his head at the oil painting of the ocean. "Breakfast is at six."

"That sounds gr—"

Margaret walked out and shut his door. Halfway through the kitchen she stopped, placing her hand to her chest and taking two deep breaths. Her corset felt tighter than usual. She had rarely seen a man's naked chest, and never up close, not even her father's. Mr. Banning's golden skin flashed before her eyes. The man was impossible, a vulgarian. From the black-and-white hair that sprouted from her father's unbuttoned collars she had assumed all men were hirsute, but Mr. Banning's chest was almost hairless. Was that why this man had no mustache or beard, because he couldn't grow one? She thought his beardless face clean looking.

Margaret walked slowly to her bedroom, amazingly tired, trying to focus on the next day's meals, but she kept seeing an impudent grin, smooth skin and wriggling toes. She hoped he left directly after breakfast.

Chapter Two

"No need to hurry off, John," Jeremy said over griddle cakes, warm maple syrup, strong coffee and fried eggs. "You're welcome to stay another night."

A muscle went into nervous spasm in Margaret's spine.

John set his coffee cup down in the saucer. "That's kind of you."

"It's nothing. Love to have the company, don't we, girls?" His grin was large as he looked at his eldest.

Victoria agreed with her father while watching Margaret's polite, cool nod. Not until hours later, however, while the women prepared dinner, did Victoria broach the subject of John Banning. "Nice-looking man, isn't he?"

Margaret looked up from the hot potatoes she was dicing and glanced to where her sister sat at the kitchen table. "Who is?" Her eyes were still red from the onions she had chopped.

"Mr. Banning."

"I thought you were enamored of Mr. Henry."

"I am. And I will marry George when he asks, but that doesn't take the eyes out of my head."

"Are you so sure he will ask? Seems he would have proposed prior to your leaving San Francisco."

Victoria stabbed one of the tomatoes she was supposed to be slicing. "You're hardly an expert on courtship."

"Most definitely and most thankfully, I'm not."

Victoria rolled her eyes. "So, what do you think of Mr. Banning?"

Margaret dumped the potatoes into a big white bowl. "He is unmannerly."

Victoria smiled. "Even his face?"

Margaret mixed her mayonnaise into the potato salad. "I haven't given his face any thought."

"It was kind of him to help with the dishes. Most unusual, too," she said, her brow furrowing.

"I thought it was bothersome. Where did you disappear to at that time?"

"I had a letter to write."

"Really, Victoria, George is hardly going to miss you if you write him most everyday."

Since the same thought had crossed Victoria's mind she did not respond, but she resented her sister speaking aloud her fears. "Well, I think you could be more friendly with Daddy's guest. This Mr. Banning seems a very pleasant man, and it's a rare male who will step into the kitchen and take up a dish towel."

"Oh, for heaven sake, Victoria, he only wanted to embarrass me and make me uncomfortable for commenting on his appetite!"

"Not at all, Miss Warren," John said quietly.

Both women jumped. Victoria stared at the man standing casually in the doorway to the dining room, while Margaret flushed, absolutely mortified that he'd caught them talking about him. She was going to appear the unmannerly one around this man.

"Any luck finding employment?" Victoria asked.

He shook his head, his gaze leaving Margaret's eyes and trailing down her pink neck to her gray, high-necked dress. "There are two miners to every position. I'll try again tomorrow. Maybe someone will sleep late and I'll get lucky."

"Maybe our own brother-in-law," Victoria said. Margaret shot her a quelling glance and the younger woman shrugged. "I love him dearly, but I know he'd rather work in Daddy's saloon than down in a tunnel."

"Wouldn't most men?" asked John.

"Mining is a great deal more respectable than inebriating the male population," interjected Margaret.

"More dangerous, too," said John.

Margaret turned from the counter, her small paring knife clenched in her hand. "Then why did you come to Bodie?"

"For something dangerous," he said softly. His eyes locked with hers. Both appeared unaware that Victoria was holding her breath in amazement at this unexpected challenge from her sister toward a man she didn't know.

John broke the quiet tension in the room. "I'll wash up." He sauntered through the kitchen to his room and Victoria watched her sister's shoulders sag in relief.

At dinner John smothered his ham with so much mustard that Margaret almost gagged.

"You might want to fall back on your carpentry," Jeremy said, spearing a pickle and chewing on the end of it. "There's a great need for carpenters with all the people moving to town. Even the mines need them."

"I want to work at something else."

Margaret studied his hands as he cut his ham. The fingers were long with clean nails. A carpenter. She had thought him a vagabond prospector. She knew by the way the sun had seen his skin he'd not been a desk worker.

"I know how you feel," said Jeremy. "I was happy to put my butcherin' days behind me, but then, I'd been in the business for forty-five years—my father and grandfather before me. No sons of my own to take over. Though I could see Margaret attacking a bull with an ax."

Margaret immediately stood, shoulders far back, and collected the plates, sliding her father's unfinished dinner out from under him. Her fingers closed on John's plate, but he grabbed it back, staring at his ham and mound of potato salad. Margaret tugged. John wrenched the plate out of her hand and the ham slid off it and plopped onto the white tablecloth. A blob of mustard oozed into the fabric. John looked up at Margaret, bewilderment in his eyes. Margaret gritted her teeth and backed off.

"Due to wormy peaches the peach cobbler is inedible." Margaret took her stack of plates to the kitchen.

John stabbed his ham with his fork and set it back on his plate. "Wouldn't she have noticed the worms before she made the cobbler?"

Jeremy and Victoria gazed stoically at him.

"Son, how about joining me for a drink at the saloon?"

"After I do the dishes."

Jeremy stared at John as the man swirled a bite of ham in mustard. Why would this young, vital, self-assured and very handsome man want to wash dishes with a shrewish spinster? Jeremy had invited him to stay another night because he liked the man, but also because he wasn't intimidated by Margaret. He'd thought maybe John Banning could keep the woman in her place, but he sensed something else was happening. He glanced at Victoria and saw the smug, amused look in her eyes, her mouth lifting in the barest hint of a smile. Jeremy slowly turned back to John. Could it be...? No. Impossible. But Jeremy began to feel warm, an unusual occurrence for him at his age, when he was always cold and aching. "By all means, if you feel so inclined, enter the she-bear's den."

John finished chewing his last bit of ham. "I do."

"May I ask why?" Jeremy asked, very quietly.

"I think someone needs to check on that cobbler." He stood and carried his plate and glass into the kitchen, leaving an intrigued Jeremy and a widely smiling Victoria behind at the table.

"Here I am—ready to help," John announced as he entered the kitchen.

Margaret turned from the leftover ham she was wrapping. "Mr. Banning, thank you sincerely, but I don't need any help."

John set his dishes on the counter and smiled at her. "I know you don't need my help, but I either wash dishes or trot off to the saloon and soak myself with your father. I thought a sober evening would be best for getting up early and looking for work."

Margaret's eyes narrowed. "You may dry this time."

John picked up the towel. He kept up with her for the first five minutes, hop-stepping around the kitchen to put the dried dishes on the appropriate shelf. But suddenly the towel was filled with plates and silverware and here came a platter. He looked quickly at Margaret and could have sworn she smirked.

"I don't suppose you know where my sister is, Mr. Banning?"

"Somewhere avoiding this."

"It would be more efficient, Mr. Banning, if you took the dish nearest you."

John scowled and wiped a plate, while watching a bowl, teacups and a teapot come down on the towel. He reached for one of the teacups, a pink-and-white thing close to Margaret in the corner farthest from him. The cup had a delicate gold handle and looked silly hooked on the crook of his large, callused finger. His mother would appreciate the fineness of it. He smiled at the impracticality of ladies' things.

Margaret stretched her arm across his to place another teacup down in her undeterred rhythm. John's gaze flicked from the cup he held to the pale, slim wrist exposed below a few inches of rolled-up gray sleeve. So slender, the skin so white and probably soft. And warm?

A crash followed by a feminine gasp made John jerk his gaze to the broken teapot at their feet, his elbow still feeling the bump it had taken to push the pot to the floor.

"Mr. Banning!"

John met accusing sea eyes that flicked up at him from where Margaret crouched. He hurriedly extracted his finger from the little cup and set it down gently. He dropped to a knee in front of Margaret and picked up a piece of thin pottery. "God, I'm sorry." Silence. "Really, I am."

Margaret looked into his face. "Was this intentional, Mr. Banning?"

He blanched. "Hell, no!"

"The profanity is not necessary. And I'm well aware of my father and brother-in-law's interest in nettling me."

John's eyes narrowed on her upturned face, her serious eyes. "If I wanted to nettle you, Miss Warren, I wouldn't do it by breaking your crockery."

Margaret saw sincerity and affront in his brown eyes. She believed him, yet doubted the wisdom of doing so. What did she know of liars or men? She had avoided the latter for as long as she could remember. Knowing no other option, she nodded her head in acceptance of his innocence, not realizing how amusingly regal she looked.

"When do you drink tea?"

"In the afternoon."

"So does my mother, every afternoon. Tea, cakes and the best gingerbread I've ever tasted." He watched as Margaret picked up the last sizable piece of pottery. The rest would have to be swept up. "Where is your mother, Miss Warren?" he asked softly.

Her eyes, stormy dark now, rose to meet his. "She died five months ago."

"You must miss her. My father just died. A week ago."

Astonished, Margaret stared at him. His pain was a tangible thing in the few feet of space that separated them. "I'm very sorry." But she wasn't really; she was scared. She was scared of him, of his grief, his proximity and his handsome face. She stood suddenly, crunching a shard of teapot under her boot. She dumped the handful of pieces into the garbage, swept the rest up in her dustpan and returned to her cooling dishwater without sparing a glance toward the man she felt watching her.

"You're just going to dump all this cobbler?"

Margaret looked over her shoulder at John, looming above the pan of dessert.

"It won't go to waste. Danny doesn't mind worms."

John lay on his cot, hands behind his head and knees bent, thinking of Miss Margaret Warren. She was all soap and starch and polite manners. It amused him to irritate her, to see her actions frustrated by a refined sense of civility. He wondered again what would happen if the feelings ricocheting inside her escaped. She'd probably be a veritable tempest if she stopped pulling away plates and throwing out dessert and instead said what she thought and felt. The quickly disguised flare of hurt in her eyes when Jeremy had mentioned her wielding an ax had stirred him almost as much as seeing her bent over that shattered teapot. The desire to touch her soft, voluptuous lip had surged through him. She had a mouth much too full for a strident spinster. And her form was very appealing, straight and slender, full breasted. John took a deep breath and warned his thoughts from her person.

He felt the same compulsion to tease and annoy Margaret Warren as he had his mother. They were both bossy, fastidious women who found fault easily with someone like himself. His mother hadn't done more than irritate him until she'd shut the door in his friend Holly's face, scared to death he was going to marry the unwed mother. The third time she'd arranged, without his permission, for him to escort Bridget McGee, they had fought until they were not even speaking. And then Pa had fallen off that damn ladder, broken his neck and died.

John let the pain wash over him and in its wake he wondered how his brother and mother were. Two days after Pa's death, Pat had thrown himself into the family business, setting up appointments with architects, ordering wood at the mill, all with a fury that hurt John to see. His mother followed him around the house, waking him at night, perching on his bed in the morning until John felt suffocated. He was glad he was in Bodie, where no one expected anything of him.

He rolled over on the narrow cot. The curtain of sleep began to descend and he soon dreamed of Margaret Warren, only her hair was long and unbound and she wore something white and loose and she smiled at him quite unlike Margaret Warren.

John was whistling when he came into the house the next evening. He walked first to his room through Jeremy's empty bedroom and set a couple of packages on his cot, then washed his hands and face in the bowl on the small stand beneath an oval mirror. By the time he came to the kitchen Elizabeth was whistling her own improvised harmony. He greeted the ladies with much cheer and got it all returned except, of course, from Margaret. "I start to-morrow at the Standard," he announced. The younger women congratulated him, and even Margaret looked pleased. "I believe your father had a hand in my good fortune."

Elizabeth smiled. "He did name his saloon The Fortune."

"Would you like some lemonade?" asked Victoria.

"I'd love some."

Victoria left the pie dough she was mixing and went to the cellar. John walked to the table where she had stood. "Can't tell you how relieved I am. Thought I might have a very long wait." He picked up the forks and tossed the flour, added a little more water, then tossed some more. Elizabeth turned from checking on the baking chicken and watched him, the potholder held loosely in her hand. "My shift is not the best, but I didn't expect any better. I've got three in the morning to three in the afternoon."

Margaret saw Victoria come back with the lemonade and stop and stare. Slowly, she turned and saw John pat the dough into a ball, place it on the board, flatten it with his hand and then roll it out to a thin circle. "Strange hours, but I suppose it's so a man can have some time with his family." He gently lifted the dough with the rolling pin and laid it in the pie pan. "I stopped by your father's saloon and he invited me to stay on here for fifty cents a night instead of moving to the mine's lodging house. If it's all right with you ladies I'd like to do just that, seein' as how the food and company can't compare anywhere else." He looked up questioningly at Margaret, who was staring at him. They were all staring at him. Margaret looked shocked, Elizabeth highly amused and Victoria both. John glanced down at himself. He was decently clean. His pants were buttoned. He finished folding down the edges of the pastry and wiped his hand on a rag.

"Do you do top crusts, too?" asked Victoria.

John's gaze flicked down to the pie pan and then back up. He blushed. "My mother..." He shrugged. Margaret was smiling, even her eyes, and she was beautiful. "Would you actually laugh if I made the whole dinner?" His voice was soft, directed only at Margaret. Her smile faded, then bloomed again.

"Could you?"

He nodded. And she did laugh, her sisters joining her in soft waves of amusement. John turned to leave, but Elizabeth grabbed the bowl of sliced peaches off the table and thrust it into his hand. "Go on," she said.

John sighed. "You all love this, don't you?" Three heads nodded. He looked into the bowl. "You got your sugar and flavorings in here?" Nods and grins. He dumped the peaches in and then made a top crust with deft movements. When he was finished, Elizabeth popped the pie into the oven and Victoria handed him a glass of lemonade.

Dinner was a lighthearted affair. The women were tickled, Jeremy and Margaret left each other alone, Danny rambled on about working down in the mine, and John accepted Jeremy's repeated invitation to board with them. While the women cleared the table, Jeremy asked John to join him and Danny at the saloon, after the dishes.

Margaret accepted John's presence by her as she did the dishes. Although she did not slow down for him, she didn't try to overwhelm him with her speed, either. For the first time her body was not painfully tight when in the same room with him. For once he did not barrage her with questions and chatter. This time she was the one who desired answers. "Why did your mother teach you to cook, Mr. Banning, if I may ask?"

His lips curved in a small smile as he dried a glass. "Now, you can't tell anyone this." He left her side to put away the glass and came back to see her watching him, her hands still. He realized that Margaret Warren took everything seriously. She jerked back into action after following his gaze to her dishwater.

"I won't speak a word of it," she said quietly.

And he realized Margaret Warren could be trusted with all confidences to her death. "I have an older brother, Pat. My mother wanted a girl, but she had me. Pa said I looked like a girl when I was a baby, with blond curly hair and a pretty mouth. If it wasn't for Pa and Patrick I would probably be wearing a dress right now, but they made sure I got educated in everything male. So, now you see."

And Margaret did see, standing so close to him, meeting his dark brown eyes, her hands falling still again.

"I'm very much a man even though I can cook, clean, sew and write with the prettiest script," John said. Margaret's eyes were huge. He leaned over and kissed her.

His mouth was soft, his lips were closed, and Margaret was stunned. For one second she stood still, then she pushed her hands against the counter and stepped away from him.

"Mr. Banning!"

He did not apologize. He did not smile. He slowly straightened and his eyes were darker than before.

Margaret dried her hands on her apron and lifted her chin, her heart pounding furiously. "I am duly chastised for prying into your personal life, Mr. Banning. I will do it no more. I will forget this incident as I know it will not happen again." She returned to his side, picked up a serving bowl that held half an inch of light green water from the green beans and dunked it in her soapy water.

John's mouth hung open until he snapped it shut. Such composure. He had expected a slap, at least a royal raging; that is, he had anticipated something like that after the kiss, for the crime had been purely unmeditated. He stared at her as she calmly proceeded to wash. Did she really believe the kiss had been some kind of punishment? She turned to him, her eyes reminding him of San Francisco and the Bay.

"Mr. Banning, I soon will have no place to put a clean, wet dish."

He looked at the filled towel and slowly chugged into the process of drying. They worked silently. When all the dishes were washed she helped him dry and put away. Standing next to him, she stretched to place the refilled salt and pepper shakers on a high shelf above the sink basin. John dried the forks while looking at her raised arm and down to the mound of breast slightly flattened as she reached. He grew warm. He knew he was being stupid as he ducked his head under her arm and put the hand holding the dish cloth on the small of her back. He felt the shock jerk through her body right before his lips touched hers. She strained away and he held her with his other hand, still clutching several forks, low against her abdomen.

Margaret had barely pushed the shakers with the tips of her fingers so they were safely over the edge of the shelf when his tongue flicked across her lips. She twisted her face away, shocked nerves tingling down her spine to her toes.

"Get out!" She backed away from him. His behavior was unpardonable. She straightened her shoulders and snapped her feet together. Just when she almost had her reserve back he said the most outlandish thing.

"You're very pretty, Miss Warren."

He put down the cloth and the forks, smiled gently at her and walked out.

* * *

John saw Jeremy standing behind the bar, elbows on the counter, cigar in one hand and a drink in front of him, talking animatedly to Danny and a red-haired, red-faced man. John stood next to Danny, ordered a beer from one of the bartenders and listened to Jeremy, Danny and Red-hair discuss the practicality of having free lunches in the saloon.

"I'm getting good business as things are, and if we changed, I and my help would have to be more of a watch-dog to see if people were eating without buying drinks. Don't think I'd like that." Jeremy turned to John and winked. "Them dishes get washed?" John nodded. Jeremy turned so that he was facing away from Red-hair. "How do you find my Margaret?" he asked softly.

John tipped the beer glass to his mouth and swallowed while eyeing Jeremy. Soft lipped? Clean smelling? The talk, shouts, laughter and clink of glasses rose around him as he remembered the flush of color in Margaret's cheeks, the bolt of anger in her green-blue eyes and the vein of desire he had discovered within his own body. He knew that he absolutely should not have kissed her that second time, but he had wanted to crack that damn composure of hers. He had, and though it was mean of him, he had enjoyed see-ing her floundering, upset and unsure. He wondered which of those she would be feeling when she unwrapped the packages he'd left on her bed. Too late, he realized Jeremy was reading his face, interpreting his own answers.

"She's a fast dishwasher," John said lamely.

The red-haired man left them to find more stimulating conversation.

Jeremy straightened and tapped his fingers on the bar. "She's also unmarried. She needs a husband." John drained his beer and Jeremy refilled his glass. "I'll give twenty percent of this saloon's profits, which are very nice, to the man who marries her. Forty percent if he takes a hand in running it."

"Why don't you take an ad in the paper?" John asked.

"I would if I thought I could get a decent man that way. I do want a good husband for her. If she picked her own he would be a pompous ass, but she's not even looking, thinks she doesn't want to get married. She doesn't think about where that leaves me. Or maybe she thinks I want to have her bossing me around for the rest of my life."

"I'm not your man," said John. He took a large swallow of his second beer and looked around the saloon. He admired the cut glass chandelier Jeremy had put in, the shining mahogany bar and the display of sparkling glasses and bottles above the back bar. He liked the warmth and friendliness of the saloon, the voices engaged in conversation, the endless number of stories that one could hear in the course of a night and the flap of shuffling cards. He would be happy helping run this place. If he wasn't going to go back to carpentry then he needed another business. He didn't want to be a miner all his life. "I didn't come to Bodie to find a wife," he said. "I came to get away from family responsibilities." He'd worry later about what occupation would follow mining.

Jeremy nodded. "I'll drink to that." He took a swallow of his whiskey and pointed to Danny while wiping his mouth. "Danny here is the one running after responsibility. This boy followed us to Bodie to marry my Lizzy-beth."

"I don't blame him. She's a sweet girl."

"Speaking of her, I better leave. She isn't feeling well," Danny said, getting up.

"Oh?" Every time John had seen her, Elizabeth looked very well and very nice, with a devoted and still infatuated smile for her husband.

"Funny how the sugar and spice don't get mixed in equal portions in each child," ruminated Jeremy. "And that youngest of mine is probably in the family way, not ill."

Danny looked a little shocked, then shook his head. "She would have told me."

"Don't bet on it. And it happens more often that you'd expect. Much more."

A dim light shone under the door of the bedroom Margaret and Victoria shared. Margaret opened the door and saw her sister curled on her side, asleep, a novel marked with a letter from George still clutched in her hand. Margaret looked down at her sister in the candlelight. She could remember Victoria as a pudgy two-year-old, cookie in hand, as if it were yesterday. She touched her sister's dark brown hair and pushed a strand off her cheek before she picked up the candle. Though sometimes maddening and incomprehensible, her sisters were her anchor in this life. And life was full just being able to love them. As for her father and Danny, and maybe George, it was her duty to love them and guide them.

She sighed and then slowly walked to her dressing table. What to do about Mr. Banning? she thought, methodically removing her hairpins in the light of the candle. By the time all her hair was down, her scalp was tender, and her mind agitated. She rubbed the pads of her fingers over her lips, where she still felt the wet glide of his tongue. She took off her clothes away from the mirror as her mother had taught her and put on her nightgown. Why couldn't he just go away? Why had he kissed her? Why twice? She rubbed her lips again, with the back of her hand this time and until they burned. The first kiss she could label as a male reaction to being alone with a woman, but the second? Either he was filled with lust, or he wanted to make fun of her, unless she had done something to encourage him. She was too friendly by far, she was certain. That would be remedied. The man was odd. He had such big hands and yet he could make a flaky piecrust. Despite his friendly veneer, she sensed he was uncontrollable, unlike her father and Danny, who were easily influenced in spite of their snappish ways.

She sat at the dressing table to brush out her hair and saw her lips rosy red from her own hand. She lowered her eyes to her silver-backed brush. It had been ten years since she'd been kissed. That kiss, in the hall of her friend's house during a party, had been much like tonight's in its quickness and unexpectedness, but then she'd been so flattered and even delighted, until her mother found out from Elizabeth, whom Margaret had been foolish to tell. A late-night interview followed. *"Who was it? Did you give him a proper dressing-down? No? You're shameless! You probably enjoyed it! What must he think of you? Don't think the other boys don't know. You won't go to any more of that girl's parties!"* Margaret had protested and had been hit on the side of the head with the back of her mother's brush, just like the one she held now. She had attended few parties after that, and then only adult ones and by her mother's side.

Margaret picked up her brush and weighed it in her hand. The effort to brush her hair exhausted her. Or had she already been tired? Depression had clung to her ever since her mother's death. Each month the effort to maintain her temper and guide her family grew more draining. Moving to Bodie had not helped. The wildness of the town invaded everyone's personality but hers and made her feel utterly out of place.

She walked to her side of the bed and set the candle on her small table. Brown paper packages nestled among her pillows. She sat on the bed and carefully picked one up, feeling the heaviness. She unwrapped it to find a lovely, delicate teapot. Its pink flowers were similar to the broken ones, but of a richer color, the blossoms wilder and more profuse. There were four matching cups and saucers in the second package. The note stuck down in the pot read, "To the lady of the house, from the kitchen help."

He shouldn't have, but how thoughtful, how pretty. She couldn't accept it, but how could she return it without being rude? That he had picked out something she liked amazed her. And how could he have afforded it? Her fingers gently twined around the teapot handle as she pretended to pour. What manner of man was this? She appreciated the gesture, but the man was too troublesome, too threatening. She carefully wrapped the tea set back in its paper.

Chapter Three

Margaret finished setting the table for breakfast as her father walked in, his finger stuck in his collar in an effort to stretch the starched material.

"Father, I'd like a word with you."

Jeremy grimaced, took a seat and glanced briefly at the newspaper laid above his plate before resignedly raising his gaze to Margaret.

"You must tell Mr. Banning to find lodgings elsewhere."

"And why is that?"

"The man takes advantage."

"Of what? I *invited* him to room here!"

Margaret's neck stretched. "He has overstepped his bounds with me."

Jeremy sighed. "Daughter, washing dishes is hardly the thing I'm going to take offense at."

"I'm not speaking about dishes."

Jeremy rubbed the sides of his nose with thumb and forefinger and shook his head. "Daughter, what are you trying to tell me?" Jeremy could not remember if he'd ever seen Margaret look so uncomfortable. His eyes narrowed on her face. "Did he touch you?"

Margaret was relieved that her father was finally treating the matter seriously. She nodded.

"Did he kiss you?"

Pleased to hear the amazement in her father's voice, she nodded again. Now her father would have to ask John Banning to leave.

"When?"

"Last night."

Jeremy's eyes widened. "After we got home? He came to your room that late?" What was the boy thinking? That was hardly the way to charm Margaret into marriage.

"Certainly not!"

"Do you mean to say that Banning kissed you before he came to the saloon?" Margaret flushed. This was much better than Jeremy could have hoped for. "Well!" he managed to say.

"You see why he must leave."

Jeremy's expression reverted to casualness. "Oh, Margaret, don't get so perturbed. You're an...attractive woman," he said, his eyes running down her hair combed tightly off her head, her narrowed eyes, her frown and her dowdy brown dress. "It's not so surprising he would want to kiss you. You should be flattered."

Margaret's mouth opened.

"I suppose the first time is a little shocking, but—"

Margaret raised her hand. "I don't want to hear any more."

Jeremy nodded agreeably and picked up his newspaper, a small smile on his lips. "Oh," he said, halting Margaret's withdrawal to the kitchen, "I told Banning to help himself and fix a breakfast to eat in the mine, and that you'd wrap him up some food in the future." Jeremy had said no such thing, but he couldn't resist pushing Margaret into one more involvement with Banning. He had never felt so jubilant in the face of his daughter's silent fury. John Banning must be genuinely interested in Margaret, and though Jeremy couldn't understand why, he was eager to help the man.

Jeremy wondered, when he discovered his breakfast consisted of runny eggs and burned bacon, if he'd survive until he had Margaret married off. But the biscuits that Victoria made were light and golden.

Margaret's hands were filthy with soot from the lamps she was cleaning when John Banning came back from the mine. He entered his room through her father's and Margaret listened to the clink of the pitcher against the bowl and the pour of water. There was a splash and a sigh, another splash and a satisfied moan that made Margaret cringe. She looked up at Victoria, who was sweeping the floor. Her sister was smiling. "I didn't realize how thin the walls were," Victoria said.

"No one else is so noisy," Margaret responded.

John stepped out of his room, saw the two women and smiled. "Afternoon."

Margaret nodded and Victoria stashed her broom in a corner while asking about his first day.

"It's going to be different. I've never worked underground before. And I haven't been so dirty since I was a child, but I washed up some at the mine. They have us change there and leave our work clothes so we don't take out any high-grade ore in our pockets."

"They have to expect that because of the wages they pay," said Victoria. "Can I make you something to eat?"

"Don't trouble yourself. If there's any coffee left I'll take that."

Victoria poured him a cup. "Well, I've got to get those groceries, Mag. I've put the chore off and off, and I know you need those things this evening."

Margaret stiffened, her sooty hands clenching a lamp. "I was planning on getting them myself, Victoria, on my way to the—" Victoria stepped out the back door and slammed it behind her. The latch did not fasten and the door swung back open. Margaret stared at it askance, unable to right it until she cleaned her hands.

"How are you this afternoon, Miss Warren?"

Margaret's eyes flicked to John Banning, who was leaning back comfortably in his chair. "Fine, thank you." She returned her attention to cleaning the lamps, since it was not a job she ever stopped in the middle of.

John pushed his coffee cup in front of him, leaned his forearms on the table and watched Margaret rinse the glass lanterns in a bucket in the basin. He marveled at the small waist under her brown dress and white apron and wondered how a woman could get a dress to fit so tight. His mother had used his pa's help.

Margaret's shoulders lifted with bunched muscles. She resented his quiet presence in her own home. Why didn't he get up and shut the door? She glanced behind her and saw he was not looking at her but at the wedge of sunshine that had found the wood floor of the kitchen through the open door. "Nice day," he said softly, his eyes moving up to hers, astonishing her with their piercing, alert light. She said nothing and quickly turned back to her work. "Still mad at me, I see," he said.

"I am not *mad*, Mr. Banning," she said crisply. "I am forewarned and therefore wary." She set the last of the now clean, dried lamps down on her wood counter and went to the door, which was hanging open and crooked. *The screw must be loose again*, Margaret fumed. If John had not been

standing there she might have given the door a swift kick.
This was the second time the darned thing had loosened.
Last time she had tightened the screw with a knife and that
had been a week ago. She grabbed the doorknob, lifted the
door and set it correctly in its frame—until it was opened
again. She left the room to return seconds later with the two
rewrapped packages of the tea set. She placed them on the
table. "This was a very thoughtful gesture, Mr. Banning.
Nevertheless, I cannot accept such a generous gift."

John leaned back and propped his heel on the rung of his
chair. "And I won't accept it back," he said, meeting her
eyes.

Margaret's fingers tensed into fists and then released. She
picked the packages up and walked directly to his room,
where she deposited the items on his cot, which, to her surprise, was made. She turned to leave but he filled the doorway. His eyes were narrowed, his beautiful lips tight. She
drew herself up. "Mr. Banning, I intend no offense, but
we scarcely know one another, and I cannot possibly accept—"

"You're not obliged to let me kiss you because I've given
you something."

Margaret flinched and her face flamed. "Of course I'm
not!" He took a step forward and Margaret stepped back
until the tops of her calves were against the cot.

"That's what you're scared of, isn't it? That I'll kiss you
again."

Margaret clasped her hands together in front of her.
"Mr. Banning, the teapot was lovely. I just don't feel it is
proper to accept it."

"I'm glad you liked it. And," he continued, moving
forward, "I'll even take it back if you—" he stepped directly in front of her "—let me—" his gaze lowered to her
lips "—kiss—"

Margaret turned abruptly, her shoulder bumping his raised hand. She pushed past him and only turned to look at him when she stood in the doorway to the kitchen. "I don't make bargains with demons, Mr. Banning."

He chuckled and watched her shoulders go back. "What are you? A saint in hell?"

"You have the location correct." She turned away.

"Wait. I brought you some candy." Margaret turned and stared at the green stick in his hand. "It's not poisoned." He pulled one out of his pocket and bit off the end. "Haven't you seen stick candy before?"

"Well, yes, I've just never had..." She felt foolish accepting even such a small thing. "I, well..."

"Take it."

Margaret did.

"You're supposed to suck them, but I can't stand how drawn out that gets."

Margaret sniffed hers. Apple. She licked it and looked up self-consciously. He winked at her. She lowered her eyes, put the end of the stick in her mouth and gently sucked, feeling very childish to be eating such a thing, but the snappy flavor made saliva pool in her mouth and she sucked harder.

The back door squeaked and shuddered open. "Margaret, I got a pound of cherries for a great price. It wasn't on your list, but I couldn't resist. Mag?"

Margaret briskly stepped into the kitchen, shoving the candy into her apron pocket. "That's fine, Victoria."

Victoria pretended not to notice that Margaret had stepped out of John Banning's room and that the man followed her sister into the kitchen. She clasped a letter in one hand while she pulled vegetables out of the basket with the other. "Can you finish? I have to... to go read this." She fluttered the letter in the air, which she had managed to take out of the envelope somewhere between setting the cabbage on the table and pulling out the greens. Margaret nodded and watched her sister almost run to their room.

Margaret cast a quick look to where John stood in the middle of the kitchen, arms crossed on his chest, watching her. She looked away and went to the back door, which was again hanging open. She lifted and pulled and set the door right. When she turned from the door John was right behind her. "Excuse me," he said politely. He opened the door, went through it, left it open and sat down on the back steps in the warm summer sun. Margaret's brows almost crossed over her eyes, but she preferred to have the door open rather than engage in words.

Margaret channeled her energy into her knife and made short work of chopping the beef Victoria had brought home into stew meat. She threw the chunks into a pot and seared them brown. After she finished throwing together her stew she made John a breakfast of bread, cheese and fruit and put it in a tin for him to take to the mine. He was whittling a small chunk of wood, a worthless activity in Margaret's estimation, but at least it kept his hands from worse things. And he was whistling an annoyingly happy tune. He turned his head at the sound of her footsteps. Margaret stood in the open door and held up the tin.

"Your breakfast."

His brows rose markedly. "That was very nice of you. Thank you," he said sincerely.

Margaret lowered the tin. Why was he so surprised? Hadn't her father told him she...? Her hands tightened on the tin. Obviously not. "I'll set it on the table," she said stiffly. She straightened the kitchen and then interrupted Victoria's letter writing with instructions for the rest of dinner, since Margaret wouldn't be at home to oversee the meal.

* * *

Darkness had fallen by the time Margaret walked home from the Millers' sick household, after being thanked repeatedly by Mrs. Miller for cooking enough food to last a couple of days, going to the market and scrubbing the kitchen. All four of Mrs. Miller's children had the chicken pox, and her husband was useless. He'd spent the evening in one of Bodie's saloons "to stay out of the way," or so he said. Margaret pitied Mrs. Miller, whom she'd met at Sunday worship services. Stepping into her house and her life had reaffirmed Margaret's desire for spinsterhood. What could be the purpose of risking life to bear children with a man who took no interest in them? Her own father had rarely been at home. When he wasn't in his butcher shop he was in the saloon. If he was home he was buried in the newspaper. He never did a thing around the house. Margaret and her mother had done everything, even arranging for repairs. In the months since her mother's death he had been acting even more childishly.

Her mother had claimed God rewarded the good after death. Cleanliness, morality and piousness were their own reward. Each night you looked over the day's achievements—the clean, orderly house, the mended clothes, obedient servants and sober husband—and took satisfaction in them. Margaret had always tried to emulate her mother and even more so after her death, for her family needed the guidance, but she felt she was lacking in something, for her family was disintegrating around her.

Margaret paused in the moonlit road and pressed a hand to her aching lower back and shut her eyes in deference to her pounding head. When she was this tired memories of her mother always occupied her, as if fatigue unlocked a door in the top of her head and Melissa Warren stepped down and called out, *"Do you have clean sheets on the bed? Stand up straight, dear. Don't let your father do that! Keep Victoria away from the dessert—she's getting fat. Move along. Mirrors are for detecting errors, not admiration. I see Elizabeth is as irresponsible as ever. Do talk to her, Margaret.''*

Margaret thought of her youngest sister, who seemed to enjoy the physical side of married life, was pregnant already and exerted no control over Danny. The man was weak and pleasure seeking and Elizabeth was leading him to his own ruin by not being strong with him. If Margaret was married to the man she'd pull him out of the saloon by his ear and be by his side when he was paid to prevent him buying any more stocks. Margaret didn't understand what her sister saw in Danny. A handsome face wasn't enough. No, a husband should command respect and... She pictured John Banning, then shook her head. He wouldn't go away. Yes, she admitted, he seemed a strong man, but he'd do everything his own way. And the same confidence that made him seem capable also made him arrogant and intolerable. But Elizabeth would have been much better off with John Banning. What a shame that Danny had followed them to Bodie.

Margaret climbed the steps to her house. Hearing voices raised in merriment, she hesitated with her hand on the doorknob. At this hour? At her house? She pushed the door open and saw them sitting around the dining table playing cards. Her sisters, her father, Danny and, of course, Mr. Banning. All the men had their backs to Margaret. Elizabeth shrieked as she threw her cards down and scooped a small pile of coins to her. The women were drinking out of the teacups Mr. Banning had given Margaret and the men were drinking whiskey. Margaret felt she had been gone weeks instead of hours.

Elizabeth looked up and smiled brightly. "Margaret! I won!" Her father glanced behind him quickly and Danny turned and nodded at her. Mr. Banning turned very slowly, rested his arm across the back of his chair and ran his eyes from her greasy face, down her food-and vomit-splattered dress to her dusty shoes. His eyes flicked back to her face. Margaret's stomach tightened in ten conflicting directions as he held her eyes. His were warm and something else, maybe amused.

"We're learning how to play poker," Elizabeth explained.

"I see that."

"Don't frown so. Gambling is really very fun and it's not like we're playing with strangers in a public place," her sister explained.

Margaret just stared, too exhausted to deal with this transgression. Never had she felt so outnumbered.

"Mag, you look weary. Would you like a cup of tea?" offered Victoria.

Margaret was about to assent when Elizabeth spoke.

"Yes, in one of these new cups Mr. Banning got you! They are lovely."

Mr. Banning winked at her. Margaret stiffened. "No, thank you. You'll see the lamps are turned out when you finish?" She turned and went into her room.

"Whew," Danny exclaimed. "I expected a little more venom."

"Oh, Mag's not so bad," said Elizabeth. "She just wants us all to be good." She crossed her legs and leaned her elbows on the table. "Whose deal?"

"It's late. I think we should stop now," suggested Victoria.

Elizabeth protested, but Jeremy heartily agreed and rose from his chair.

Inside her room, Margaret stripped off her filthy dress and stuffed it into a hamper. She poured some water into her pitcher and washed her face, neck and arms. The cool water felt so refreshing that she unfastened her corset and dipped her hand inside her camisole to sponge off her chest. She unpinned her hair and sat on the bed to massage her scalp. Her stomach relaxed and the pain in her head lessened as she slouched over, her elbows on her knees. She heard chairs scraping against the floor, the clatter of dishes being cleared and the back door opening and banging shut. Feeling safe in her room, she sighed. At one time she'd felt safe in her whole house, but since that stranger had come things had changed. In the morning she'd be stronger and would deal with his influence. The whiskey, the cards, the money all flashed through her head and she felt a vitalizing spurt of anger. She stood up, her lips compressed, and took off her camisole. She pulled on her long white nightgown and then shed the garments beneath her waist. Footsteps separated from the rest of the commotion in the dining room and kitchen and came through the parlor. They came slowly, too heavy to be her father's. Every muscle that had relaxed and loosened in Margaret's body immediately tightened. The footsteps stopped outside her door and Margaret knew who it was.

She clenched her hands at her sides as she stared at the door. The knock came softly. Margaret shook her head in amazement at his scandalous behavior. He knocked again and called her name. He really did not care what her family thought of him, and he actually expected her to open her bedroom door to him.

"I have something for you," he said through the wood of the door.

Margaret took a fortifying breath and stepped to the door. "Go away."

Long pause. "Not yet."

"I'm not decent, Mr. Banning," she ground out.

He chuckled. "I don't mind. Hurry up, your father's coming."

Furious with his persuasion technique, Margaret snatched her gray flannel dressing gown off its hook, tugged it on and wrenched open her door. Without meeting John's eyes she looked to her right and did indeed see her father making his slow way through the dining room toward them, his eyes fixed on her and Mr. Banning.

"Mr. Banning needs assistance to his own room, Father."

Jeremy looked from Margaret's angry face to John's amused one.

"I just wanted to give your daughter my winnings," John said, holding up his hand and making the coins clink together in his palm.

"Whatever for?" snapped Margaret.

John grasped her hand, turned it palm up and poured the coins into it. "For my meals. Good meals, too."

Jeremy came up beside John. "Thank the man, daughter."

Margaret pulled her hand back and rolled her eyes. To be receiving instructions in manners from her father! She looked from one to the other and calmly spoke. "I know you two are enjoying yourselves, but I think you're deplorable." She stepped back and shut the door in their faces.

Jeremy studied the closed door for a second and then turned to John, who was doing the same. "Are you sure this is the way to go about it?"

"Go about what?"

"Why are you purposely irritating her?"

John shrugged. "Can't help myself. She's there and I'm here." He moved away through the parlor and to his own room, thinking about the way Margaret Warren looked with her hair down.

Jeremy looked back at Margaret's door but there was no sound. He sighed. Maybe the man knew what he was doing, but he was afraid not. His daughter wasn't a mountain to be climbed but a difficult woman who needed an excessive amount of charm and patience. He shuddered. What did he know? Melissa, her mother, had liked money and security and nice words. Elizabeth had fallen for good looks. Victoria was swayed by a good and generous nature. As far as he could tell, Margaret was impressed by nothing. Maybe she did have to be hit over the head and dragged to the altar.

Margaret was in the kitchen the next morning running coffee beans through the mill when Victoria came in and stood beside her. Margaret immediately noticed her sister's suppressed high emotion. She stopped running the mill. "What is it?"

"George asked me to marry him in his last letter. I'm leaving for San Francisco this morning. I've already packed."

Margaret walked to the nearest chair and sat down. She hadn't expected this so soon. She glanced up at her sister. Victoria would not be dissuaded; her eyes sparked with challenge. She was beautiful in her excitement, with flushed cheeks and glittering eyes as she waited for Margaret's response.

"George Henry is a good man," Margaret said slowly. "He deserves you. I hope you'll be very happy."

She must have said the right thing, for though her heart had a hole in the bottom of it and she already felt lonely,

Victoria beamed and pulled a chair close to her sister and sat down. She grasped Margaret's hand. "Thank you, Mag! I know this is so sudden. And you must think it awful that he's not coming for me, but really this is so much better, since he won't have to leave the store to come get me and instead will be able to spare the time for a short honeymoon. And he's bought us a house already! All he had to do was miss me. See how fast he's moved!"

Margaret nodded, her smile bleak.

"Don't look so sad! You can visit us after George and I have a little time alone."

Margaret's mouth turned down at how happy Victoria sounded about her "time alone." Why was she so different? The thought of being alone with a man almost made her want to tear out her hair in horror.

Margaret cleared her throat. "When does your stage leave?"

Victoria glanced at the clock on the wall. "In forty-five minutes."

"Oh, Victoria! I'll never have time to get you a gift! The stores aren't even open yet. You could have given me more warning. Does Father even know?"

"I'll tell him now. And I don't need a gift, just see me to the stage. And, Mag, promise me something? Say you'll give John Banning a chance? He's a good man and a match for you."

Margaret's face drained of color. "You know how I feel about marriage. I don't have a romantic inclination in my body. If that's what you and Elizabeth want, then fine. I'd rather be an aunt than a mother, and I think both you and Elizabeth will need a maiden aunt."

Victoria frowned. "We won't do half as poorly as wives and mothers as you're so certain of, but of course, you'll always be welcome at my house. *My* house! Doesn't it sound grand? I have to go tell Father now."

Margaret perked the coffee and whipped up biscuits for her father and Victoria. She packed several sandwiches and some fruit into a basket for her sister's thirty-six-hour trip, then ran into her room while her sister sat on the edge of her father's bed telling him all her plans. Margaret did have time to give, if not to buy. She went straight to her jewelry box of intricately carved rosewood. The box and all its contents had been her mother's. There had been no question among the family that Margaret should receive her mother's belongings. She opened the lid and stared down at amethysts, sapphires, diamonds, pearls and gold. Margaret pulled out the small pearl studs and shut the box with a snap. All she'd ever worn were the pearl earrings and the citrines she had on now, whereas her sisters had admired the collection since their infant eyes were dazzled by the sparks of color around their mother's neck and dangling from her ears. She pushed the lid back up and pulled out the amethyst necklace and earrings, Elizabeth's favorite. She wrapped the box in a dishcloth and stuffed it into the basket with the food, having to take out most of the fruit to accomplish a snug fit.

"Write," she ordered Victoria at the stage stop.

"Be happy," Jeremy said against her ear during a tight hug.

"Kiss George for me," Elizabeth said with a giggle.

Victoria, smiling broadly, climbed into the stage. Margaret stared after the dusty black coach long after it pulled away until she could no longer see the cloud of dust it traveled in. At home she straightened the mess left in her bedroom by the hurried packing, did the breakfast dishes, chased cobwebs around the house, dusted every surface and mopped the floors. The housework completed, her throat dry, Margaret put the kettle on and sat down. In this first moment of inactivity Victoria's departure hit like a rock thrown into a well, fast, deep, and irretrievable. Margaret poured boiling water over the black tea leaves in her teapot and worried about Victoria's stage ride and her married life. Would George be kind and considerate, or forceful and demanding? Would she get pregnant right away as Elizabeth had?

She was pouring her second cup of strong tea when John came back from the mine. He sat down at the kitchen table with her and watched her pour in cream and ladle in sugar. "You like it sweet. I wouldn't have guessed that. My mother takes it with so much lemon I've accused her of permanently souring her disposition."

Margaret didn't look at him, just raised her eyebrows.

"Something wrong? Something more than the usual?"

"Victoria left this morning to marry a grocer in San Francisco."

"You don't look happy about it."

She looked up. "He should have come for her and married her here."

"Why? So you could scare him off?" Their eyes held.

"So I could have seen her married. So her father could have given her away. So she wouldn't have to ride that dirty stage all by herself. What if it gets held up?"

"I'm sure you mentioned all these worrisome thoughts to Victoria."

"Not a one," she said softly.

"Well, well. Congratulations."

Margaret lifted her chin. He was smiling as if very pleased with her. "Whatever for?"

"For holding your tongue. I bet you'll get a letter pretty damn quick."

She sat up straight and felt like kicking him under the table. She'd never felt like kicking anyone under the table before. "Mr. Ban—"

"I brought you another piece of candy." He pulled a red stick out of his pocket.

Margaret's eyes followed the candy. "Why?"

"Because I wanted to. This one's cherry. I like it better than the apple. See what you think." He handed the candy to her.

Margaret slowly took it. "Just to tell you which is better." She stuck the end in her mouth, concentrating on the flavor bursting inside her cheeks, and missed John's wide grin.

She sucked hard and her cheeks went concave. John's grin slipped and faded while lower parts of him began to warm.

She pulled the stick from her mouth. "I don't know. They're both very good. What other flavors do they have?"

She looked at him openly, very interested, completely unaware of the envy he felt for that stick she held tightly and licked savoringly. He shook his head. "I can't believe you haven't had these before. Every kid gets them." He immediately regretted his words when she flushed, looked ashamed, and all the childlike delight in her face disappeared.

She shoved the candy into her pocket and cleared the table of the tea things. Embarrassed to be so interested in candy at her age, she busied herself with starting dinner.

"I didn't mean to offend you. Just seems strange you've never had stick candy." John watched her stiff back, missing the relaxed woman of a moment ago.

"Mr. Banning, I'm sure you'd find many things about me strange," she said over her shoulder.

"I look forward to discovering them all."

Margaret shook her head over the greens she was rinsing of dirt. "Mr. Banning, my tongue's no match for the cleverness of yours."

He came to stand beside her. She ignored him, but he could feel the coils of tenseness vibrating off her. "Why do I make you so nervous?"

"Why do you try?" She met his eyes for the briefest second. His gaze was warm and searching.

He broke into a huge grin and whacked her on the bottom with the palm of his hand. "Because you're the most challenging diversion Bodie's got!"

Margaret straightened like a maypole, her vegetable greens falling out of her hands.

John whistled on his way out the door, tugging his hat low over his eyes while he trotted down the steps. His hand tingled warm where he had touched her. He grinned again, damn sure she was boiling with rage. He'd spoken the truth—she was the best entertainment he'd found in this town. She was so easy to get a reaction out of, to tease, and yet it was so challenging to get her to reveal herself. He'd never have guessed that candy would have broken down so many defenses. He suspected her childhood hadn't been much to boast of and thought he could show her a hell of a good time to make up for it.

There wasn't much else he wanted to do in Bodie. A saloon was a saloon and he'd been in countless since he was sixteen. The town was full of whores, but John had only paid for a woman once and thought the one-sided pleasure a far cry from mutual lust. The problem with Bodie was that most of the women were married or whores. There were but few single working girls or widows looking for companionship. Just Margaret, lonely and unhappy, though she didn't know it. John kicked the dirt in front of him and sent up a spray of dust in the September afternoon. His body's natural urges were gathering, asserting their importance. He decided a long fast walk before dinner was needed.

Chapter Four

Danny and Elizabeth joined them for dinner that night and John noticed Margaret seemed relieved. She hadn't spared him a word since he'd returned to the house, and the one glance he got was cold.

A new strike had been discovered in Bodie and Danny told them all about it.

"Sounds small," John interjected.

"Nothing's small in Bodie."

"Well, I wouldn't buy any stocks in it yet."

Danny shrugged and Margaret skewered her gaze on him. "But you did, didn't you?"

Danny's hand fisted around his fork. "Bodie has produced more ore this year than all the rest of California combined. This place is inexhaustible," he pronounced.

"Nothing is inexhaustible but God's power," Margaret responded, leaning toward her brother-in-law.

"Any day that vein could disappear," John said quietly.

"Every vein in every mine sure as hell won't!"

John shrugged. "The only vein I've seen is the Standard's."

"So, you've bought a few stocks in it?" asked Jeremy.

John shook his head. "I want to own more than a few pieces of paper when I put my money down on something."

"Well, you can all do a little investing my way," Elizabeth blurted out. "Because I'm going to produce a baby."

Jeremy shouted and smacked Danny on the back, who stared at his wife with an open mouth. Danny went with Jeremy to the saloon after dinner and had to be carried home by several friends. He didn't make it to work in the mine the next day.

The beginning of September was decorated by the continued blooming profusion of the rabbitbrush. The bright yellow flowers shooting out of the shrubs were clipped by Margaret and set in vases in her parlor, the strong scent permeating the house. The other strong presence permeating the house was John Banning. It had been a few days since he'd so rudely touched her and Margaret hoped she'd lost her entertainment value. His noise as he slammed doors, laughed loud and shouted occasionally bothered her as much as his touch. She'd never admit it to anyone, but even his smile disturbed her, as full of admiration and warmth as it seemed to be. She had to restrain herself from looking behind her to see who he was smiling at. She'd done that once, which had given him so much amusement that she'd left the room.

He surprised the frown right off her face one afternoon when he set a bag of tools and hardware down on her kitchen floor, took the back door off the frame and proceeded to rehang it. She followed him about the house as he oiled all the doors and then back to the kitchen, where he lifted a chair upside down and sawed off a small piece of an uneven leg.

"Thank you very much," Margaret said as he put his tools away. "Did my father mention these repairs to you?" she asked hesitantly.

"Why? Was he supposed to?"

"Oh no, but I've told him several times about the door. I never felt you were under any obligation to make repairs around this house."

"Jeremy never said a word."

Margaret nodded. She wasn't used to someone doing something without being nagged. "Is there anything you'd like in return?"

He stared at her steadily for a moment. "You already cook for me." He stood up with his tools and nodded at her before leaving the room.

Margaret sat in the chair he'd just leveled and tried to get a grip on the fact that he didn't want anything in return from her. He must feel indebted for the free meals since her father was only charging him for sleeping in the small room. The thought that he felt obligated didn't take away the pleasure of his help.

She put a large basket over her arm and walked to the market to select fruit for a coffee cake to tempt Elizabeth, who looked peaked, and to thank John for his repairs. Margaret slowed her step up Main Street. Ahead of her a crowd of men swarmed around the front of a saloon. From the midst of the shouting men rose an erratic swirl of dust. A fight. Margaret stopped long enough to notice the excited faces of the watching men as they cheered and encouraged and wagered. Disgusted, she caught her dress up in one hand and crossed the street, running to avoid being trampled by a mule team loaded with wood.

In the fruit market Margaret saw her friend from church services, Mrs. Hoyt. "Scandalous!" hissed the older woman, nodding her head toward a young woman dressed all in black with a brightly painted face who was flirting with the proprietor while paying for apricots and cherries. The slim, mustachioed man was thoroughly enjoying himself until he noticed the two pairs of eyes glaring at him over pursed lips. He straightened and gave the woman her change without further banter. Margaret averted her eyes and Mrs. Hoyt twitched her skirts out of the way as the woman left the store.

Their fruit purchased, the two women stood outside the store on the planking. Mrs. Hoyt brushed at the dust coating her sleeve. "One of the more distressing things about this town is how close we have to come to the disreputables. Will you be bringing your sisters to services tomorrow? I haven't seen them in a while."

"One returned to San Francisco. The other is not inclined to come. My influence weakens the longer we stay here."

"Go home, brew some tea, take a rest and start over. You can't give up, dear. They depend on us. I hear you have a young man residing with you. A relation?"

"More like a boarder."

"Well, bring him tomorrow. Reverend Hinkle's sermon will only do him good and you don't want to miss influencing anyone under your roof."

Margaret nodded, said goodbye and turned toward home, her basket of apricots and peaches feeling heavy on her arm. Would she get John Banning to church services? Could she influence the man? She stopped in the dirt before crossing the road and smiled to herself. If anyone was being influential under her roof it was Mr. Banning. Since he'd come there'd been poker, kisses and candy in her house. She'd need to have Reverend Hinkle hold services right in her parlor to exorcise Mr. Banning's influence.

Hurriedly she crossed the street before a jangling, loaded freight wagon.

By the time Margaret returned home she had seen three dirty boys heckle and throw rocks at a Chinese man, heard every oath known to man as she passed open saloon doors every few yards, and acquired a fine coating of dust on her skin and clothes. She sorely missed her pleasant neighborhood in San Francisco, which she'd never had to leave to do her marketing.

She made two coffee cakes filled with apricots and swirled with brown sugar and cinnamon. She put a piece big enough for three into John's breakfast tin and took one cake over to her sister. One look at Elizabeth's house and Margaret moaned. "How can you live in this?"

Elizabeth shrugged, took her cake and poured a glass of milk. "I don't feel well, Mag." Margaret raised her eyebrows at her sister, who still sat in her dressing gown at five o'clock in the afternoon. Margaret spent an hour dusting and straightening her sister's cottage. "Mag, you shouldn't," said Elizabeth.

"I won't be able to sleep knowing you have dust balls everywhere."

"Are you being nice to Mr. Banning?"

"He's living in my house. I think that is pretty nice."

Elizabeth looked away. "You're being your usual standoffish self," she sighed. "Father can't take care of you forever, you know."

Margaret stood as straight as the broom she held. She opened her mouth and closed it. The impertinent chit. She put the broom away and left.

John left the saloon before Jeremy and walked home in the dark. There was something about being in a dark hole all day that made him seek the warmth and sociability of

The Fortune and put off sleep. John regretted staying as long as he had, but there had been a poker game, and then the debate about stocks on the Noonday Mine. He still hadn't bought any stocks yet and doubted he would. He liked to spend his money on tangibles, like tea sets, he thought, grinning. In San Francisco he spent money on restaurants, where he took his lady friends, or gifts for his family. He needed very little to be happy, so he had a large savings in the bank, but he had no compunction about spending when he did want something. He was probably one of the few in Bodie who hadn't indulged in a fantasy of fortune, but riches were not the reason he'd come to town. He needed time to breathe, time to get a grip on his pain every time he picked up carpentry tools. He'd done the work around the Warren house as quickly as possible, no enjoyment in the feel of the tools in his hand, just a sense of repayment for Margaret Warren's meals and her endurance of him. He'd wanted to repair her back steps, but when he'd picked up a hammer in the hardware store he'd broken out in a sweat and had dropped it back into the barrel.

The house was dark and he went in the back door. He shook his head. Another of Miss Warren's displays of disapproval. She thought the men should sit around their own hearth until they went off to bed. He felt his way through the kitchen, stumbled over his own foot and cursed the fifth whiskey he'd drunk. In his room he shucked off his clothes, crawled under his blanket and fell instantly asleep.

He dreamed he was in the mine, picking and shoveling. Alongside him worked his father. They were arguing. His pa asked for the hammer and John threw the hammer wide, but his pa reached for it and fell off the platform, down into the shaft, tumbling over and over and over. John woke yelling, sitting up on his cot.

A glow of light illuminated his room. He'd left the door open. "Mr. Banning, are you all right?" He couldn't answer—he was still seeing his pa, but he heard bare feet pad close. He looked up at the candle Margaret held, the bright light burning out the images in his mind, but not the feelings.

"Nightmare?"

"Yeah." His voice cracked. He was shaking and damp with sweat.

"I'll make you some tea."

"Don't." He dropped his head to his hands. She didn't go away. John was roiling with guilt, pain and rage.

"Do you want to talk about it?" she asked, concern heavy in her voice.

He raised his head and glared at her. "No! It's nothing someone who does everything right could even understand!"

Margaret stepped back. "What do you mean by that?" She prided herself on being a good listener. He threw off his covers and stood up in his long underwear and poured himself a glass of water. She caught a whiff of him. "You've been drinking."

"So? Go back to your own room. I don't want your condescending sympathy or your righteous manner."

"Well, I beg your pardon," Margaret snapped sarcastically. "I was awakened by a scream and I came to see if you were all right, not to be insulted! You can find another place to live if you're going to indulge in drunken rages!"

"Oh, so the mighty composure cracks! The lady's not so pleasant anymore. What, do I have to get nasty for you to drop the control?"

"I don't know what you're talking about."

He kicked his chair across the room and Margaret jumped. "Ouch, damn it! I'll leave in the morning! You won't have to put yourself out any longer." He held his foot and hopped to the bed, the rage draining out of him as the pain continued to shoot up from his toes.

"Good!" Margaret turned in the doorway, taking the light of her candle with her.

"Margaret," John called. "Margaret," he yelled loudly when she didn't respond.

She popped her head back in the doorway. "Stop shouting," she demanded through gritted teeth. "You'll wake my father!"

"Well, come closer so I don't have to yell."

She took two steps forward so she stood just inside the doorway. John's eyes dropped to the mounds of her breasts under her thick white cotton gown and he started wanting things for the pain inside his heart. But she wouldn't be coming any closer. He stood and walked to her, favoring his right foot.

"I'm sorry for yelling at you. It was just a really bad dream and it set me on edge."

Her chin lifted. "So, you're changing your mind about leaving?"

He felt his stomach sink. She really wanted him to go. "Yes," he said softly, that old demon rebellion rising in him. He circled her neck with his hand and yanked her mouth to his. She squealed beneath his lips and he softened his touch on her mouth but held her neck in a vise. "Kiss me," he whispered, his arms aching to crush her. He rubbed his lips against hers. She'd hate him if he touched her breast, but it was poking him in the chest and he wanted to enclose it in his hand and squeeze. Heat and longing raged through him. He'd been too long without this, and too long near this woman whom he desired. He released her neck, and holding her shoulders, he pulled her close to keep her breasts torturing him. He trailed kisses down her cheek. "Tell me you want me to stay," he begged.

She shook her head.

He couldn't let it end like this. He had to make her stop being mad. He lowered his head to kiss her neck, dropping his left hand to enclose a warm breast, but at the moment his left arm dipped it was singed by the candle she still held. He yelped and jumped away and Margaret flew from the room.

She slammed her bedroom door behind her and shoved the back of a chair up under the knob. Her candle had blown out in her flight. She stood in darkness and listened to the blood rush through her ears. She never should have gone to him at night in her nightgown. She was foolish to let her guard down. He did want something from her. But why her? She knew there were women in town who'd gladly give him what he wanted for much less than the price of a tea set. She sat on her bed and breathed deeply to calm herself, but she couldn't rid herself of the feel of his mouth so briefly against her neck, or his fingers beginning to squeeze her breast, or the sound of his voice as it went soft and pleading.

On the other side of the house, in the room next to John's, Jeremy took a long draw on his cigar as he lay in bed listening. So, there were some strong feelings on Banning's part, he thought. He smiled, imagining living alone. He never had. He'd moved from his parents' home to one with his wife. He rose and pulled his dressing gown over his white nightshirt, then knocked lightly at the door that joined his room with John's. The door swung open soundlessly and Jeremy stared up at the dim, shadowy figure of the younger man.

"Marry her, boy," Jeremy urged softly. "Her room will be yours. And half the saloon, too. Notice, I've increased the percentage."

"I don't want your saloon, not like that."

"But for some reason, one which I'm supremely grateful for, you want the girl. Let me be done with her! You'll make her a good husband, but if you refuse I'll find another, a man who'll take her for the saloon."

John tightened his hand on the door. Damn the old man for forcing this! Did he sense that John couldn't watch another man marry Margaret, couldn't bear to imagine another man having the right to touch her and please her? Would Jeremy really be so heartless as to marry his daughter to someone who only wanted the saloon? What kind of hell would she endure with a man who didn't want her? Maybe someone else would make her cry, would hit her or hurt her or neglect her.

John squeezed his eyes shut. He would love to have that saloon. He wouldn't have to turn back to carpentry, never have to work with his brother again and be tortured remembering how it had been when Pa was with them. Margaret would hate him being half owner of The Fortune. But if not him, someone else, and he didn't want that. It was him he could imagine her with, talking, laughing, loving. Yeah, much loving. He was about to step off a cliff, was aware of the danger and just couldn't stop.

"All right," he said slowly, "I'll marry her, but not for the saloon. I'll just marry her." Then he suddenly felt a great flow of relief and he chuckled. "But good luck getting her to agree!"

Jeremy snorted. "Don't be stupid, son. You can't support her the way she's accustomed to on a miner's wage! What if she has a baby every year? What if the mine closes down next year? No, the saloon and her go together. I'm letting you in for nothing down but the marriage vows! You can sell out later if you want, make yourself a bundle to invest in something else, but I'm not going to leave my daughter poor. I know what kind of girl I have. She'll be the one to provide if anyone in this family ever needs a thing. How is she going to do that on four dollars a day?''

John shook his head. ''She'll hate you for this, and me, too.''

Jeremy flapped his hand. ''You can make her understand. If you're not up for it I'll find some weak-kneed man she can order around and kick out of bed.''

John felt hot anger flush his face. He didn't like being manipulated this way, but he couldn't stand one more image of Margaret sharing a bed with someone else, or her father speaking of her so insensitively. ''I'll take your damned bargain then. And damned I'm scared it is.'' He shut the door in Jeremy's face before he shook the old man.

Margaret stared at her father's nose while he snipped straggling hairs from his mustache. Then she flicked her eyes to his white-shirted shoulder as he snipped a hair from his nose. If she wanted to talk to him alone, this was what she had to do, watch him groom himself. He'd already run out on her in the morning when she'd tried speaking with him in the house devoid of John Banning. Now that man had just left for the saloon and her father was soon to follow.

''Well?'' she demanded, having waited as long as she could for his response to her plea for Mr. Banning to leave. She had asked nicely this time, hoping a show of meekness would get her further.

Her father carefully combed his hair, keeping the center part perfectly straight. ''Daughter,'' he finally said, ''the man likes you.'' He put down his comb and turned to his flustered daughter. "Don't you think it's time you thought of a husband and children?"

Margaret clenched her fingers in her skirts. "I don't want either."

Jeremy pulled his tie into an elegant knot and reached for his coat. "That's very selfish of you. Who do you expect to support you for the rest of your life?"

Margaret's head reared back as if she'd been slapped. "You need me, Father," she said very softly. "You need me to cook and clean, to take care of you."

Jeremy almost smiled, but he didn't, opening his bedroom door instead. When he was composed he turned to her. "You make wonderful meals, but I can satisfy myself at a chop stand or diner. All I need is a bed, a comfortable chair, a cigar and some men to share my time with. I've done my time with women. I've married, I've fathered, now I'm ready to grandfather." He looked at her pointedly and then turned and walked into the parlor.

"You know I don't want to marry," she said slowly. "You know how that scares me," she said even more softly.

Her father sighed and faced her. "What choice do you have? You can't live with me forever. Now this John Banning would be good—"

"I can't marry him! He's not even offering. Besides, he's...he's..." Her heart was pounding too fast. She felt breathless. "You don't care what he does to me! What kind of father are you!"

Jeremy frowned. "Margaret, he's a good, decent man. I would choose no less. He will make a fine husband. And you *will* marry him."

Margaret inhaled. "What do you mean you 'would choose no less'? *Did* you choose him? Did you hire him off the street, or at a bar table, to come home with you and marry the daughter you want to be rid of?"

Jeremy was silent a second too long. "Of course not."

Enraged and humiliated, Margaret wailed. "How much did you offer him?"

"Margaret, you are being ridiculous. He's just a nice—"

"Will I see him as a partner in your precious saloon as soon as the wedding vows are said?"

"Well, that would be standard. He'd be my son-in-law. I'd like to keep the business in the family."

"Don't lie to me! You didn't bring Danny into the saloon! That's this one's prize, isn't it? Well, I won't marry him! I wouldn't even if I was desperate for a husband. He's a cruel, wretched man. And you're cruel for trying to sell me like this to a—a base, common laborer. He'd probably take to beating me if I married him. He can't even support himself but lives off us, paying only a pittance. How do you expect him to support me? Oh, I forgot—the saloon! You know I hate that place, and yet you'd make me a barkeep's wife!"

Jeremy hadn't seen his eldest daughter out of control since she had discovered her mother's final pregnancy. Very few times in Margaret's life had her composure cracked, and though her tantrums were a mite frightening, they were the only times Jeremy felt much empathy for her. So he stood and listened to her rant, saw the fear beneath the hysteria.

"What kind of man would live off us? Do you know anything about his family or where he came from? No! A carpenter! He could build brothels, for all you know. I won't marry him, let alone even speak to him. I hate him! I hate his looks and his manners. He's coarse and lewd, and he frightens me. He's pushy and bossy and I don't like him!"

"Margaret—" his voice was very gentle "—you have no one else."

"I don't need a husband," she screeched. "I have you, and Elizabeth, and her child, and Victoria will have children, and I'll be—"

"None of us truly needs you."

There was a second of silence and then her voice rushed on louder than before. "Yes, you do! I'll take care of you all."

"Margaret, we don't want you to take care of us. We want you to have your own life."

This final, very calmly stated rejection was too much. She couldn't even scream or rage anymore. Her father wanted to be rid of her. He didn't care that she didn't like the man.

"I'll kill myself first."

Jeremy sighed. "For God's sake, Margaret!"

"I mean it. I will borrow Danny's gun and I will shoot myself in the head. And I'll do it in the kitchen."

"Margaret, calm yourself."

"You don't know what he tried to do last night!"

"I'm sure it had to be something a man would do to his wife. And I suspect you really are ready to marry him now, or you wouldn't be this upset."

"Oh, my Lord."

Jeremy grabbed her arm. "Enough." He looked her in the eyes until she began to slow her breathing. "Now, he wants to marry you and you will do so by Elizabeth's birthday, November fifteenth, or—" She shook her head furiously and Jeremy paused a moment. "Or I sell this house. And, if you don't remember, you have no funds of your own, so you will be on your own without a home." Margaret's eyes rounded at the cold, callous threat. Her father released her arm. "I'll have some coffee, then I'll be off and I won't be back for supper."

She followed him into the kitchen but stopped frozen in the doorway, her eyes widening in horror at seeing John sitting at the kitchen table facing her, a mug in his hand. Her father cleared his throat. "Think I'll do without that coffee." He escaped out of the house while Margaret continued to watch John watch her. He did not look his usual placating, amused self.

"I thought you'd left," she said in an agonized whisper.

"I decided to wait for your father." He dropped his angry gaze from her face and pushed his coffee cup away. Standing, he picked his hat off the back of his chair and shoved it down on his head. Margaret tensed as he strode out the back door, waiting for the slam, but he shut the door with a soft click. She wasn't fooled; she knew he was going to make her regret uttering every last one of the defiling names she'd called him. She was scared, yet she felt helpless. What did a woman do when her own father was pushing her out of her home and into the arms of a man she didn't understand, didn't want and was frightened of? Limp as a rag doll, Margaret sank into a chair and laid her arms and head on the kitchen table.

Chapter Five

Two weeks passed and Margaret began to feel safe. The day she'd lost her temper and humiliated herself in front of John Banning she'd gone to Elizabeth's, where she'd made dinner for her sister and Danny. She'd had Danny walk her home on his way to the saloon. Both men in her house had been gone. The arrangement had been so comfortable that Margaret had repeated it everyday. She thought that if her father didn't need her, as he'd insisted, then she wouldn't bother with his meals, but she learned from Danny that her father, to prove he did not need her, never ate at the house anyway. Nervously, she avoided dwelling on the ultimatum he'd given her, hoping he'd change his mind. She did not mention his threat to a soul. She stayed in her room in the morning, working on Elizabeth's baby quilt until her father left for the saloon. She was at Elizabeth's house by the time Mr. Banning came back from the mine.

Tonight, according to Danny, both the men she avoided were at The Fortune. Margaret had taken advantage of the opportunity and filled her tin tub with hot water. Outside an icy sprinkle of rain fell through the gusts of a biting wind. The steaming heat on this cold September night felt blissful, sinful, but even she deserved it. She soaked and sighed until she heard knocking on the front door. She ignored the noise. The knocking turned to pounding. Whoever it was would eventually leave and look for Jeremy at the saloon. No friend of hers would pound so rudely.

"Margaret, I know you're in there!"

She sat up straight in the tub. Banning. Her arms crossed over her breasts. She had locked the front and back door and he did not have a key. She sank back into the tub. The banging stopped and she began to relax. The pounding began on the curtained kitchen window and Margaret jumped, sloshing water onto the floor.

"Margaret, it's cold out here." Short silence. "Come on," he coaxed gently.

Margaret gritted her teeth. He was ruining her bath.

"I'm getting mad. Do I have to break the damn window and climb through?"

"Don't you dare," she shouted.

There was a long silence. Margaret started washing. While she soaped and rinsed her hair she thought of things to rid her of her torment, which came in the form of a honey-haired man. A blizzard. A saloon fire. A mine explosion. An open window followed by pneumonia.

"I had a better idea," drawled a voice behind her.

Margaret screamed, hands flying to her breasts, and looked over her shoulder. John Banning stood in the doorway, unsmiling. He waved the house key he held. "The old man gave me his key. Said he best make me a copy."

Betrayal surged through Margaret. She felt everything she had being pulled out from under her. "Get out."

He walked to the tub and crouched at the side, facing her. He glanced down at her crossed arms and drawn-up knees. "I do have the advantage now, don't I?"

Margaret looked straight ahead. Her eyes flicked to her towel, which lay across a chair pulled near the tub, within arm's reach. But an arm would have to move from her chest to grab it. If she didn't risk it, how long would he have her sit here?

"I bet you want that towel."

"Not as much as I want you to leave."

"Well, I'm hungry, but I don't expect you to wait on me since you're busy bathing and naked and probably getting cold with all that wet hair." She shivered. He stood up and grabbed her towel, holding it out for her, just far enough away that she would have to stand to reach it.

"Don't be cruel."

"You've already labeled me that. And lewd, and common."

So here it was, she thought, the revenge for every word. Where would it end?

"Come on." She shook her head. "Then sit." He dropped the towel where he stood and moved to the counter, whistling while he made himself a sandwich. When he was slicing the meat, Margaret rose out of the water, carefully stepped over the side of the tub and lunged for the towel. She wrapped the towel, which only came to mid-thigh, around her and turned toward him. He was watching her, leaning against the counter, the knife grasped in a hand on his hip.

"Nice."

Hot anger and embarrassment coursed through her. She turned her back to him, marched to the kitchen door and jerked it open, one hand holding her towel in place.

The front door flew open, banging against the wall, and Jeremy and another man stomped in, removing their hats, their voices loud and exuberant. Margaret stepped back out of sight and flattened herself against the wall, her anguished eyes meeting John's surprised ones.

"Margaret?" called her father. He started toward the kitchen.

John, chewing on a piece of meat, strode past Margaret. He winked at her pale face.

"Oh, John! Margaret gone to bed?" asked Jeremy.

"Yeah."

"Wanted her to see Tom Rogers. We knew him in San Francisco. Oh, well. Any coffee?"

"I was just about to make some. I'll bring it out to you."

"Thank you! Step over here first and meet Tom. He used to be a produce man. Now. . ."

Margaret looked at her nightgown and robe on the table, her mound of clothes over a chair. Her mouth was dry, her body freezing. As if winged, her feet moved to her clothes. She couldn't possibly stroll past her father and Mr. Rogers if she was supposed to be asleep. This was a nightmare. She could at least wait for the men to leave with some clothes on. She pressed her hips against the table to hold the towel partially up and raised the gown above her head.

Large warm hands settled on her bare shoulders, squeezed and slid up her arms, pulling the gown out of her hands. He tossed it back onto the table. "Stay like this," he whispered against her ear.

She wrenched the towel up tight and turned. "I will not!" she whispered furiously, wishing she could scream the words.

"Don't be difficult," he said in a normal voice.

"You say something?" yelled Jeremy from the front room.

Margaret stepped away from her garments. She didn't want her father to see her unclad, as well.

"Just talkin' to myself," John called back. He gave Margaret her dress. "You can stand on this," he whispered. She glared into his smile, took the dress and threw it on the cold floor against the wall, where she stood on it while John made the coffee. She refused to meet his gaze while he ate his sandwich and watched her.

He walked toward her, wiping his fingers on a dishcloth. Every muscle in her cold body convulsed with fearful anticipation. She shook her head furiously, but he did not stop until the toes of his boots touched her bare feet. She tried to press herself into the wall.

"What an opportunity," John murmured. He threw aside the dish towel and his gaze slowly traveled down her body. Gooseflesh dotted her chest and the curves of her breasts. He wanted to tug the towel away and show her how gentle he could be. He stepped back. What was wrong with him? How could he let this woman get to him so? She hated him and he desired her. She was repulsed by him and he wanted to marry her. Any other woman and he would have shrugged and walked away. Why did he want to punish Margaret for feelings she had a right to have? The answer was obvious, and admitting it drained away his anger. He liked this troublesome woman and wanted her to like him. He wanted her to desire him. He wanted her to kiss him. He stepped close again and his breath brushed across her face, but every time his lips came to hers she twisted away. He kissed her cheek, her nose, her closed eyes, her neck, while her breath grew more shallow.

"I won't hurt you," he whispered against her ear. He nuzzled her neck again and her skin was cool. His tongue touched her pulse. He had to thread his fingers through her damp hair and hold her head to take her mouth. His kisses were light; he didn't want to scare her any more. He slid his tongue along the compressed joining of her lips and she bucked her head back, banging the wall. John pulled away and looked down at her. Her eyes opened, staring at his neck. Every fiber of her body was straining away from him. He should let her go, but she was something to behold in that towel. He spread his fingers out over her collarbone, then drew them lightly down to the exposed swell of her breasts. She began to tremble. She was going to hate him. She already did. Over and over he brushed her chest with the tips of his fingers, watching the gooseflesh converge across her flinching skin.

Margaret turned her face to the wall, squeezed her eyes shut and mashed her lips between her teeth. Silently, she recited the Lord's Prayer to distract herself from the effect of his touch, which brought her blood to the surface of her skin in a way she'd never felt before. His voice interrupted her recitation. "You're so sensitive," he whispered, and his lips were against her neck again. She started the prayer over but lost her place as her nerves shivered under the wet trail left by his tongue. His hand slid down her towel-covered ribs and clasped her hip. "You're beautiful, Miss Margaret Warren." He mouth touched hers. Every kiss and caress he made were the gentlest. His tongue barely tasted, dotting her with a light dew. Her head came away from the wall.

"Please..." she begged.

John pulled his head up. He'd never thought to hear that tone in her voice. She wouldn't meet his eyes and he didn't really expect her to. She was shivering in his arms, her face was pale. He didn't want to let her go until she clung to him.

"I'm sorry," she whispered.

He couldn't think straight. "For what?"

She met his eyes, hers confused. "I shouldn't have said all those mean things about you. I was just so mad."

With fingers softly rubbing back and forth over her collarbone, he pressed his forehead to hers. "Why? Because I kissed you that night? Because I touched your...your breast?'' he whispered, looking down at the creamy mound now.

"Yes.'' Her defenses were scattered by standing so close to him, nearly naked, her hair down. She felt crazily intimate with him, and she confided in a whispered voice, "I hated my father pushing me away and onto you. It was humiliating. I lost my mind for a minute and I am sorry. Please stop punishing me like this.''

John swallowed and pressed his forehead harder against hers. He moved his hands from her collar to her shoulders and gripped them hard. "You gotta understand one thing, Margaret. I'm not doing this to punish you. Yeah, I barged into the kitchen while you were bathing to embarrass you, but I didn't come over here and start begging kisses to get back at you. I just want you that way something fierce. Don't you feel something, anything?'' He lifted his head from hers and looked down into her huge, uncertain eyes.

"John, how's that coffee coming?''

John jumped, his face jerking to the door. "It's coming right out!'' he yelled too loudly. He looked back at Margaret, at her nakedness, her face suddenly flushed and her eyes agitated, skittering from his gaze. He briefly squeezed her waist through the towel, then stepped away and handed her the nightgown and robe. "You can wait in my room until they clear out of the parlor.''

When he returned to the kitchen Margaret was in her dress and shoes and was pinning up her hair. He stared as she threw a shawl over her damp hair and folded her gown and robe. She stuffed them behind a sack of sugar in the pantry. Ignoring him completely, she grabbed an old cloak off a hook by the back door and walked outside, quietly closing the door behind her. He stood in the middle of the kitchen holding the coffeepot and staring at the cold, cloudy bathwater. A minute passed and he heard her come

in the front door. In response to her father's question, she
told him she'd been at Elizabeth's. She sat and chatted for
a few minutes and then politely excused herself and went to
her bedroom.

John shook his head. She was a hard cracker. The only
other woman he'd met who was so willful and stubborn was
his own mother. He dumped the tub water out the back
door and sat up late thinking about Miss Margaret Warren, but not as late as the woman herself sat up.

Hands knotted in her lap, Margaret fumed and furied at
John Banning, her father and even herself. At herself for
the feelings that had arisen as that strange man had kissed
her neck, his body so close she'd felt his heat warm her. She
was sick and scared of herself. She couldn't seem to control him, but she absolutely had to control herself. Shaking, she pulled out one of her etiquette books from her
dressing table and reread the section on greeting persons of
the opposite sex. The passage was dull enough to calm her
nerves. Then she remembered how tender he'd been, how
he claimed to want her ''that way.''

She didn't understand why he was attracted to her, but
she had to admit she'd felt flattered even while she didn't
believe him, certain it was the saloon he wanted, not her.
Her face heated just remembering his last question, which
she'd not answered. She didn't know how to deal with a
man who was interested in her for any reason, but she knew
she couldn't hide from him at Elizabeth's any longer. That
had been foolish and had left her weak and vulnerable to an
attack by him. She'd face him in the morning; she'd make
breakfast and every other meal and never let him see how
scared she was.

A black night two weeks later, John walked Danny
home, wondering how a man with such a pretty wife could

get so drunk so often. He grabbed Danny's arm as the man weaved toward the wooden pole support of the Bodie Pharmacy. Danny laughed as he bumped into John's shoulder. Down the road Danny scooped up a handful of the October snow and shaped it while John knocked to warn Elizabeth they were coming in. She met them smiling in the small entry just before her husband's snowball hit her in the face.

"Oh!"

Danny laughed, falling helplessly against the wall. John saw why Margaret was so vehemently against drink, and even men, when they had to be put to bed like children, threw snow into a pregnant wife's face and embarrassed you at your bath. John, Jeremy and probably every other man in The Fortune knew that Danny had lost his job in the Standard Mine a week ago for missing two shifts. The line of unemployed men was too long for the mine managers to cut the men much slack. Danny hadn't told his wife, and John and Jeremy had been sworn not to. Now Danny caught Elizabeth and twirled her around in a wild dance while he sang. His wife looked tired and irritated, but John waited to intervene until Danny whacked his head on a doorway. John led the dizzy and cursing man to his bedroom. Elizabeth pulled off his shoes and coat and threw a quilt over him. Danny protested until the lamp was turned out and he fell unconscious.

"Thank you," whispered Elizabeth when they'd left the room. "Can I make you a cup of tea or coffee?" He shook his head. "Are you sure? It's cold out."

"I'm fine. You best get back to bed."

She hesitated. "How's Margaret?"

John arched an eyebrow as he looked down at her. "I'm sure you know the answer to that better than I do."

Elizabeth held his gaze. "For two weeks she was here for every meal, now for two weeks she's been back at her house cooking and cleaning. She won't tell me a thing." John said nothing. "She doesn't look well. She's lost weight." John sighed and slapped his cap against his thigh. "I'm sure it has something to do with you," she added boldly.

John frowned. "And what makes you think that?"

Elizabeth smiled. "No one in my family has gotten under her skin like you did the first night you were in Bodie."

John shook his head. "Being under her skin is not such a pleasant place. She doesn't have a word to spare me." He put his cap back on, walked to the door and stepped out.

Elizabeth ran after him. "Mr. Banning, wait."

He turned on her front steps. "Get back inside. You'll catch pneumonia."

"I know she's difficult, but—"

John pushed her back inside, followed her, closed the door and leaned against it to hear out another of Jeremy's hardheaded daughters.

"On the inside she's really very loving. And . . ."

"And?"

"And she's scared, I guess. She tries to be like our mother was and that's what shows, but she's not as hard in her heart as Mama often was. And Mag, she got the worst of Mama's meanness. She was like a wall between Mama and Victoria and me." She looked hopefully at John, but he was giving nothing away. "If you'll just be a little kind and very patient with her—"

John rolled his eyes and straightened from the door. "I see you've inherited your father's matchmaking tendencies. Good night, Mrs. Clutter. Get some rest. I think you need your own patience with your own husband."

John walked briskly to the Warrens', unable to ignore Elizabeth's words. What had their mother done to Margaret that made her so tense? When he was near her, when he touched her, she never had the look of a disinterested woman. No, she acted threatened, and very aware of him, and he wondered if that was a symptom of her fear or of an arousal she was trying to deny. Maybe she was more scared of herself than him. Lustfulness was not something she would want to set as an example. If she was feeling any such thing she'd hid it well the last two weeks, but then he hadn't come within three feet of her. He ate her meals but didn't bother to wash any dishes, knowing that would torture her. They'd only spoken when absolutely necessary and her voice had never reached lukewarm. The last thing he needed was a frightened, frigid woman. She wasn't cold, a voice inside him countered, she was warm and responsive, but, as Elizabeth had warned, John sensed that coaxing Margaret would take a hell of a lot of patience. He'd told Jeremy he'd marry her, but he wasn't so sure he was ready.

He shook his head, chuckling ruefully, then kicked a chunk of powdery snow into a small spray. He worked in a dark, damp hole where the pay was lousy when weighed against the risk to life and limb. And he had a growing, churning lust for the face, the body, the being of a woman who disliked him. He should either go back to San Francisco, back to work he had once liked, or marry the damn woman and see what happened.

The next morning, while John was at the mine, Margaret decided to ask Danny and Elizabeth if she could live with them. The idea came to her while she ate her oatmeal, and though she didn't much care for the plan, it was an option if her father was truly going to sell his home out from under her. Elizabeth would need help when the baby came. The baby. Margaret was suddenly excited about the coming little one.

Two hours later Margaret was thinking she'd be better off living alone. She declined a cup of coffee as Elizabeth poured one for Danny.

"You quit your job?" Margaret asked for the second time, but he'd answered in the affirmative the first time. "What are you going to do?" She was perched on the edge of her chair.

"I'll work in the saloon."

"Why ever for?" She knew why. She didn't wait for him to give her an elaborate lie for an answer. "I think you and my father should sell it! You'd both make good money and could invest in something honorable."

"That wouldn't be a smart financial move in this town, Margaret," Danny said wisely, as if he knew all about financial wizardry when he'd worked with his back and his hands all his life on the docks and in the mines.

"Well, it definitely wouldn't be a wise move for your drinking convenience."

Danny scowled.

"Are you sure you wouldn't like some coffee, Mag?" Elizabeth asked.

"For five percent of your salary I'll cook your evening meals for you, if you provide the funds for the food."

Danny looked incredulous while Elizabeth gasped in pleasure. Margaret knew more than five percent would be spent at the restaurants in town if the cooking was left to Elizabeth.

"That would be wonderful, Mag! Can you start tonight? I'd love some dumplings!"

Danny looked from Margaret to his wife and back to Margaret. He sighed and nodded. "Five percent."

"Oh, Danny, make it ten. She's family." He glared at Elizabeth, who beamed back. "Cherry pie, chocolate cake, roasted fowl . . . Danny, I'm pregnant."

"Are you mad, woman? Absolutely not."

Elizabeth shrugged and glanced at her sister before looking back at her husband. "Well, let's invite Mr. Banning to dinner," she suggested smoothly.

Danny's scowl lifted to a smirk.

"Let's not," snapped Margaret. She rose from her chair. "I have some menu planning and shopping to do. I'll be back later." She left feeling jubilant. With her five percent—and she'd make sure Danny paid her—she'd have a bank account growing weekly. If and when that irresponsible boy of a man named Danny Clutter couldn't provide for his wife and child, Margaret would.

Chapter Six

Margaret walked out of the butcher shop, where she'd purchased a fat chicken to go with her dumplings. She stopped on the plank walk outside the store and readjusted the leeks in her basket. A bone from the chop stand next to the butcher shop flew past and hit the road in front of her. A yellow dog, one of the many mangy dogs in town, lunged for the fresh bone. A black dog of equal size and scrawniness sidled up and growled. The first dog's jaws locked down on the bone while the black one snapped. Before Margaret took two steps away, men began to converge around her and the dogs, shouting as the dogs bared teeth. The bone dropped to the ground and the dogs snapped and bit. The air filled with yelps and growls and the shouts of men as they wagered on which dog would walk away with the bone. Margaret couldn't see past the male bodies and had to push her way through them, rubbing against their dusty and grimy clothes.

"Please, move!" she demanded several times in the midst of the throng, prodding the slow ones with her basket. She could see her way through the last of the men when an arm snaked around her waist. She jerked her head up and saw Mr. Banning. He shouldered the rest of the men out of her way and pulled her along.

"Thank you. That was most unpleasant. I've never seen human beings flock like flies."

"They're bored and unemployed. It's a bad position for a man. There are too many miners for not enough mines."

She began walking. A roar went up from the crowd. "They don't sound too depressed." Margaret glanced at him. "What were you doing? You're not unemployed. Did that increase your wager? Perhaps you'd better go back and see how well you predicted."

"I don't wager on dog fights," he said, sticking by her side. "I *would* wager that you are lonely in that house by yourself." That took the zip out of her stride. "In fact, I'll wager that within the week you'll be begging me to come dine with you."

She looked up into his smile. "Mr. Banning, I wouldn't beg you for anything."

His smile grew. "Anything's a big word, Maggie."

"Don't call me that." She resumed walking.

"I'll wager for a kiss that you're begging me to come to dinner within the next five minutes."

"That's ridiculous. And I don't gamble."

He stopped walking and she sped ahead of him. "Maggie, I have your corset," he called after her.

She froze.

"The pretty white one with the lace where—"

She spun around. "Stop."

He cocked his head and mouthed the word *dinner* and rubbed his belly.

She shook her head, her face scarlet.

"Can I keep your underwear, Maggie, as a reminder of—"

"Will you *please* come to dinner, Mr. Banning?"

He flashed her a smile. "Do I win the wager, Miss Warren?"

She glared at him. Some of the men in the steady stream of traffic had slowed and were watching the two of them curiously. "Maggie—"

"Yes!" she hissed.

He trotted up to her. "What're we having?"

She stared straight ahead as she marched to Elizabeth's. "You stole that corset from behind the sugar sack, didn't you?"

"Pretty rude of me, wasn't it?"

"Yes!"

"I wanted something to smell you by," he said softly.

Margaret's stomach cramped way down low. She wanted to look at him, see if he was laughing at her, but she didn't dare.

Margaret wouldn't let John help her in the kitchen, so he amused Elizabeth by losing to her in a game of gin and one of checkers. Danny came home on time for dinner sporting newly pomaded hair and a heavily waxed mustache. "Your hair!" Margaret couldn't help exclaiming, wrinkling her nose at the perfumed smell of the pomade.

"Now he looks like a real bartender," replied Elizabeth defensively.

"Isn't that nice," Margaret responded.

The table conversation revolved around the town's namesake, W. S. Body, whose remains had been discovered outside the town.

"Imagine if he was your pa and you had to see him dug up like that just so the town could bury him in the cemetery, even if he did discover this place," Danny said.

"It was indecent for his bones to be on display to the public," agreed Margaret

"I wish I could've seen him," said Elizabeth. "I've never seen a human bone before," she added as Margaret frowned at her.

"You didn't miss much. It's kind of pitiful to think of all the airs we put on when we're all reduced to a similar-looking skeleton," said John. Then he turned to Margaret. "These are the best chicken dumplings I've ever had. I'm glad you insisted I come to dinner."

Danny looked at his sister-in-law with bewilderment and Elizabeth asked what was for dessert. After the peach pie, Danny returned to the saloon and Margaret started cleaning the kitchen.

"Go on to bed, Elizabeth, you look exhausted," she told her sister when she started to clear the table.

"Lord, I am and I don't do much all day. It's just being, you know—" she glanced at John "—pregnant," she whispered.

"I understand. Go rest." Margaret bit her lip as Elizabeth left the room. A familiar fear gripped her, the same one she'd always had when her mother was pregnant. John was soaping the dishes when she returned to the kitchen. He glanced behind him and moved away from the small basin. He held up his hands. "All right, I know you like to wash. I'll dry." She stepped up and took his place, but he stayed close. "I want my kiss now."

She didn't look at him but could feel his warmth and his breath. "You don't get one."

"I will."

"Be still with your sappy predictions."

"It's going to be a long, nice one."

She threw down a spoon and he smiled. They worked in silence. John took his time drying and Margaret ended up helping him. He stared at her a good deal of the time and she was getting jumpy. "God, you're easy to unnerve. I wonder why no one else does it."

"You're the only one who wants to kiss me," she snapped.

His brows rose.

He walked her home in the cold night. "Look at those stars!" he said, and automatically she looked up. The stars were brilliant in the clear sky. She smiled, not able to remember when she'd last looked up to see the stars, and then she felt him watching her. Self-conscious, she turned away.

"Nice folks, your sister and Danny." Margaret didn't respond. "Nice dinner tonight." A few minutes later he said, "Nice walk." Several minutes after that he stared pointedly at the woman walking next to him. "Nice silence."

Margaret stopped and whirled on him. "I'm glad you think everything is so nice. I don't. Elizabeth didn't have any money to pay me for the food I bought today. She laughed it off, said she was temporarily out of pocket, but I know when she's trying to hide something. I don't think Danny gives her any money. I think he spends it all himself. He was always irresponsible, but he's gotten worse, and now he's got a baby on the way!" She turned away.

John watched her stride off. He was struck by how frivolous he could be compared to Margaret, who cared so much about things. She was really worried about her sister, not just trying to give Danny a bad time or pick on men who drank and gambled. A small, admiring smile tugged the corners of his mouth up. He jogged to catch up with her and walked in silence beside her.

On her porch he took her arm. "We can go inside, stoke up the fire in the stove and kiss in front of it." She looked aghast. "I see you don't like that idea, so we'll stay out here." Gently he pushed her against the door and stepped close. "Say you want me to go."

"I want you—" His open mouth covered her open mouth. He kept the kiss soft and she closed her mouth. Undaunted, he held her head. He dropped kisses along her cheeks, over her nose and back to her mouth.

"Kiss me, Maggie. Kiss me," he whispered against her lips.

She shivered, cold everywhere except where his hands cupped her cheeks and his lips caressed hers. He was so gentle, he didn't even touch her with his body, and for that her relief was great. She twisted her face away. "Why do you do this?"

"Push you?"

"Kiss me."

His chuckle was half groan. "Because I like to kiss you. You're soft and sweet." He rubbed his lips back and forth across hers. "And I like *you,* Maggie." He kissed her neck and she arched abruptly as heat sizzled through her.

"I don't want you to like me," she gasped. "I want you to leave me alone."

He sighed and pressed his forehead against hers. "You make this so damn hard. You need me, Maggie." She shook her head. "If I wait for you to realize it, we'll be sixty years old."

She shoved at his shoulders. "I don't know what you mean. Please go. Please."

He held her hands, then transferred both of them to one of his and cupped her chin. "Are you scared of me, Maggie?"

"Stop calling me that! My name has never been Maggie."

He gave her face a little shake. "Are you?"

"Yes," she whispered.

"Why?" No answer. "Is it because I make you feel things? I hope I do." He kissed the tips of her fingers and she began to tremble. "Your father wants me to marry you." She tried to pull away, but he held fast to her wrists. "No, no, stay here," he said as she continued to struggle. "I didn't want a wife."

"I don't want a husband," she retorted.

He grinned. "Yeah, I know, but maybe I can change your mind."

Margaret stiffened. "Why bother? I've never given you any encouragement! I've barely ever been nice to you. You just want the saloon!"

"Hold still! Damn!" He pressed her against the wall with his body. "I think you would make me a good wife."

"Thank you very much, but I think you'd make me a horrendous husband."

"And why's that?" He couldn't help it; he felt himself growing peeved. "Did you mean those things you said about me to your father? You think I'm a cruel, base, common laborer?"

"No," she whispered, "but I think we're very different. We don't suit each other."

"I like the differences. I think we'd make a good match."

"I don't want children."

"You don't want children, or you don't want sex?"

"Neither."

John smiled. "You're just scared."

She trod on his toe, but his boots were so thick he only chuckled.

"Mr. Banning, stop this at once. I don't want to marry you or anyone. And I don't see why I should have to marry and have children."

He looked down at her. She was serious. "I believe you feel that way now, but what are you going to do when your father sells this house and another family moves in?"

She didn't answer.

"And he *is* going to. He wants a daily progress report on our courtship. He said we can keep everything in the house. He's already taken what he wants. So, are you going to go hire yourself out as a maid or a cook and live in someone else's house in the cramped little room they're willing to spare you, when you have a strong, able man right here, willing to take you on for the rest of your life? It's something to think about, isn't it? So is this."

His mouth came down hard and fast. His hand had undone the top buttons of her coat while he'd spoken and now he reached inside and squeezed her breast. His finger circled her nipple, which hardened instantly. Inside her mouth his tongue surged. She tried to push it out but only rubbed against his wet flesh, exciting them both and fueling the reluctant passion within her. She couldn't shut her mouth. Her body was wedged between the wood door and his equally hard thighs. She felt flushed, hot, and her nails dug into her own hands where he still held them. He caught her tongue and sucked on it while his fingers gently pinched her nipple. And then it happened. She became the conduit for lightning. Heat from his mouth and hand struck down her body, grounding her, paralyzing her. All thought stopped as her mind swirled in dizzy rapture. She existed only for her own hot blood and his silky thrusting tongue and his squeezing fingers over a part of her breast that hurt like no pain she'd ever felt before. She whimpered as John's hands fell from her and he stepped back. They stared at each other, John breathing uneasily. "Go inside," he ordered softly.

She did so without argument and John stared at the door after it slammed shut. He groaned, then smiled and stretched his arms over his head with a loud sigh. She was not a cold woman. He sat down in her porch chair, pulled it up so he could rest his feet on the railing and leaned back with a proprietary air. Soon this house would be his. Not that it was a great house. The construction was shoddy, but Margaret was part of it. He thought of the homes in San

Francisco he'd built with his brother and father. Beautiful homes. One day he'd build one for Margaret.

The front door flew open and a strident voice yelled, "Get off my porch!"

John jerked in surprise and his chair teetered on its back legs and then crashed to the porch. The front door slammed shut again and John lay on the planking, his legs dangling up over the seat of the chair. She was a delightful woman.

Two weeks later Margaret was walking home from Elizabeth's after putting the kitchen in order. She had worked hard and was tired and the weariness felt good. She was near the corner of Fuller and Green streets when someone large fell into step beside her. Margaret's grip on her basket tightened and she looked up into a shadowed face.

"Need help with that basket?" asked an ingratiatingly friendly voice that stunk of alcohol.

"No, thank you," Margaret answered tightly.

"You're Jeremy Warren's daughter, ain't you? What's goin' on at your place? Your daddy's livin' in a hotel, and you got a miner under your roof that you ain't married to."

Margaret refused to answer and walked faster. The man gripped her arm.

"Slow down, honey. I'll walk you home."

"That's not necessary." She pulled her arm away from his hand.

He reached for her again and she broke into a run and didn't stop until she had slammed and bolted the door of her house. She wasn't sure, but she thought she heard male laughter on the wind.

For her birthday, Elizabeth had a party and she invited her friends, who were mainly Danny's friends. Margaret prepared a meal with funds she had cornered Danny for on the street. She roasted stuffed Cornish game hens and little potatoes, boiled several bunches of fresh leafy greens to dump in a bowl and sprinkle with vinegar, and baked bread and little apple-filled tarts and a huge white cake with white frosting. She was still in the kitchen when the last guest arrived.

Her food was very much appreciated even though she insisted the bottles of spirits be cleared off the table when dinner was served. Margaret ate little, uncomfortable among the unfamiliar people and the too familiar John Banning, who sat directly across the table from her. Hal, a mustached man with mutton chops, his lips loose with drink, raised his glass to Margaret when he had finished eating. "You're a true credit to all womanhood, Miss Warren."

His praise was echoed by the others and Margaret nodded stiffly, uncomfortable with admiration.

"A woman who can't cook has no business bein' born," continued Hal.

"Wait just a minute," said Danny, looking at his wife. "I can't agree."

"Well, some ladies do compensate for that lack," amended Hal.

Elizabeth smiled prettily and batted her lashes. Margaret agreed. A woman should cook well and keep her house, but Elizabeth was sweet and joyful.

"There's more to life than a well-prepared meal," John said quietly.

"Yeah, what about them hurdy-gurdy girls? They'd starve if they could only cook but didn't have no money to buy food," added Saul, the youngest man at the table.

"They'd have husbands buying their food," interjected Margaret.

"What if they don't want husbands?" asked John softly.

Margaret looked away from his dark, deep eyes.

"All women want husbands," asserted Hal. "They're all swayed by romance and pretty words. Take Natalie here, she has a story clipped out from the newspaper and folded in her Bible, of all places, about a man and a woman who meet on the train and marry after writing letters to each other for years. They hadn't even seen each other, but 'their intellectual attainments had formed a bond of marriage.' Don't that beat all? They hadn't even seen each other!"

Natalie smiled. "The woman wore a red rose on her hat and the man wore a red silk handkerchief around his neck so they could find each other."

"That is nice," Elizabeth said softly. "And they did marry after meeting?" Natalie nodded. "I'd like to read that story."

"Well, I'm sure he exposed his financial status in black ink and white paper," John said. All the women turned to him. "And I bet you this red handkerchief man was pleased with the looks of his bride."

"Amen," agreed Hal.

"You don't think there can be a marriage of minds, Mr. Banning?" Margaret asked. "You don't believe some could elevate their love above the physical?"

John leaned forward, forearms on the table, eyes leveled at Margaret. "For the intimacy of marriage, Miss Warren, I do believe a little physical attraction comes in handy to perform the—"

Margaret stood abruptly and excused herself from the discussion to clear the table with the help of the only other woman besides Elizabeth. Natalie Baker was unmarried and Margaret wondered what she thought of the discussion, but the woman had drunk too much wine and Margaret didn't dare converse with her for fear the woman would let the plates she held slide off each other onto the floor.

Elizabeth insisted on champagne as well as coffee with the cake. Margaret began to worry. Her sister was poisoning herself with drink while she carried a babe. She pulled Elizabeth aside and voiced her feelings on the matter. "It's my birthday!" her sister protested. "And I'll only sip." But she sipped and sipped and sipped. Margaret wanted to go home. The hour was late, everyone was inebriated and spoke three times as loudly as necessary, and Mr. Banning had wangled a chair next to her and stared at her too often.

He had come knocking at her door every evening in the past two weeks, but she had never let him in or stepped out with him. Her father had not once visited her to remind her of his threat and she truly thought he might have recanted his proclaimed fate for her. If not, as Elizabeth's birthday was the deadline, she might find tomorrow unpleasant. How would he go about removing his eldest daughter from her home? While she imagined him trying to pull her out of the house she watched Elizabeth fill her glass with more champagne. Margaret slid it away. Maybe if it stayed out of sight Elizabeth would forget about drinking it. A few minutes later her sister reached for the glass and looked puzzledly at Margaret when she found it on the far side of her sister.

Someone proposed cards. Elizabeth begged for poker. She'd only been able to play a few times since John had taught her. No one needed any convincing. Margaret was dealt a hand. "No." She pushed the cards away.

"Oh, come on," urged Elizabeth. Margaret shook her head.

"Could you move aside then?" asked Saul.

"Why?"

Hal laughed loud. "He takes his gambling very seriously."

"I know how you ladies are," Saul argued. "You like to band together. You'll probably give Mrs. Clutter some tips."

"I don't even know how to play the game!"

Several voices jumped in offering to teach her. Margaret agreed reluctantly, not wanting to leave Elizabeth's side. She felt Mr. Banning looking at her. Elizabeth squeezed her arm happily. Margaret sighed and listened to Danny explain the game with numerous interruptions from the others. The game sounded simple enough, until they started talking about wild cards.

She stole Elizabeth's drink away again while everyone studied their cards. Margaret didn't care about her cards. She had a pair of threes and would discard the rest. She noticed Elizabeth looking around and then her sister studied her cards again. Margaret lifted the champagne over John Banning's whiskey and his hand came down over the top of his glass. She looked up at him. "Please," she mouthed silently. He slowly moved his hand, his eyes holding hers. She poured Elizabeth's champagne into his whiskey. She did not draw any more threes and folded.

Hal dealt the next hand. Saul filled Elizabeth's glass again. Margaret let her take one sip and then filled Mr. Banning's glass to the top. He'd stopped drinking. Miss Barker raised the bet. Margaret swallowed the rest of Elizabeth's champagne. She gritted her teeth to keep from coughing. The bubbles fought to come back up in a belch but she repressed it by squeezing her lips together. The game continued, the champagne kept pouring, and Margaret continued to drink.

Chapter Seven

Margaret felt the birthday party drawing out into eternity as she tried to protect her sister. Elizabeth took a sip of champagne now and then but became preoccupied studying her cards and trying to win a hand. She won one and concentrated harder, forgetting about the drink at her side, but this was only after Margaret had swallowed four glasses of the vile stuff and was feeling out of her mind. She found herself staring at people, and it was increasingly hard to sit up straight. When she noticed she was slumping she'd shoot up and feel as if she were thrusting her bosom too far out, a perpetual jack-in-the-box.

Finally, Elizabeth's condition caught up with her. She excused herself by pleading tiredness after thanking everyone for coming. She urged them all to stay and continue playing, and no one refused. Margaret rose and swayed and gripped the back of her chair. She was drunk. How could someone like this precarious feeling? Elizabeth looked at her sister quizzically as Margaret struggled with her coat. The armholes of the thing kept moving from her hands.

"Have you been drinking?" Elizabeth asked in an amazed voice.

"Just go to bed," Margaret whispered loudly. Her sister seemed immune to the drink she had imbibed. Though her cheeks were flushed she moved quite assuredly.

"I'll ask Mr. Banning to walk you home."

"I'd be happy to." John spoke behind Margaret, holding her coat in just the right position so she could shove her arms into it.

Margaret didn't object. In fact, she held his arm as they walked down the road. She was sure she'd fall down otherwise. Tonight she'd be a perfect victim for that nameless man who had accosted her the previous night.

"Ever drink spirits before?" John asked.

"No, and I see I didn't miss much. What is so attractive about losing control of one's body?" John chuckled and didn't respond. Halfway home a light snow began to fall. Margaret stopped and watched the flakes in the moonlight. "It's snowing and it's not cold out."

"It's cold," John assured her.

She looked at him. "You mean I just don't feel it, because of the champagne?" He nodded. "Oh." They resumed walking. The air cleared her head and she felt light and gay. She stopped and studied the footprints they made in the snow. "Look how big your feet are! I can step right inside them." She pushed him ahead of her and followed in his tracks. She giggled. John stopped and waited until she caught up with him. He tucked her arm tightly under his and walked the rest of the way holding her close.

Margaret slipped on her wet wooden porch. She couldn't fit her key into the lock but wouldn't give it to John to try. "I'll do it!" She started laughing when she kept missing the keyhole. "I don't know why this is so funny!" When she finally got the door open she tripped over a rug and stumbled all the way across the parlor until she hit the wall. Nothing hurt. Paroxysms of laughter shook her. She tried to light a lamp, but every time the match went out before she got the wick lighted. She threw the matches down. "You better do this." She struggled out of her coat and tossed it onto the sofa while he lighted the lamp. Her shawl fell to the floor and her hat landed on a small table.

"At least you're not a mean drunk," he said, shaking out the match.

"I just had a little too much champagne. I'll splash some water on my face and I'll be just fine." She walked to her bedroom and then turned around in the doorway. "I need a light." John handed her a candle and watched her walk through her room. A moment later he heard water splashing and then laughter. He walked slowly to her door. She was looking down at herself where she'd soaked the front of her dress. "What a mess," she said, giggling.

John leaned against the doorjamb, enjoying this different Margaret who could laugh about a mess. She hummed as she tried to wipe the water dry with a towel.

"Your fire's out. I'll build you a new one before I go to the mine," he said, watching her. He didn't want to leave at all.

Margaret looked up and walked crookedly to her hamper. She tossed the towel inside it. "There you go again."

"What?"

"Looking at me like that. You've been looking at me like that all night."

He smiled. "How could I not look at someone who was pouring champagne into my whiskey?"

She took a step toward him. "But this look isn't reserved for my fouling your spirits."

"Oh? What is it reserved for?" And he crossed his arms and gave her the full force of his look, his eyes heating, darkening, lowering.

Margaret stared back. "Kissing," she announced loudly.

John burst into laughter. Margaret joined him but had no idea what she was laughing about. It just felt good. He shook his head and turned and left the room. She followed him. "Where are you going?" she asked.

John raised his head from where he was crouched in front of the wood stove. She sounded so disappointed. "I'm going to start that fire. You're shivering."

"I am?" She looked down at herself. Sure enough, her arms were trembling.

"Why don't you go get out of that wet dress?"

She frowned.

"Go on," he urged roughly. She was acting like a kitten wanting to be petted and he was too willing to oblige, but it was so obvious she was only half here. He started the fire and then sat on the sofa and listened to her bang around in her room as she changed. He heard a great deal of muffled giggling and wondered if she was trapped with her dress over her head.

He wasn't far off the mark. Margaret had gotten her dress off, though the buttons had given her much trouble. Her nightgown, however, was stuck somewhere over her head and her arms were not shoved all the way through the sleeves yet. She'd spun around the room a couple of times in a blind, drunken mirth as she wriggled the garment down.

John pounded on the door. "Are you all right in there?"

Margaret opened the door. He assumed she didn't realize how askew her hair was, her chignon sitting lopsided, the pins half in and half out. "I'm fine," she said, trying to be controlled but sounding bright and silly.

"Button yourself up," he said, motioning to her gown.

Margaret shook her head. "Oh no, more buttons," she groaned.

John grinned and did them up for her. She stood real close and stared at his mouth the entire time. He knew what she wanted but wasn't about to give it to her when later she'd claim he'd taken advantage. He pushed her away. "Go get in bed," he ordered.

She pouted. John's eyes widened.

"I don't feel like going to bed."

"No? What do you feel like doing?" he asked with exasperation.

She tilted her head, her mussed hair falling even more to the side, tendrils of chestnut curls wisping over her face as she looked at him. Her eyes were deep and dark and admiring.

"Get to bed!" he shouted, causing her to jump. "You're going to hear about this tomorrow." He strode out and slammed the door.

Margaret shrugged away her confusion and crawled under the covers. She blew out her candle and then shivered and turned and huddled on her side. Beneath her closed lids blackness whirled. Her eyes popped open and she gasped at the dizziness that had assailed her. She rolled to her back and propped her head up with the pillows. That felt okay. She looked straight into the dark room until her eyelids grew heavy and sank shut. Again the blackness rushed up at her, worse this time. She'd have to try to sleep with her eyes open. But the dizziness came upon her in spite of open eyes. She had to sit up to banish it. Soon tiredness overwhelmed her and she lay back down.

John made sure the fire in the parlor was high to keep Margaret warm in the next room. He opened her door to let the heat in and heard a miserable groan and the bed creaking. He grabbed the lamp from the parlor and strode back to her dark room to find her hanging over the bed, reaching for the chamber pot. He scooped the bowl out, removed the top, pulled her to her knees and thrust the bowl under her chin. She retched miserably. John covered the pot when she was finished and set it on the floor. Margaret sat back down and moaned. After wetting a hand towel in her pitcher, he sat beside her and wiped her face with the cold, wet cloth.

"Can I take your hairpins out?" he asked gently. She nodded her head. He pulled out the pins and set them on the table next to the bed. She leaned into his chest.

"I'm so tired," she whispered. "And cold."

He pulled the covers up over her body, but she still shivered. Undoing his boots, he slipped into bed behind her. His calves brushed against the hard shoes that she'd forgotten to take off. He debated whether to remove them and decided he'd hold her first until she warmed up. He couldn't leave with her body temperature dangerously lowered by alcohol, he reasoned. He wrapped her in his arms and she burrowed her backside into his warmth. He held her hands in front of her breasts. Her fingers were icy. He told himself the pleasure he received in having his groin cushioned against her soft bottom was incidental to his mission of warming her. He wished he'd drunk less or more instead of just enough to lower his control and heighten his desires. In seconds she was asleep and John tightened his arms around her. He had to get up, go to work. He needed more sleep than he usually got, but he'd gone to the party to see Margaret, stayed late because she had and was still with her because she felt so good. But now he wanted to do so much more than just hold her. Tantalizing himself with the ways he wanted to touch her and see her, John fell asleep.

"It's considerate of you to accompany me, Reverend Hinkle. Miss Warren's never missed one of your sermons.'' Mrs. Hoyt's black wool skirts swept the icy planks as she walked to Margaret's with the Methodist minister. ''I know something must be wrong. I can feel it.'' She gingerly picked her way across snowy and muddy Main Street.

''Maybe the cold was too much for her.''

''Not possible. Miss Warren would not let a little discomfort keep her from attending to her spiritual needs.''

Reverend Hinkle helped her up the slippery steps of the Warren house and Mrs. Hoyt knocked loudly. ''Margaret!'' she called out.

Margaret woke with a warm body, icy face and splitting headache. She heard her name inside her aching head and tried to focus bleary eyes. A heavy weight held her down, preventing her from sitting up. She lifted the covers, looked down and gasped at the sight of John Banning nestled against her, his leg and arm thrown over her, his face snuggled between her arm and breast. John groaned as he stretched and woke.

Margaret didn't meet his eyes but sat up and swung her legs out of the bed. Leaning over, she groped for her slippers under the bed and felt her brain falling out the top of her skull. She groaned, got the slippers on her feet and limped to her dressing gown across the room. The pounding on the door was echoing the pounding in her head and she squinted with pain as she opened the door.

''Margaret, finally!''

Margaret backed up in surprise and Mrs. Hoyt appropriated the space, entering the parlor, the minister following her. ''Are you all right? You look terrible! What is that smell?'' She raised her gloved hand to her nose. ''My dear, what have you been doing? You smell like drink.'' Her voice trailed off in a whisper and then she stiffened, eyes riveted on a spot behind and to the right of Margaret.

Margaret jerked her head around but felt as if her eyeballs had been left behind. She saw John Banning leaning against the doorframe of the bedroom, his unbuttoned shirt showing long underwear underneath, his hair mussed, his feet shoeless. Margaret's stomach lurched and her head felt squeezed in a vise.

"My Lord!" exclaimed Mrs. Hoyt, staring and blinking.

Reverend Hinkle took Mrs. Hoyt's elbow. "I believe we're intruding."

"I can explain," Margaret responded, raising a hand to her aching head.

"Oh!" the woman went on, staring over her shoulder as she was pulled away. "To think I thought so highly of you."

"I've done noth—"

"Miss Warren!" called Mr. Reeves, a pharmacist and friend of her father's. "You're still here!" he exclaimed, stepping up onto her porch. His family, a sedate-looking woman and two little girls remained in the snow-covered yard. "Morning, Mrs. Hoyt, Reverend Hinkle," he greeted.

"What do you mean?" Margaret and Mrs. Hoyt asked simultaneously.

Mr. Reeves removed his hat and looked confused. "Your father told me the house was for sale. He assured me you would be moved out today. I want Mrs. Reeves to see the inside."

"I see," Margaret said tightly.

"Oh, Mag," called Elizabeth, pulling herself up the stairs and crowding the small porch. Mr. Reeves stepped aside for her. "Congratulations! I'm so happy for you! Is this a party?"

Margaret raised her fingertips to her throbbing temple.

"What has happened?" asked Mrs. Hoyt, looking from Elizabeth to Margaret and voicing everyone's curiosity.

Elizabeth smiled widely, happy to pass on the news. "My father just informed me that John Banning is going to marry my sister!"

Margaret blanched as everyone on the porch turned to stare at her.

"Indeed?" Mrs. Hoyt asked.

"Excuse me, please," Margaret said softly, and shut the door in everyone's face. She locked it. Immediately some-one pounded on the door.

"Miss Warren, is this house for sale or not?"

Margaret turned huge eyes to the man still standing in her bedroom doorway. His dark brown eyes were calm, sleepy, maybe even amused, and definitely studying her. She glared at him with bloodshot eyes while she shuffled past him into her bedroom. She sank onto the bed. "I can't believe this. I shouldn't have answered the door, but they might all have just barged in," she said, hoisting up her dressing gown. "My father is passing around different stories about me, and Mrs. Hoyt saw you, saw *us*, like this," she said, glanc-ing down at herself. "And she smelled me," she wailed softly, wrinkling her nose.

"She's a snitty, gossipy biddy. What do you care what she thinks?"

Margaret looked up at him. "You don't even know her," she said, holding the palm of one hand to her forehead. "You don't realize what this means." He still leaned in the doorway.

"Mrs. Hoity-Toity won't be coming for tea?"

Margaret stared at him as though she were watching a hideous bug crawl across her floor. "She'll tell everyone. No one decent will speak to me."

John combed his fingers through his rumpled hair. This was bad. He hadn't wanted her to be embarrassed or exposed to ridicule. Now she was going to be impossible. "I'm sorry." He walked toward her. She held up her hand, stopping him. "Your father is forcing you to make a decision. We can't go backward, Maggie. What happened happened."

"Stop calling me that!"

"You can always marry me," he said. "That should ease everyone's mind. Then Mrs. Hoity-Toity will speak to you again, if that's what's so important."

Margaret walked to her dressing table, picked up her brush and swiped at her tangled hair with it. She winced at the pain to her scalp. "I'm not a fool. I know Mrs. Hoyt is an intolerant and difficult woman, but she has certain standards of decency that I respect."

"Like spreading vicious gossip? Like casting judgment as if she were God?"

Margaret glanced at his reflection in the mirror. His arms were crossed against his chest. She'd never seen his mouth turned down so. His brows drew together and his dark eyes met her curious ones in the mirror.

"Since we're going to be accused of fornicating I'd like to at least have had the pleasure."

Margaret couldn't help the smile that cracked her lips. "Mr. Banning," she admonished, shaking her head, but inside her something was nodding. He must have sensed it for he walked up behind her. The mirror frame cut off his face just above his mouth. He placed his hands lightly on her shoulders and Margaret stiffened but didn't try to throw them off. She stared at his full mouth, waiting for him to speak, feeling intimately connected to him since he'd slept in her bed all night with his arms around her. Everything seemed upside down. Usually she tried to keep her life planned and orderly, and then she felt safe. But with John Banning around nothing went according to plan, and she felt adrift. So she waited.

Shock rippled through her body as she stared at his mouth and felt his hands slide over her shoulders, down to her breasts. She spun around, tripping over one of his feet as she lunged away from him. She faced him from across the room, her chest heaving, her eyes wide.

"Why are you so damn scared of me?" he hollered.

"Stop yelling at me!" She clenched her fists at her sides.

His jaw tightened. "I'm sorry," he said quietly. He looked at her, his eyes snapping. "I'd just like to know why you're scared of me. Or is it that I repulse you? There are some women I wouldn't want touching me, so I can understand. Not that I like that idea." He shook his head at himself. "Just tell me something so I can get the hell out of here and see if I still have a job at the mine."

"I don't like you touching me. I thought you knew that by now."

"But why? Because I scare you or repulse you?"

Margaret crossed her arms. "Scare."

"Why? You looked flattered when I said I wished we'd done what we are being accused of. Hell, last night I thought you might ask me to kiss you!"

"I wouldn't!" She turned away and poured herself a glass of water. "Why are you so... so... interested in me, anyway?" she demanded softly after she put her glass down.

John looked at her from head to toe. I think I'm in love with you, he thought with a trace of wonderment and self-disgust. "For some reason I like you," he said. He shrugged. "It's incomprehensible to me, even," he added flippantly. "Must be for the same reason I like my mother's cat, even though she's always scratching me. I'm not trying to compromise your damn morals, so I don't see what the problem is!''

Margaret sat down on the bed and stared at the floor. She felt like a fragile, burgeoning plant, just up from the soil, that was being deluged with a bucket of water. She wanted to scream at him, but she didn't want him to leave. She shook her head at herself.

''I guess it's worse to marry me than to have your reputation ruined or to find a new home and support yourself.'' He sat down on the end of the bed, his back to her, and pulled on his boots.

Margaret lifted her head. Because no other men had ever pursued her, she couldn't understand what John Banning found likable in her, but he did find something. He'd proven it too many times. She was somehow pleasured by his persistent interest and guessed he was right—she was flattered. She absolutely believed that a large part of his attraction was the saloon, for if he married her he'd be well-off with the profits from The Fortune. Margaret's eyes narrowed. She didn't think John Banning was a spendthrift, and his responsibility would leave less money in Danny's irresponsible control. She would be able to rest assured that Elizabeth and the baby would always have enough. Marriage would protect her reputation, protection she'd need now that the rumor would be spread that she was a loose, immoral woman. How many men would think she'd be available? Men like that stranger in the street the other night. She cringed. She'd have John here to protect her, to keep her company, to do for. She did not like an empty, quiet house. The bed shook as John rose and walked around it.

''All right, I'll marry you.''

''*What?*'' He stared at her, his brows rising into his hairline.

"Today."

"What?" he repeated.

"Don't 'what' me. You offered."

"But I didn't think you'd ever accept!"

"So, your offer was not sincere?"

"I meant it," he said quietly.

"Good. But I don't want any...conjugal relations." She said the last two words hastily.

John relaxed. "I knew this couldn't be true." He smiled. "You want me to marry you to protect your reputation, but we're not going to be intimate?"

Margaret nodded.

John laughed. "No. I can't do that."

"It would only be for a few months, until Elizabeth has her baby and is getting around again. We can leave here then and separate."

"You're talking about a temporary marriage?" he asked incredulously.

She nodded again.

"That's a sham! I want to really marry you, not pretend! And I don't want to leave here."

"Well, you can come back!" She moved away from him and snatched up her soiled clothes from the floor. John stared at her as she shoved them into a hamper.

"Margaret, I can't participate in this. The vows are for a lifetime, the bond is physical." He took a deep breath and slowly let it out, making his shoulders relax. Her eyes rose from the rug, glanced at him briefly, then flicked back down. "If we marry, it's because you choose to make the union complete."

She faced him and he thought she looked as if she were fourteen years old. She was trembling and he wanted to tell her not to worry, she didn't have to marry him, but she knew that. He didn't understand exactly what she was so afraid of—sex, him, being forever with him?

"I don't want any babies," she said very firmly, thinking she was stark raving crazy to be even considering this. She didn't have to marry him, but it would solve many of her problems in one swoop. It would also give her a new crop that she was ill-equipped to deal with. She was confused and she tried to get her thoughts to come clear, but she was guided by a compulsive drive to keep this man bound to her, to have him help her with her worries about Elizabeth, to have him alleviate her loneliness.

"I can prevent that," John responded softly, the realization that this woman might really accept him sinking in. He felt very solemn all of a sudden.

Margaret turned away from him and nodded. She looked terrified, still and pale. John felt nervous. He took a step toward her. "I'll be real good to you," he said hoarsely.

She flinched as he took another step closer. "I need to get dressed," she said.

John left the bedroom and leaned against the closed door on the other side. Soon, he thought, he wouldn't have to leave for her to dress. He could watch. He could help. His blood began to warm. It would be in a boil by tonight. He snatched his hat up off the sofa in the parlor and strode out the door in search of the minister.

Chapter Eight

The ceremony took place at four o'clock. Elizabeth had been hopping around for the previous hour trying to get Margaret to change into a prettier dress than the gray wool she wore. Margaret would not change her clothes or curl her hair or bejewel herself, or anything else Elizabeth nagged her about. She didn't care if John Banning did think she was dowdy. Maybe he'd forgo the evening's ritual. Reverend Hinkle and her future husband walked into the parlor and Margaret felt every muscle in her body tense. She found it difficult to move her mouth to greet either of them.

"I'm glad to see you make this right," the minister said. Margaret winced.

Danny walked in with a bottle of champagne under each arm.

"Get that poison out of my house!"

"You didn't object to it last night. Seemed quite fond of this 'poison,' in fact," Danny said blithely.

Margaret reddened and could feel Reverend Hinkle staring at her. Danny smiled and went to stand by his soon-to-be brother-in-law. "Protect me, John."

John sighed. His bride was growing rigid with fury and embarrassment. He'd have to remember to thank Danny for guaranteeing a rough wedding night. "Where's Jeremy?" he asked, to take the attention off Margaret.

"Here I am!" Jeremy announced, walking in with a long, flat, gift-wrapped box. "You didn't think I'd miss the day I thought I'd never see, did you? Especially after all the trouble I went to to bring about—"

"Shall we get started?" John asked no one in particular, to interrupt the old man's speech. His bride looked as if she were about to have a fit of apoplexy.

Margaret stared at the collar of the new white shirt John wore throughout the very brief ceremony. Neither had a ring for the other. Margaret had not thought of it, but it seemed appropriate that he not give her one. She wasn't sure yet that she wouldn't run out on him before the sun set.

"I pronounce you man and wife," intoned the minister. "You may kiss the bride." John turned and clasped Margaret's shoulders. Margaret tensed and clenched her hands as he turned her to face him. He took so long about it that she raised her eyes to his. She could feel the others staring at them and she felt hot. Never closing his eyes, he lowered his mouth and pressed a warm, soft kiss against her lips. He grinned widely on pulling away. "Mrs. Banning," he said.

Margaret's knees buckled. She heard laughter as Mr. Ban—John—her husband caught her with his arm around her waist. Everyone smiled and offered congratulations. Danny popped both corks, Elizabeth ran for glasses, and John guided Margaret to a chair. She sat, not daring to speak, flooded with regret that she'd done something so mad. She pushed away the glass of liquor John held out to her.

"A toast, Mag. You must," Elizabeth urged.

Margaret took the glass.

Reverend Hinkle cleared his throat. "May you both find contentment in each other's regard and God's blessings. Here's to a long and fruitful union."

Margaret blanched. John twined his arm through hers, looked into her eyes and nudged her frozen arm. They both drank from their respective glasses. Margaret barely sipped and set her glass on the nearest table. Elizabeth came over and kissed Margaret soundly on the cheek. "I'm so happy for you, Mag. John is just the perfect man for you! Oh, I wish Mother could see this! Wouldn't she be surprised?"

"Yes, wouldn't she." Margaret could almost see her dark-haired mother standing in the corner, frowning, waiting to pull Margaret aside and give some last-minute warnings for the ordeal ahead. Margaret squeezed her eyes closed and banished the ghost.

"Congratulations, son," her father said to John, slapping him on the back. "Keep him happy, daughter. I made Danny a partner in The Fortune, as well, so there's no use fighting it anymore. Your family is entrenched in the business."

Margaret skewered him with a narrow-eyed gaze while John wondered how everyone in her family could be so insensitive at times.

"Yeah, I'm twenty-five percent owner!" Danny announced happily. "It's great to have you in the family, Banning. I guess Lizzy is going to have to do her own cooking. We'll have to talk about the saloon. You're the boss now. I'm sure you'll be wanting to take over the books and glad I am of it, too. But we'll talk about it later." He winked. "We'll leave you alone now. Elizabeth said you wanted a private dinner." He smirked and then left with Elizabeth and her father and the minister.

Margaret scowled. He hadn't had to make it sound so intimate. Margaret had known she wouldn't be able to eat a thing, so she refused all of Elizabeth's suggestions concerning a dinner with the family. She glanced up at John, who was perched on the arm of her chair. Oh Lord, she thought, maybe she should have agreed to a celebratory dinner in a restaurant. It would have put off going into the bedroom. John looked down at her, the light in his eyes alerting her to the fact that he was already thinking about it. Margaret fluttered her hand toward his thigh. "Please move," she demanded somewhat breathlessly. "This chair was not made to support a body so." John moved to the sofa across from her. "I don't want you working in that whiskey mill. I want you to convince them to sell it."

"Think it would be a good idea to let Danny have the chunk of money his share would be? Think he'd invest it wisely? Think he'd save it?"

Margaret pressed two fingers against her temple. He was thinking and she wasn't. "Well, I want you to make sure he goes home and sees to Elizabeth. Don't let him drink overmuch and—"

"Margaret, can we talk about this later?"

"No! This is important. This is why. . ." She didn't dare finish that thought. She had a strong sense that John would not like the way she was using him thrown in his face, even though he was using her for the saloon.

John sighed. "You want to fight real bad, don't you?"

"I don't!"

He smiled at her. "Think if you keep me real busy with all that you want, I won't be able to get in what I want tonight?"

She flushed scarlet and stared at him silently. He leaned forward. She stood and turned toward the kitchen. He followed. She whirled around, scared he'd attack her from behind, and took a step backward as he approached. She backed up farther and banged into the wall, wincing as her spine took the brunt of the hard wood under flowered wallpaper.

John shook his head. "Would you relax? I'm not going to hurt you."

"Yes, you will," she whispered.

John glanced away from her solemn face. He'd never been with a virgin before, so how in the hell would he know if it would hurt her. His brother hadn't shared any specific details of his sexual life with his wife, Amy. John had heard that for women it *could* be painful the first time. He looked back at his wife and found her watching him. "I don't want to hurt you," he said hoarsely. He could have drowned in her wide eyes. He'd have to put everything he had into making her feel good tonight so she'd never look at him with fear again. He wanted to start now, but the sun was barely down and she'd balk less if he steered her toward the bed when it was closer to bedtime.

"Why don't you make us something to eat?"

Margaret snapped off the wall. "Yes!" She turned into the kitchen and released a held breath. She brewed a fresh pot of coffee and John poured himself a large mug when it perked dark. He stood leaning in the doorway, watching her, and Margaret forced herself to concentrate on putting a meal together with every ounce of energy she had. She fried two thick steaks and diced potatoes with onions. She sliced a loaf of bread and threw together an apple pie. When she went to place the dishes on the dining table he stopped her.

"Let's eat in the kitchen."

"Why?"

"That table's too big out there."

Margaret reluctantly set the small, rough table in the kitchen. John ate everything she put on his plate and finished off the potatoes remaining in the bowl. Margaret ate four bites, one of each thing. She didn't respond to his attempts at conversation except in monosyllables. She'd forgotten why she'd married him. Her mind buzzed dully. She couldn't think logically, could only respond mechanically to the physical requirements of cooking and cleaning.

For the first time, John had to wait for dishes to dry. He cleared his throat when she soaped a plate over and over, her rag rubbing in mesmerizing circles. She jumped, glanced at him and dumped the plate in rinse water.

"Maggie?" he said softly.

She couldn't force herself to look at him. Her skin tingled with hypersensitivity, as if any minute she were going to be caressed or slapped. The hair rose on the back of her neck every time she felt John looking at her. She tried to calm herself but could only feel the impending doom approaching her in that front bedroom. Soon, much too soon, they'd be in some state of undress, together, close, his body inside of hers. She thought she was going to scream just thinking about it. And she didn't even understand why she was so very afraid, except that she was sure she was going to be hurt, invaded, left vulnerable, have all her dignity taken away, then be cast aside after.

They finished the dishes and silently stood side by side.

"I don't think there is anything I can say to calm your fears until you see how it's going to be."

Margaret's fingers clamped on the wood of the counter.

"So why don't you go on and get ready for bed," he said softly. She barely nodded and turned away. John watched her leave the room, wondering what had happened to the woman who had tried to bargain with him this morning. His wife looked like a girl, a terrified girl about to be torn to pieces by a gang of marauders.

Margaret made it halfway across her room in the lavender light of evening before the numbness cracked and she sagged to her knees. She reached her bed by crawling. "Oh, God," she whispered, "what have I done?" She tried to pray, but she couldn't. Her mind wouldn't be still; she could find no peace, no center of herself to give to God and she knew why. She'd taken the sacred vows of marriage and wanted to make a mockery of them. She was unwilling to complete the union; she wanted to leave her husband in Bodie when it was convenient for her. She'd repeated words about forever when she planned to use this man to her advantage and leave him. No matter how noble her reasons, she was still a liar. And she planned on seeing to it that this man would subvert the will of God and make sure she did not get pregnant. No wonder she could not pray.

She rose to her feet. Enough with self-pity. She lit a candle. She'd made a bargain and she had to honor it. She undid the top five buttons on her bodice without looking at herself or touching any of her body, only the thick gray cloth and black buttons, just as her mother had taught her. Across the house she heard his footsteps. She froze, looked down at herself, saw the curved neckline of her camisole and the swell of breast beneath. He'd already touched them, she thought, and it hadn't hurt—she hadn't been forever humiliated. She noticed her ringless finger still poised on the sixth button, and regret swept through her that he hadn't bought her a ring. How much did he truly care about her? Oh, he said many pretty words, but she'd lived with his eagerness to bed her for too long to trust a single thing he said. He was right. When they got this out of the way, when she saw how it would be not just during but after, then maybe she could relax her guard.

Ring? Lord, she was a fool. What did she need with a ring when she was so reluctant? Rings were more trappings of the vows and the binds. As if it were yesterday, she could see her mother pointing to her own wedding band and bitterly commenting, *"Makes you a slave. This gives them the right to everything of you. Even if they care for you they can't control themselves. We can only inhibit them so much and then we're pregnant again and again."*

Margaret closed her eyes. John said he could prevent that. But now that she'd given her mother voice she couldn't shut her off, not when the only information she had about the act was in the words her mother had passed down. *"It's so disgustingly messy, Margaret,"* Melissa Warren had confided one teatime the day after her father had gotten his "male needs satisfied." Margaret drank her tea with cream and sugar and her mother had sat across from her in their parlor pouring dark, strong-smelling tonic into her own. *"They turn into hard-breathing animals."* She'd pressed a hand to her generous bust. *"And Lord, but they have a fixation with a woman's chest. I think the lot of them weren't weaned soon enough. What he does to my poor bosom, well, I hope you never have to endure such a thing!"* Margaret had listened in horror, watching her mother pour more tonic into her tea and wondered how she'd face her father over the dinner table. It always took her at least five days after one of her mother's accounts to look her father in the eye again.

Margaret dropped her hands from her bodice. She couldn't bare that part of her yet. He'd only touched her with his hand there, but suppose he wanted to...to...? She swallowed. There was so much she didn't know and she suddenly wished she'd spoken with Elizabeth about what went on in the bedroom, but she'd never thought she would need to know the details.

"Oh, Mother," she moaned. "Why did you tell me all those things? I wouldn't be so childishly scared if I hadn't heard how much you hated it." She sat on the bed and then jumped back up. She'd be there soon enough. She took her hairpins out one by one and listened to her heart pound faster and faster as heavy footsteps came closer and closer.

He knocked. She heard restless shuffling. He knocked again, each rap slower this time. "Come in," she called breathlessly, her hands tightening around hairpins until they skewered her flesh.

John opened the door slowly. He stood in the frame and regarded his wife. He didn't comment that in twenty minutes she'd managed to unbutton five buttons and take her hair down. Instead he said, "You have beautiful hair." He admired the thick chestnut length, shining with a healthy luster in the candlelight. Even in the dim light he could see her blush. He glanced around the room and felt as though he'd be violating her inner sanctum if he stepped inside. He was an intruder. There was nothing of him here, nothing but his masculine body. Behind this closed door she could pretend he didn't exist even after he'd made her his. He didn't want her to be able to put him aside so easily. No, he wanted her seeped in him, who he was, how he felt, his things, his touch, his voice. She'd already invaded his mind, his heart, his present and future. He stepped into the middle of the bedroom, clapped his hands together and said, "Let's do some rearranging!"

She blinked and the vulnerable, young-girl face before him shimmered with the adult woman coming back.

"Let's start by moving the bed to my room."

Her head jerked back. "That room is tiny!"

He shrugged. "Cozy. And we're low on wood, so we'll close this side of the house off. I'll try to get more wood, but everyone else is trying, too. If we use only the small bedroom and the kitchen we might never spend a cold night in Bodie."

"You expect us to live in only two rooms all winter?"

He grinned. She was sounding more like the woman he wanted. "Yeah. What do we need more for?"

"The bed will take up the entire room!"

His grin broadened. "Sounds like my kind of bedroom."

Margaret made an irritated noise between a choke and a gasp.

John rolled up his white shirtsleeves. "Ready?" She shook her head. He cocked his. "Well, maybe we should wait until tomorrow to move furniture and just concentrate on getting to know each other better tonight. It *is* our wedding night."

Margaret had turned to the bed before he finished speaking and grabbed the pillows off the crocheted coverlet. She faced him with her arms full. "Let's get it situated now," she said. "I don't like things waiting to be done."

She strode past him with her armful, ignoring his chuckle, knowing her motives were as obvious as the dress on her body. In the small room off the kitchen she placed her pillows on the desk and sighed. There would be no escape from him in here. She shuddered. That must be what he wanted—her within arm's reach at all times. She folded up the cot and carried it into her father's room. Back in her room she watched John take apart her bed frame. Her crocheted cover was thrown in a chair. The mattress was tilted against the wall. He stood up, saw her, winked. "Want to take an end?" She nodded and they carried it to their new room.

"This desk has to go," he said after they'd set the headboard against the wall.

Margaret was still looking at the headboard. The bed was going to take up three-quarters of the room. She helped him move the desk into her father's room, her muscles straining. She'd started perspiring by the time they finished getting all of the bed moved, but it felt good to be working. Nothing was better for tension than vigorous housework in her estimation. John planted a quick kiss on her cheek when they'd placed the mattress down on the frame. He moved away so fast back to her old bedroom that she didn't have time to get nervous.

"What do you have to have from here?" he asked her when she joined him in her room.

"The dressing table and mirror and the wardrobe."

"The wardrobe will never fit. Have to put it in the kitchen." He carried the vanity by himself and Margaret ran after him with a rug. She rolled it over the small strip of floor next to the bed, under his feet, which he lifted one at a time, and all the way to the wall. He set the table down, looked around and nodded his head. "Cozy," he pronounced. He pulled Margaret up by her hand and led her back to her bedroom, where he brought her hand to his mouth. The kiss grazed her knuckles and sent tingles up Margaret's arm to her throat. She pulled away, but he didn't seem to notice and walked to the big oak wardrobe. He grabbed it with the palms of his hands, almost embracing the article. He gave it a shake. "This one will be tough."

"Let me take my things out first." She stripped the wardrobe bare and carried all the items to the new room and laid them on the bed. Before she got back to John she heard a bang. She ran to the bedroom and saw him with the tilted wardrobe. "Careful! You should have waited for me. You're going to put a dent in it and it's a beautiful piece of furniture!"

John grunted and Margaret ran to the other end and lifted. She did not budge her end off the floor. John's arms were quivering. "Leave it here," she said.

He shook his head. "It's going to be freezing back here."

"So? It'll get full of cooking smells in the kitchen. I'll be dressed in bacon or maple syrup in the morning."

John laughed. "Balance it while I push her back up."

Margaret steadied the heavy piece until it was upright again. Together they shoved it back against the wall. John looked down at her, his hands still on the oak. "You're sure? I can get Danny to help me tomorrow. We could even move it to the parlor so it would be closer but you wouldn't smell like breakfast," he said, grinning.

"I'm sure, but . . . thank you."

He nodded, his eyes never leaving hers. "Thank you for letting me make these changes."

"You're welcome," she said, her gaze dropping for a second to his beautiful mouth, then flying back to his eyes. But his were lowered, fastened on her mouth, and she watched his face descend. This kiss was slower than the last, but soft and warm. She neither retreated nor responded. John started to pull away, got two inches from her, then lowered his mouth again. His mouth opened, hers didn't. He dropped his hands from the wardrobe and brought them around her, but before he touched her she stepped away. "Maggie?" he whispered, taking one step after her.

"I have to put my clothing back in," she said brightly, and turned away, her hair lightly bouncing on her back.

John let his forehead thud against the hard oak wardrobe. He still had quite a bit of work ahead of him. He meant to help carry her clothes, but instead he watched her make three trips back to their room, returning each time with an armful. His eyes never left her as she put everything neatly back into the wardrobe. He feasted on her loose, long hair, which when down made her look young and free, not the strident spinster he'd first met. She'd buttoned up three buttons sometime when he wasn't looking. Now, where she'd left the others undone, he could see the small hollow at the base of her throat that he was dying to kiss. Lust was building in him and he knew he was making her nervous by staring, but he couldn't think of anything else to do except shut his eyes and imagine her as she would be in just a short time, naked and under him. Feeling himself harden, he opened his eyes and watched her shove a hatbox onto the top shelf of the wardrobe. She glanced at him, then shut the doors and moved right away to the chair where her white crocheted coverlet lay bunched. She picked it up and started walking. John jerked out of his trance.

"Wait! Can we use something else on the bed?"

Margaret looked down at the covering she held in her arms. "Why? I made this," she added softly. She'd had it on her bed for the nine years since she'd made it at fifteen. She couldn't imagine sleeping under anything else.

"I can't see myself lying under that frilly thing. Is there something else you've made that would be more suitable for the both of us?"

Margaret's arms tightened on her bundle. This was just too much. Did everything have to change? He was going to get her body, did he have to have everything his own way? She didn't look at him but marched into her father's room and with one hand threw open a trunk on the floor. John was right behind her. He knelt in front of the trunk and picked through the blankets and quilts.

"This is nice," he said of a red one.

"Fine."

"Or how about this?" he said, holding up a white-and-blue one like the one on her father's bed.

"Fine."

He held up a green-and-cream quilt with red flowers. "This?"

"Fine."

He threw it back down and glared at her. "I'm trying to be fair. I just want to compromise."

"I'm not stopping you," she snapped. "Use any you want."

"Margaret—" he ground out the words "—try to understand. I don't want it to look only like your bed. I want it to look different than before. I want it to look like *our* bed."

"I don't think that I'm going to forget that it's *our* bed."

They glared at each other.

"Why did you agree if you can't stand the thought?"

"I'm an idiot!" She jumped up and threw her crocheted cover at him, hitting his face and chest. "I don't care what you use. I will be in that room as seldom as possible!" She stormed out of her father's room and down the hall.

John swore softly and went after her. He caught her by the arm in the middle of the hall and yanked her around to face him. He thrust the crocheted cover into her stomach. "Here! Use it if it's so important!"

She flung it back at him. "No! I wouldn't have it soiled by your body. I don't know why I thought you worthy of it!"

John's mouth gaped open. Margaret strode down the rest of the short hall and into their bedroom, slamming the door behind her.

He stalked up to the closed door, the cover clutched in one fisted hand and dragging on the floor. "You're a real viper when you get down to it!" he shouted through the thin wood. He spun away and made to throw the cover down the hall, but then pulled it back at the last minute. He bunched it up and stuffed it in the trunk in Jeremy's old room. Wadded up in the corner it looked pretty harmless. He shook his head. *Great, Banning,* he thought to himself, *call your wife a viper when you want to seduce her.* He gently touched a forefinger to the edge of one white crocheted flower. This was special to her, but he didn't want to lie under it. It hit him. Virgin white, delicate and feminine, just like herself. And he was going to go into that bedroom and take her, and she didn't want to lie under him. He sighed and pulled out the quilt he wanted, the dark-blue-and-white one, shut the trunk and got a package out of the desk they'd moved in here.

He shut the door between the kitchen and the rest of the small house. He knocked on the bedroom door. No answer. He opened it and saw her sitting on the foot of the bed, brushing her hair and staring at the wall, which her knees were almost flush against. The only place to sit was on the bed. There was no room for a chair between the vanity and the bed. And the small chest of drawers next to the vanity needed all the available room to get a drawer open. He spread his chosen quilt over the bed and then sat on it. The movement bounced her. He removed his boots and dropped them to the floor.

"I'm sorry about calling you a viper," he said quietly. No response. She continued to rhythmically brush her hair. "Can I do that?" he asked softly. Her hand stilled with the brush in her hair. She shook her head and continued brushing. He leaned forward and set his brown-wrapped package next to her hip, nudging her with it. "I bought you a wedding present."

Margaret turned slightly. "You didn't have to do that."

"I know."

"I didn't get you anything." She turned so she could see his face.

He shrugged. "Open it."

Margaret turned more fully toward him and gingerly touched the brown paper. She glanced up at him. He lounged back against her feather pillows, one stockinged foot on the bed, his wrist propped on his bent knee. He neither smiled nor frowned, just met her gaze. She looked back to the gift and slowly untied the twine, then unrolled the paper, which had been wrapped five times around what felt like several objects. Onto the bed the gifts fell, a bottle of perfume, hard candy sticks in every color of the rainbow and a carving knife in a long flat case. "Oh," she sighed, touching the knife handle with her fingertips. Carved in relief were heavy antlered stags. Margaret picked up the knife. Its weight was heavy but not cumbersome. Her fingers tightened around the handle and she lifted the knife to her face. She could see her reflection in the blade, her disheveled hair, her wide eyes. As she brought the knife down to her lap, the blade was pointed up, the tip almost reaching her chin. What a strange gift.

"Thank you," she said softly. "I do like it. And perfume... I've never gotten..." She didn't want to confess that no one had ever bought her perfume. She laid the knife across her lap and unscrewed the top of the perfume bottle and sniffed. Violets and spice rose around her and she closed her eyes. She wet her finger with the scent and put some behind her ears the way she'd seen her mother do. Not looking up at John, she touched more to the hollow of her throat the way she'd seen Elizabeth do. She felt her cheeks heat with a blush.

John could not smile. He was devastated just watching her. When she broke off a piece of cherry candy and pushed it into her mouth, his restraint snapped. He lowered his hands to the bed and crawled to where she sat, again holding the knife pointed up. Inches away he stared down into her eyes. She didn't look scared, she looked powerful, as though he should be scared. He touched his nose to hers, then nudged his nose against her lips. She didn't flinch. Slowly, still on hands and knees like a supplicant before a shrine, he pressed his lips to hers. He courted her with soft, gentle kisses until his arms trembled. When he opened his mouth she yielded her lips to his tongue. He felt the prick of the knife point under his chin and froze, not knowing if he'd lowered his head while kissing her or if she had purposefully poked him. He waited, unmoving, his tongue in her mouth, the sweet cherry taste of her and her perfumed scent surrounding him. The knife pricked again. He winced and pulled away, sitting back on his heels. There was a light in her eyes, which were more green than blue tonight. A small drop of blood glistened, on the point of the knife, but John didn't mind that she'd hurt him, that she looked a little wild. She wasn't cold or terrified. He wiped the blood from the small cut under his chin with the back of his hand.

Margaret's eyes narrowed as she watched. She was surprised he wasn't angry with her. She was scared no longer. And she wasn't sorry she had pricked him, though she did not understand why she had. It seemed only fair somehow, since he was going to hurt her as he took her virginity. She wiped the blood from the knife onto the brown paper with a graceful swipe. "Turn out the lamp," she said softly when she'd finished. Let's do it now, she thought, while I don't know who I am.

Chapter Nine

John turned out the bedroom lamp but left the lighted one on the kitchen table. Its soft glow illuminated their room. He wasn't going to make love to her for the first time in total darkness.

When he came back to the bedroom, Margaret had placed her gifts on the vanity and had taken her boots off. She was sitting on the bed, unbuttoning her bodice, and didn't look up at him but pushed her dress down her arms while she listened to the rustle of his clothing coming off. She stood and slipped the dress over her hips and legs, not rushing, but not hesitating. When she sat again in the stillness a spasm of fear that he might be already naked and watching her quaked through her briefly. She reached under her petticoat and pulled down her drawers and stockings without baring herself to him. At the same time she peeked across the floor, her hanging hair hiding her eyes, and saw his naked feet and calves. Icy fear squeezed her stomach. This wouldn't be the end of her, she reassured herself. She reached behind her and untied her corset, pulled it off, set it on the heap of her clothes. Never did she leave her clothes in a pile like this, but she wasn't about to walk past a stark naked man and hang them up. Feeling sufficiently disrobed, she yanked the covers down on the bed and crawled in, pulling them over her. Her eyes shut tightly before her head landed on the pillow.

"Move over," he said quietly.

"I want this side." She didn't want to be pressed up against the wall.

She'd asked for it, she told herself as he pulled the covers down and she felt the cool air touch her. The bed sunk as he climbed over her, only he stopped directly above her, one knee bracing each of her hips, his hands sliding under her shoulders but his body not touching hers. Her eyes flickered open and saw his broad, naked shoulders and his lowered head as he looked down at her. She squeezed them shut again and held her breath. She shuddered with relief when she felt him roll to the side of her, but then he reached for her, his naked, hot body coming against her. His arms went around her, turning her on her side, and his legs slid down hers, wrapping her icy feet against his calves. He rubbed his cheek against her nose. Reflexively she pulled her forearms up against her chest and her heart thundered.

John pulled his face away and looked into her eyes in the dim light streaming from the kitchen. His hand lifted to her breast and felt the pounding of her heart. "So scared," he whispered.

She didn't want to be frightened anymore. She wanted to feel brave and strong. Fear made her more vulnerable to him. Then his lips were against hers, soft and brief. He kissed her nose and her forehead and rubbed his lips back and forth against her cheek. His hand moved from her back and discovered the dramatic dip of her waist and the rise of her hip.

"Relax. I want to please you. I don't want to hurt you."

Her enjoyment was the last thing she was worried about. If she made it through this without total degradation she would be content. He smoothed his thumb across her cheek and she looked into his eyes. He smiled briefly and slid his hand into her hair. Her bunched hands in front of her effectively worked to keep him from getting any closer. He left off stroking her hair and curled his hand around her throat, resting his fingers over her pulse point. The weight of his hand eased and then the tips of his fingers lightly circled her lips. "Maggie, look at me."

When she opened her eyes she saw he was worried. He took up one of her tightly fisted hands and kissed the knuckles. "What we're going to do is right and natural. We're going to join our bodies as we did our lives when we said our marriage vows." She glanced away from him, but he took her chin until she looked back. "This will bind me to you," he said hoarsely.

Margaret again looked away. She couldn't concentrate on a word he was saying. Why didn't he just do it? He was too close and he was going to get closer, closer than anyone had ever been to her. She was having a hard time breathing. All he did was demand for her to look at him again.

"Why?" she asked, panic in her voice.

He frowned and sat up, pulling her to sit beside him. "Talk to me, Maggie. Tell me why you're so scared."

"I don't want to talk about it. Just do it, but don't insist I speak of it. I don't want to hear about it anymore!" She lifted her shaking hand to her forehead, but the gesture didn't ease her dizziness. He was staring at her, his eyes so dark and probably condemning.

"All right, no more talk." He pushed her down. The blanket rested about her hips. He dropped his hand to her belly and rubbed a slow circle. She looked down at his hand, tanned brown skin against stark white camisole, and swallowed. When she looked up at his face she saw a growing tautness around his mouth. He met her gaze and she felt the heat of his eyes pierce her. It was happening now.

His hand kneaded. Margaret flinched and he relentlessly stroked her up between her breasts and slowly covered one pointed fullness. She stiffened and stared at the ceiling while he squeezed with one hand, then both. Was she unusual or did all women feel this stabbing heat when their husbands made circles around their nipples?

He eased down beside her and pressed his long length against her side. "You *feel* beautiful," he whispered into her neck. Margaret closed her eyes. She wished he wouldn't compliment her so. The words made her dizzier yet. He nuzzled her neck and she forced herself to remain still and not turn away. When his tongue tingled across her flesh she clamped her lips together. His thumbnail flicked her distended nipple and she whimpered. He kissed her slowly, thoroughly, with his hot mouth. Under the assault her face heated and the warmth spread downward. She didn't like the fact that he was making her feel things. She didn't want to feel anything for him but respect. She didn't know what these other feelings were, but she was sure if she gave into them she'd be weak and at his mercy. When he was back in the saloon he'd laugh about the woman waiting for him at home, needing him. She wanted to shove him away and jump out of this bed that used to be her bed and was now supposed to be their bed. He pulled away from her and regarded her mutinous glare.

"If you don't like me inside your mouth, how are you going to tolerate me inside your body?" His hand slid under the blanket and pressed her pelvis.

She flinched. "I didn't know it was a requisite that I enjoy this," she hissed.

His hand remained on that unnerving part of her and he glared at her, his face inches from her nose. "No, but you could try. You keep looking at me like you want to kill me."

She made her face a perfect blank. "Is this better?"

He abruptly backed away. "No." He sat up, his wide, smooth back to her, and drew up one knee. "Look, I don't know exactly what you're so scared of. And I've never been with a virgin, so I can't say how much it will hurt, but I promise I'll make better whatever pain I cause." He turned, braced one palm on the mattress and looked at her. "I've never hurt a woman in my life," he said softly. "Not in bed."

Margaret glanced at him and then away. That there had been many other women was obvious. For some insane reason it bothered her to think of him with them.

"And," he added, bounding over her and out of bed, "you've got the knife." He opened the case and slid the knife under her pillow, then lay back down by her side. "Just stick it in my back if it gets to be too much. But watch how deep you stab—this is a hanging town."

He slipped his arm under her neck and with a hand on her hip rolled her to him once again. He combed his fingers up and down the tightness on either side of her spine, leaving in their wake muscles loosened and warm. She felt herself losing her separateness from him as their bodies melded. His hand slid farther down and clasped her bottom. Margaret bit her lip when she felt the hot, hard outline of his maleness against her belly. She arched back into his hand while his mouth covered hers, still gentle, though his tongue licked with increasing frequency at her lips. Slowly, inexorably, the hand on her bottom pulled her closer until she was caught tight between his hardness and his hand and could feel nothing else. His arm tightened under her neck, his hand dropping on her shoulder. She was amazed his mouth remained gentle when every other part of him was hardening and tightening around her. She pushed against his hand as the lesser of two evils, and he pulled her back, only to let her push away again so he could meet her with a thrust of his hips. He turned his mouth from her and rubbed his cheek against hers. Margaret understood she was giving him pleasure. She went completely still. John chuckled in her ear and lifted his hand from her bottom.

Relief coursed through her until she felt his hot hand on her calf, slowly sliding up beneath her petticoat. She went rigid as he continued up her naked thigh and cupped her bottom again. Her face had become buried in his neck and she burrowed deeper as he kneaded her soft flesh. Lord, but his hot arms around her felt good, so strong. She could picture her mother's disgusted expression when she talked about sex; she knew she should be disgusted, and she tried hard, even missing what John was murmuring into her ear. His hand slipped behind her knee and he lifted her leg. He set it down over his hip and she gasped at the feel of his hot, naked skin. His palm returned through her parted thighs to her bottom, and she felt how vulnerably close her private parts were to his hand. She guessed his intention and her suspicions were too much. She began to struggle, but his arm beneath her neck cinched tight and his grip on her bottom hardened.

"Easy, easy, easy," he breathed against her ear.

Margaret stilled but remained as tense as a crowbar. His touch on her bottom lightened and, just as she dreaded, his hand slipped downward. The barest touch of his knuckles passed over the God-given covering of hair. They passed again and again, each time a little closer to the shrinking flesh below, until his knuckles finally pressed into the place she didn't have a name for. Margaret's head snapped back and she gave a moaning cry.

John bent his forehead to her chin. "My wife," he said. Margaret choked as his hand spread and covered her from hard pubic bone to soft, curving flesh. "I want to love you, every bit of you, not hurt or humiliate you." His hand began to move on her and she shuddered. His mouth took hers again, still gentle, and she twisted her face away, wishing he would hurt her so she could resist. "I love how you feel everything," he said throatily. In further illustration his finger slipped down over an acutely sensitive spot between her thighs and she cried out. His finger moved farther and circled the womanly entrance of her.

Margaret reached down and grabbed his forearm. "Please, don't." His eyes scanned her face and she felt burned, but he smiled gently and pulled his hand from between her thighs. With her eyes locked to his, she lifted her leg off him and he let her go. He pulled his arm from beneath her and propped his head on his hand. Margaret stared up at him warily. She didn't like the strange, satisfied smile he wore. She was feeling more comfortable, her body cooling off now that he wasn't touching her, but that didn't last.

His hand rose and touched her breast while his eyes remained on her face. She looked away when he plucked her nipple through her camisole. He rolled it between thumb and finger, and Margaret bit her lip and clutched her pillow. Arrows of sensation shot down her body into the place he'd touched between her thighs. She shifted to ease the feelings, but John left her breast and again lifted her petticoat, his hand cupping what she was trying to protect. His mouth came down on hers, hard and brief. He invaded her body with a finger and then brought his hand to his mouth. She watched in wide-eyed worry as he wet his finger. "Jus to ease things a bit,'' he whispered. His hand descended once again and then she felt wet fingers nudging her as his mouth covered hers, his tongue thrusting in now as his fingers pushed below. Her fingers curled into the bed and she arched her back up and her head down trying to escape both invasions. She began to count to one hundred to distract herself from what was so alien, so troubling in pleasurable sensation. She faltered at twenty when his hand slipped away and he stopped kissing her, only to roll on top of her. Twenty, twenty, twenty, she cried to herself, hearing him tell her to relax as if from a distance.

He nuzzled her breasts through the white cotton. ''Can I take this off?'' She shook her head vehemently. He opened and closed his mouth over one taut nipple. Her body rocked beneath his as he suckled her. ''Oh, stop!'' she wailed. He did, and rose above her. She buried her hand under her pillow and closed her fingers around the ivory-handled knife. She struggled to get control of herself. Thousands of women did this. She was acting like a child. Whether it was degrading or not, painful or not, she could endure it. Slowly, she opened her eyes.

''Trust me,'' he whispered.

She did not respond, just stared at him with huge eyes.

''Oh, Maggie,'' he sighed.

Margaret stared at the deeply shadowed ceiling as he pushed her petticoat up over her hips until the garment bunched around her waist. His hand kneaded the inside of her thigh, slowly pushing her legs farther apart. Margaret lay still for fifteen seconds, which she counted off in her head, then she shoved her petticoat down and snapped her legs together until they hit his bare, hot skin.

John looked up at her. His eyes had gone black. Margaret met his gaze defiantly, but he didn't seem to mind. He trailed a finger from her knee, up her thigh, pushing the petticoat before him. "You're beautiful everywhere," he whispered. The deep, hoarse voice sounded different than his. Margaret flinched as the finger traveled up her belly. Then his whole hand spread out over her hip and he moved over her. He rested his elbows on either side of her face and his hands played in her hair. He was heavy and hot, his eyes too intense. His mouth lowered and he trailed soft kisses down across one cheek, to her mouth and across the other cheek, while his hardness bumped her below. "This won't always hurt." He kissed her deeply, but he couldn't distract her from the pushing invasion that began below. She felt herself stretching, unexpected pleasure opening her mouth wide and arching her neck up, but quickly there was an uncomfortable pressure. "No other way," she heard him whisper. He thrust through the barrier and she cried out.

"Is it bad?" he asked, deeply imbedded but still.

"Don't talk." She forced the words out, feeling overwhelmed by the physical intimacy.

He rolled to his side, keeping them joined, her leg pulled over his hip. Her eyes opened in surprise. "I won't go as deep this way," he explained breathlessly.

Margaret found the sensation less disagreeable immediately. Though he continued to thrust, the shredding pain was gone. Only an ache and a burning remained, and she was spared the heavy, dominating weight of his body. He quickly pulled out of her and rolled her almost to her back again, rubbing his hardness on her belly. He groaned and she felt wetness against her skin. It took her a few seconds of agonized calculation before she guessed what he'd deposited on her stomach, though what he'd done was better than getting her pregnant, she reasoned.

When John lifted his head from where he'd been cradled in her neck, he looked down the length of her naked legs. He pulled the covers up over her and bent to kiss her.

His mouth was affectionate, soft, a thank-you without words. That more than anything softened Margaret and she felt like a shrew and helpless to be any other way. He reached over her to the floor and snatched up a kitchen towel that he must have brought from the kitchen. He began to wipe her off, but she grabbed it from him. "I'll do it."

He lay down beside her while Margaret discreetly took care of herself under the covers. She held the soiled towel between her thumb and forefinger. She couldn't take this to the Chinese laundry. She climbed out of bed, knowing John watched her curiously, and stashed the towel in a basket in the kitchen to deal with later.

She thought he was asleep when she crawled in beside him, but his arm looped over her waist as soon as she lay down with her back to him. She didn't try to remove his arm, because, as miserable as she felt because of him, he also gave her the only comfort she could find.

He should be satisfied for at least a week, maybe two, even a month. She felt desolate. This mating had caused something to crack inside her and she knew she would never be the same. She was bound to him in some elemental way that she had not anticipated. She could never look at him and not think of this, of his body joined with hers, so deep inside. Maybe he'd have some power over her that she would be unable to fight. Why else had her mother continued to let her father come to her? Why did Elizabeth let Danny in her bed when he was a terrible husband, unless somehow this act enslaved a woman to the man? She clasped her hands together and prayed for understanding. She hadn't been so scared in a long, long time. Not to know what was right or wrong anymore was devastating. This night had shaken the foundations of her beliefs. John had been gentle and kind. Was it her duty to resist and to hate it as she'd been taught? She had, but why did she feel small and cold and unfeeling? Why did she feel less than sacred for trying to be so honorable and pure?

Margaret did not sleep that first night of her marriage. She was up at two-thirty stirring oatmeal on the stove for John's breakfast before he left for the mine. Maybe if she cooked all day she wouldn't have to think a single thought about what was really bothering her. John came up behind her in the warm kitchen and put his hands on her waist, turned her around and kissed her soundly on the mouth. "Good morning, wife."

Margaret blushed and turned back to the oatmeal.

"I'll be going to the saloon after the mine."

She faced him, still holding her spoon. A glob of oatmeal dropped to the floor. "Why?"

"I want to look at the books." He poured himself a cup of coffee. "Don't worry, I won't stay long," he said, giving her a cocky smile.

"The saloon," she grumbled, despairing that the reason he'd married her had to be made obvious so soon, and disappointed that she cared. "So, you're going to do both? The mine and the saloon?" she asked, retreating behind snappishness.

He nodded.

"How will that be possible?" He did not answer her. "I think you should quit the mine, sell the saloon, go back to being a carpenter and teach Danny the trade, as well."

He shook his head and pulled on his coat. Going to the mine was his penance. He hated the dark, cold, damp tunnel he heaved a pick in but with each swing of the hard wood handle he chipped away at the guilt he had for killing his father. And each time he lighted a round of charges down in the earth, the risk to his own life seemed just. His aversion to going back to the trade of carpentry that his pa had taught him was still too strong.

"I heard that a man was crushed in the Jupiter mine last week," Margaret said softly.

"Yeah, and he was a carpenter working on the timbering."

"I'm just saying that it's not safe down there. There are fires and cave-ins and explosions."

He buttoned his coat, holding her gaze. "Wifely concern?" he asked. She lifted her chin. He grinned. She couldn't help herself; she had to be concerned about everyone's welfare if she thought them under her jurisdiction. "I'm glad to see that last night hasn't left you wishing me dead."

Margaret flushed. "Why do you have your coat on? You haven't eaten your breakfast yet!"

"I appreciate your getting up, but I can't eat this early and at least one of us needs a full night of sleep."

"Will you be home for supper?"

"Definitely." He hauled her against him and kissed her hard. After picking up the food she'd packed in a tin for him, he slammed out of the house. Margaret stared after him.

Chapter Ten

Margaret went back to bed after John left, but couldn't sleep. She rose with the sun and made *their* bed. The sheets needed changing before anything; she scrubbed out the blood herself. She could make do with one less petticoat, so she threw away her blood-smeared one. Then it was time to straighten, mop, dust and oil the wood in her two rooms. It was still morning when she finished. She'd have plenty of time to sew if she only had to keep two rooms up.

As she passed through the parlor to change her soiled skirt she noticed the hastily bought wedding gifts from her father and Elizabeth on a small table. She hesitated. Should she wait for John? She decided not to. Her father had gotten them a tablecloth—the same gift he'd gotten her seven times in her life for various occasions. Elizabeth had purchased pillowcases and had embroidered the date of their wedding on them in red thread. Margaret changed her pillows on the bed into them and felt pleased that her sister had taken the time, especially considering what little of it there had been.

Elizabeth knocked on the front door later, while Margaret was working on a baby quilt for her. Margaret opened the door and sighed at the gleam of curiosity in her sister's eyes. "Are you hungry?" she asked, leading her sister into the warm kitchen. She fed Elizabeth a big lunch and sat across from her, watching her eat while she herself nibbled on a piece of bread. Elizabeth looked big for six months along. She also looked tired and a little sallow. "How are you feeling?"

Elizabeth shrugged. "I ache sometimes. I wondered if I could borrow a pillow. I'm not as comfortable at night."

"Of course you can."

"You seem fine. Not at all different. You're just as assured and organized as always."

"Why shouldn't I be?"

"I thought maybe the consummation of your marriage would loosen you up a bit," Elizabeth said.

Margaret lifted her teacup. Did she hide things so well that her sister could not see that she felt raw and confused? "You sound as if you want me to be unhappy."

Elizabeth sighed. She looked down at her belly. "I'm sorry. I want company in my misery. I'm losing my shape. I thought you could lose your starch. Is John happy then?"

"I didn't ask him."

"You couldn't just tell?"

Margaret got up abruptly and cleared the table of the lunch and tea dishes. "I don't exactly know what to look for. He seemed . . . satisfied."

"Was it all right, then? I was truly worried. I hoped he'd be real nice. Mag?"

Margaret gripped the sides of the drawer she had opened, feeling dizzy from the concern in Elizabeth's voice. Her mother had always said Elizabeth was a silly and stupid girl. Margaret had always added "nice" to herself after her mother's words. But maybe Elizabeth wasn't such a ninny. She knew about men and women together. She knew what love was, at least some form of it. Oh, she wanted to turn and pull up a chair next to her sister and ask her every troubled question that was tormenting her. But she didn't. How did you break the habit of being an older sister? She'd always told Elizabeth what to do and when and how and why. She'd always known everything.

When Margaret did turn she appeared not to have heard Elizabeth's intimate questions. "Do you want that pillow now or would you like to go to the market with me first?"

"The market. You can help me buy for the meals I have to make without you," she said, smiling, the teasing light back in her eyes.

Elizabeth dragged Margaret into a jewelry store, a dressmaker's and Boone and Wright's General Merchandise to look at glassware. Their boots were soaked from crossing slushy streets and the wind had whipped a blush into their cheeks. Outside the market, they watched some of the town's children slip and slide and shriek on the ice slick at the lower end of Main Street where water from the Booker and Mono mines had pooled and frozen.

"In a couple of years mine will be out there," Elizabeth said softly. "Another year after that and you and John will have one trying to keep his balance on that ice."

Margaret flicked her gaze from the ice to her sister's dreamy expression. "I don't plan on being in Bodie that long."

"Oh? Does John know this?"

"He certainly does."

Elizabeth shrugged. "I'm happy wherever Danny is. I'll live here the rest of my life if he wants to."

Margaret's mouth turned down as she regarded her sister. "You'll probably have to, since he won't ever have the funds to start someplace else."

"We'll always have what we need."

"Well, I'll come visit you occasionally. Let's do that marketing, shall we?"

Margaret walked her sister home, helped her put away her food purchases and made her a cup of tea before she left for her own house.

"Mag?" Elizabeth called as Margaret pulled on her coat. "Now that John is going to help in the saloon, I thought Danny would be able to come home more. Do you think you could have John send him home when he's not needed?"

"Yes, I'll make sure he does that."

Margaret kissed Elizabeth's soft cheek and walked home in the wind, which helped push her along. She baked gingerbread during the cold gray afternoon. When a light snow began to fall, she was snug and warm in her fragrant kitchen. To leave her body unconfined, she wore her oldest, loosest house dress and no corset, since she was still a little sore from her wedding night. She planned on being polite and friendly when John came home for dinner, as if nothing had happened. But when he stomped in the door early, right after the three o'clock shift, shaking snow off, her body went quivery and she couldn't meet his eyes.

"I thought you were going to the saloon after the mine," she said, turning back to the counter she'd been scrubbing.

John doffed his cap and hooked it on the tree he'd moved from the parlor to the kitchen. "I wanted to see you first."

Margaret scrubbed harder, every nerve in her body vibrating with his presence. Why did he fill the room like no other man or woman she'd ever known? "How was your day?" she asked with false brightness.

"Nice. I thought about you most of the time."

Margaret glanced at him. He was shrugging out of his coat and she couldn't see his eyes. "I'll have dinner ready soon. I didn't expect you yet." He looked at her as if *she* were dinner and he were starving. Why did he have to be so handsome in his red flannel shirt?

Margaret snatched up a pot holder and retreated from him to the stove. She got very busy testing the gingerbread and pulling it out while ignoring John standing behind her. She set the pan on the stove and moved the saucer of butter to a warm portion at the back to soften. He put his hands on her hips and she straightened. "Smells good," he said, nuzzling her neck. Margaret pushed his hands off, but they came back, around her waist this time, circling until his arms wrapped around her and he hugged her tight against him. "Let's go to the bedroom," he said against her ear.

She pulled at his arms, but his hands moved up and cupped her breasts.

"I'm hard as a pickax handle from thinking of you all day and how you felt last night."

She tugged at his arms, but they didn't budge. "John, be reasonable! It's afternoon. And we already did . . ."

One of his hands tightened on her breast, the other pressed down into her pelvis. "I don't feel reasonable." He pulled her back against him. "I know you can't feel anything through all these clothes, but believe me, I need you. Turn around," he whispered, his hands squeezing and rubbing her belly and breasts.

"No!"

He lifted her skirts, passing his hand underneath. She stepped to the side, but John grasped her stockinged thigh. He straightened and pressed close, slid one hand around her hip and cupped her woman's flesh. Her skirts were bunched around her waist in back of her and her bottom pressed against his groin. Now she could feel his hardness. She had to pull up her own skirts in front to reach the hand that held her so intimately. When she grabbed his fingers he was rubbing his palm against her. Briefly, halfheartedly, she tried to tug him away, but the feel of his hard warm fingers in her sweaty hand unnerved her.

John unbuttoned his trousers and underwear with his left hand then inserted that hand under her skirts and tore open her drawers.

Shocked, Margaret went completely still. "John?"

"Yeah?" he said innocently.

Margaret went speechless, watching his hand until it disappeared under her dress. She braced for pain, but his touch was so light it tickled, then soothed, and never hurt. He wedged his knee between her thighs, preventing her from closing her legs. She winced as his finger slowly penetrated her, but the shock was the instant pleasure. Then he barely touched a point of immense sensation and she jerked against him, but his finger continued to caress that spot until she quivered and gasped.

"Turn around, Maggie."

She'd do anything to get away from that hand. But when she pivoted around, she didn't recognize him. His face was flushed and strained, his eyes half-closed.

"This is obscene," she hissed.

He ripped her drawers farther so he could circle his hands on her naked hips, then grasped her leg and pulled it up high over his hip. "That a man wants his wife? That she obliges him?"

"That they do it standing up over a stove!"

"At least we're warm." He opened his mouth over hers and guided himself into her body. Margaret inhaled through clenched teeth as her body stretched until he was buried deep. There was a slight burning as he moved back and forth, but the discomfort didn't obliterate the pleasure of his flesh gliding within her. She gripped his arms and squeezed her eyes shut, fighting the inclination to wrap her

arms around him. She wished he'd praise her with sweet
compliments as he had last night, even though she knew it
was weakness on her part to crave those words. His sudden withdrawal came as a shock to her, and the feeling of
his long, hot length against the underside of her thigh as he
gripped her leg and strained against her only heightened her
sense of loss. He buried his face in her neck, his breathing
labored, then eased her leg down and loosely hung his arms
around her hips.

"You must think me an animal," he whispered hoarsely.

Margaret was forcing herself to think of a confirming
response when there was a loud knock. They stiffened, their
heads turning in unison to stare at the door.

The knock came again and they heard Danny calling for
John. Margaret pushed her skirts down and shoved John
away.

"Of all the bad times," he grumbled.

"Why? You've finished!"

He looked at her regretfully. She strode past him to the
bedroom and slammed the door, only to lean against it and
bow her head. She would be eternally grateful for Danny's
interruption. She went to the washstand and lifted her skirts
to clean herself. Her flesh was tender and still burned with
a heat that went deep. She washed her hands and face and
put on clean drawers. The ones he'd ripped would have to
be mended; she didn't have such a supply of clothes she
could toss a garment out each time they had relations. She
stood uncertainly in the room and heard her husband and
brother-in-law talking about the saloon. What else?

Margaret sat on the bed and looked in her dressing table
mirror. That was a mistake. Her eyes reflected turmoil and
shame. She was in danger. Not only did she live with a man
she couldn't seem to control, but she herself was exhibit-
ing behavior that was incongruous with being the lady she

thought herself. She looked away from her bright eyes and vividly remembered the pleasant glide of his body into hers. Why had she stood there and let him do that to her? Some dark, vile part of her had wanted to see if he would really do it, and how much he desired her, and what it would feel like, and if it would stop this swollen disturbance she'd had between her thighs ever since the first time. She jumped up and paced, damning herself with each step until her thoughts came solely from her head and the rest of her body was silenced and numb. She stopped pacing abruptly and straightened, clenched her teeth and walked back into the kitchen, her shoulders tensed. Danny was gone. John sat at the table reading a newspaper, the pan of ginger-bread in front of him half-eaten. He looked up at her over the page he was reading.

"Are you okay?"

"Of course. Are you hungry for dinner?"

He followed her glance to the cake. "Danny had some, too. It was good," he said a little defensively. She glared at him and he looked back to his paper. A headache began with a dull throb behind her eyes.

"And yeah, I still want supper," he said. "I wouldn't miss a meal the best cook in Bodie made."

Margaret jerked open the oven door and took out the baked ham and little potatoes. She kicked the door shut and slammed the pan on the top of the stove.

"Are you going to the saloon tonight?"

He kept reading and answered absently, "No. Think I'll go to bed with you instead."

Margaret's headache took a sudden turn for the worse. Did he plan on doing it again? The thought of another performance made the disturbed heat in her body flare. She advanced on John where he sat reading, his hand filching more cake.

"I won't be used every time your base urges come upon you."

John looked up, his hand still in the gingerbread.

"And that cake was for dessert, not an appetizer!" With a snap of her arm she sent the pan flying off the table. John watched it bang against the pinewood floor and skid into the wall. He looked back up at her flushed face.

"Anything else?" he asked blandly.

"Yes," she hissed. "Don't touch me again tonight."

"Okay."

"And don't ever force me again!"

"I don't remember you resisting."

Margaret felt her face flame hotly. "I said no somewhere!"

"If I stopped every time you said no, we'd never do it."

She swiped the paper out of his hands and slapped it onto the table. "I said I was willing to be your wife! You'd just better ask my permission and honor my refusals."

John looked down at his newspaper and stood up. "I think you need a hot soak." He stepped around her trembling body and set the big pail of water on the stove. She glared at him.

"I don't need you to tell me when to bathe."

"I'm not speaking of washing but of soaking. I'm sure you're the sweetest smelling lady in Bodie."

"If you think I'm going to bathe in front of you to provide your evening entertainment, you're sadly mistaken."

He lifted the tin tub from the wall and set it in front of the stove. "I'm going to the saloon, after all. You have a few hours alone to soak your sore body and your sorer pride."

"My pride?" she screeched, ignoring his reference to her body.

He picked up the water buckets by the door. "Don't worry about serving me dinner. I'll be back with more water."

A cold blast of air hit Margaret in the face before he banged the door shut behind him. She kicked the tub, wishing it was her husband. She didn't want a bath. No, she wanted to slap his face, scream Bible verses at him and throw his dinner on him. Instead, she paced. She was not going to take a bath. When he came back in she glared at him over crossed arms while he poured the water into pots on the stove.

"You wasted your time. I'm not going to use it."

"Then you'll be wasting your time, too. Alone." Margaret scowled. John set the buckets down and went to drop a few potatoes into a white cloth and carve himself a thick piece of warm ham, which he stuck between two pieces of bread. He pulled down the vanilla from the shelf and poured a little into one of the pails on the stove. Margaret's eyes widened and he winked at her before he left the house.

"I'm not getting in," she said to the empty room, which smelled sweetly of vanilla. She wrapped the ham up and put it away. She wasn't hungry. The first pail of water began to simmer. She pulled out the baby quilt and began stitching. She leaned back in her chair and tried to get comfortable. Her back was so tense that she had shooting pains up her neck. Steam rose from the pots. He wasn't going to bother her tonight, but he probably would again in the morning. Did he just want her to "soak" her soreness away so he could use her without her complaining? What if she was perfectly recovered and still told him how much she hated it? She jumped up and dumped the hot water into the tub, setting one pail aside to rinse with. He wasn't going to be able to blame her reluctance on pain.

* * *

In the small office Jeremy had partitioned off in the corner of the saloon, John changed out of his flannel shirt and into a white shirt and black pants. Behind the bar he tied a white apron around his waist. Jeremy slapped him on the back. "Missed you last night." He winked.

John felt himself flush. That Jeremy could refer to the intimacies he'd engaged in with the man's own daughter embarrassed him, especially when Jeremy knew how reluctant his bride was.

Dexter, a regular, grinned across the bar at him. "Heard double congratulations are in order. A wedding and half-owner of this here saloon." He tossed two bits on the counter. "Have one on me." Several other regulars sidled forward with voices of encouragement.

Danny set a bottle of whiskey in front of John. "They treated me last night."

John could tell from the bloodshot eyes of his brother-in-law that the drinks had been well accepted. "Thank you, gentlemen. I don't imbibe behind the bar, but I'll accept a cigar instead." He got six cigars of the very best that night.

Later, after Jeremy had retired to his hotel room, John pulled out the cushioned chair in the small office. The shouts and laughter and drone of talk met no barrier in the thin wall separating him from the sight of the customers. He dropped the account books on the top of the desk and watched the dust fly. Jeremy had asked him to look over the books, get familiar with how much money came and went through the saloon and make the last day's entries. John suspected Jeremy didn't want to bother with the job himself anymore and wasn't convinced Danny was capable. With a sharp thrill John finally acknowledged the fact that he had the most control of the saloon. With his fifty percent ownership, he outweighed both Jeremy's and Danny's twenty-five. He didn't ever have to return to carpentry or his brother.

The cover of the top book was stained with some kind of alcohol. Beneath the bar was not the best place for the books, but Jeremy had stashed them there, where it was convenient for him to pull them out and get a general accounting. John pushed the lamp to the back of the desk, seated himself and opened the top book somewhere in the middle. He turned a few pages and noted the neat handwriting of Jeremy's entries, every purchase accounted for, everyday's receipts accounted for. And then in October, Danny's haphazard entries started, the receipts down, probably because he spent his share of the money before he entered it. John sighed. He was going to have to talk to Danny. He scratched his cheek and yawned. He'd rather imagine how Margaret would look in her bath. She'd be naked, tinged pink from the heat. Would her hair be down and wet or piled on her head? He would have to restrain his impatience with her and try some slow wooing. He shook his head. She wouldn't indulge him in lingering kisses and touches even if it meant she'd like the latter part of lovemaking better. In fact, she especially wouldn't indulge him for that very reason.

He sat up straight and dipped his pen in the ink. He looked at the pencil scratches Danny had made on a piece of paper and started entering. Book work was not his favorite thing to do. His brother, Pat, or his mother had done it for the family business, though John had been instructed and thoroughly tested in it. John, like his pa, had preferred to work with their customers, going over house details, which some people were apt to want to change everyday. Patiently, John or his pa would rework the plans, advise, listen, reassure. They both also liked getting up on the building frame and doing the actual constructing, while Pat stood back and watched and inspected and directed. John sighed again, longer and louder this time. He bet Pat was hurting back in the City with Pa and him gone, working with hired men, not able to trust them the way he did his family. Ma was probably doing all the book work unless Amy, Pat's wife, had taken some on. She must be about six months pregnant now, same as Elizabeth. They didn't know he was married or owned a saloon because he hadn't written them yet. If he did, his mother would probably take the next stage out to inspect his bride. He gritted his teeth. That's all he needed. Margaret and his mother would probably take to each other like coffee and cream, and then he'd have two bossy women to contend with. They'd not meet until he was ready. He dipped his pen again and got to work so he could go home and sleep with his wife.

Margaret was wide-awake in the dark bedroom when John came home. She'd tried desperately to fall asleep before he returned. The bath had done wonders for her tense, tender body and she'd been sure sleep would come quickly. But knowing he would come back and crawl under the covers anytime kept her on edge. She didn't move a muscle where she lay on the far side of the bed as he came in, listening to every rustle as he removed his clothes.

He lifted the covers and slid in beside her, his chest and stomach pressing her back, his loins and thighs curving around her backside. He slid an arm under her neck and tucked one around her waist. Sighing in her hair, he rubbed his foot along her calf. Then he fell very still, his breath even and deep.

Margaret's eyes remained wide open. Lord, he was warm! She'd never spend another cold, shivering night if she slept with him. Slowly, her back relaxed into his hard chest and her eyes closed. "Mmm, you feel good against me," he said softly, his arm tightening. Margaret's eyes flew open. "Did you enjoy your bath?" She stiffened in his arms. "Don't worry, I'm not going to use you, as you so romantically put it." He rubbed his arm reassuringly against her stomach.

His question hung between them. "Yes, I enjoyed the bath," she whispered.

"Good," he said against the back of her head. Then his arm grew heavy on her waist.

After hours of wakefulness, Margaret was surprised at how quickly she became drowsy, and admitted it was his presence that spread warmth and an unfamiliar security into her limbs, her mind, her heart.

Chapter Eleven

John was gone when Margaret awoke. She listened to the wind blow against the house and lay in bed remembering the feel of his arm around her as she'd fallen asleep. Had her mother enjoyed that part of marriage? The warmth of sleeping together? She'd never mentioned it.

Margaret made her weekly trek to the post office, hoping for a letter, and was rewarded with her first one from Victoria. She sat at her kitchen table with a pot of tea and read two pages of her sister's happiness with her husband and their new home and furnishings. She imagined Victoria would be pleased when she wrote to tell her of her marriage. She got some paper from her cold, closed-up room and sat back at the table. *John Banning and I married recently.* She wanted to pour out the particulars, but so many feelings arose inside her that she couldn't compose a coherent thought. Instead, she wrote about Danny being too much at the saloon and the cold winter that was beginning and about the shortage of wood. She posted the letter and went to visit Elizabeth. She couldn't stay in the two rooms of that house waiting for John to come home when she couldn't stop thinking about him.

* * *

In the saloon, in the deepening light of evening, John stood at the bar and flipped through Jeremy's bartender's manual. He'd just received a tour of every item on the workbench under the bar and the back bar, as well. He'd never realized how many different kinds of drinks there were. Beer, ale and porter had been his choices since he'd started imbibing.

Jeremy, standing across the counter, watched the young man who'd abruptly stood up, crashing his chair on its back.

"You dirty cheat!"

The older man he addressed slowly put down his drink. "Son, you can't just walk off and leave your claim."

"I left it with you!"

The man nodded. "And now it's mine."

The young man's face turned red. "I want my mine back," he sputtered. The older man stood and shook his head. The boy pulled his gun, though he couldn't steady his hand.

Jeremy ran down the length of the bar, his white bar towel bunched in his hand. "Whoa, there, Sonny—"

The boy spun toward the voice and his finger unconsciously tightened. The mirror above the bar shattered as the crack of the pistol sent most men diving for the oil-cloth floor and some racing out the double doors.

The boy turned back and found the older man leveling a gun at his chest. "Calm down, boy, before you get hurt."

Frustration and humiliation flamed through the boy and his finger tightened on the trigger. The older man moved quickly, knocking the boy's arm to the side and up. The bullet hit the brass lamp fixture above the bar and rico-cheted into Jeremy's chest. He was one of the few still standing. He fell quietly while the older man disarmed the enraged boy and pushed him outside. John stood up and didn't see Jeremy.

"You can get up, Jeremy." John peered over the bar and saw the crumpled figure of his father-in-law, his white bar cloth soaking with red blood pressed to his chest. John vaulted over the bar, shouting for a doctor.

When Margaret lifted the lid from the pan of pork chops, no steam escaped because they'd sat so long cooling. John had never been late for a meal. She wondered what obnoxious merriment he was involved in that he could postpone filling his stomach. And deep down she worried that he was no longer interested in her now that he had the saloon. She picked up the big bowl of mashed potatoes from the table and walked with it to the range, hoping to keep it warm. The back door crashed open before she got there and John barreled in panting, his eyes wild. Margaret dropped the bowl and the crockery cracked in two while potatoes splattered her skirts and the wood floor. She stared at John, sure he'd come to hurt her.

"Margaret," he whispered, "your father..." He cleared his throat. "You've got to come to the saloon. He's been shot."

Margaret felt as if the blood in her body evaporated out the top of her head. The man was saying more, but she couldn't hear. He grabbed her arm and pulled her around the bowl of potatoes, across the room and down the steps. "We've got to hurry," he kept insisting. Margaret ran as fast as she could, her arm still gripped in his hand. The cold night air was like a slap across the face that didn't stop stinging. They ran up the saloon steps into the lights and the warmth. The room was quiet—no piano, no laughter, no shouts, only the sob of hysterical crying. John led Margaret to the crowd of men and pushed through them until

she saw her father lying on two hard tables pushed together. His white shirt was soaked with blood and cut open,
exposing the hole in his chest. A doctor covered the wound
with the bloody shirt and shook his head.

Margaret stepped behind a sobbing Elizabeth, who was
clutching her father's hand, and looked down at Jeremy.
He was so pale and his mouth kept moving, but he couldn't
get any words out. Elizabeth bent so close she was almost
on the table with her father. "Papa, papa," she cried repeatedly. Hoarsely, barely audible, Jeremy said, "Lizzy-
beth." His breath rattled and he went completely still.
Elizabeth gave a keening cry and fell on him. Jeremy's
blank eyes stared up at where Elizabeth had been and
Margaret now stood.

Danny pulled Elizabeth away when her sobbing continued to grow more frantic. She had blood on her hands and
chest and threw her arms around Margaret and wailed.
Margaret touched her back gently but shuddered at the
hysteria. Danny carried Elizabeth out of the saloon. Margaret again looked down at her father. Someone had closed
his eyes. She looked up. So many men were staring at her.
Some said how sorry they were and she felt herself nod. The
undertaker came. She spoke with him calmly, not sure how
she could speak at all. She felt so numb. She watched as
men she didn't know carried her father away.

John stood beside her, watching her. Her eyes were clear
green-blue glass, her skin white clay. He walked her home
in the freezing night and she didn't say a word, not even
when he pushed her arms into his coat. John was worried.
He'd also been quiet when his pa died, but then, he'd been
responsible. He'd had no right to cry. But Margaret was not
the cause of Jeremy's death. Had she disliked her father, so
much? John suddenly felt he really didn't know Margaret
at all. His mother's reaction to the death of his father had

been just like Elizabeth's. His brother had ranted and raved and wept, had even punched John, blaming him. John hadn't fought back. A few tears from Margaret would be reassuring. He wanted her to care.

They didn't speak until climbing the back steps of her house. "I guess you'd say he got what he deserved for running a saloon," John said, trying to provoke a reaction.

Margaret glanced up at him in the doorway. "What?"

John frowned. She looked as if she were off in another world. Inside the door she removed his coat that she wore, laid it over a chair, then went to the broken bowl and threw it in the garbage. She wiped up the splattered potatoes and looked down at the pork chops. "The meat is cold and dry, but I'll heat it up if you want some." She turned to John, who leaned against the back door. He stared at her, arms crossed over his chest.

"Your father just died."

"I know that."

"Can you really think of food?"

"Do you want to eat or not?"

"Not. Margaret, are you all right?"

She was back to looking at the pork chops. She nodded. John shook his head and went into their bedroom and lay down on the bed.

Margaret looked at the meat in the pot until her arm trembled from holding up the cast-iron lid. She replaced it and stared at the black handle. She did that until her knees buckled and she sank to the floor, just managing to turn around. She dropped her heavy head into her hands and let her excruciating headache take over.

John listened for movement from the kitchen, but the quiet continued endlessly. He got out of bed and looked into the room. He was at her side in an instant. "Maggie?"

"My head hurts."

"What can I do?"

"Cold cloth," she whispered.

He wet a dish towel and scooped her off the floor. Settling down on the bed with her on his lap, he pressed the cloth to her forehead with one hand and undid the back of her dress with the other. "I'm just going to get you comfortable," he reassured her, but she never protested. He leaned her against his chest, pushed her dress off her shoulders and down her arms. His hand slid to the tight walls of her corset and completely unhooked the binding. Her breath shuddered free and deep as he tossed the garment across the room. He undid her hair next, searching out pins, dropping them on the bed, until soft hanks of hair poured over his arms.

For a long time John relished her warm, unresisting body in his arms, her face burrowing into his neck. "Maybe your head would feel better if you cried," he whispered against her ear.

She shook her head. Her voice came out muffled. "I don't cry. Mama wouldn't allow it."

John puzzled over her words. He'd never heard of a female who didn't cry or wouldn't allow it. He laid her on the bed and pulled her dress down her hips and legs and removed her shoes. She pushed herself up on her elbows. "Don't leave."

John's heart pounded. He'd been about to pull the blankets up to cover her. Instead he lay down beside her and she nestled close, one of her arms circling his waist. He pulled the blankets over them and then soothed her back with his hands and felt heat fill him. But the despair in her voice had not been for his lovemaking, so he just held her. He let his hand drift down over her hip and bottom while a sweet tenderness gripped him, mixing with desire, creating wants and needs he'd never had before. He rubbed his face in her hair, inhaling the scent of her, and his arms tightened around her.

"It hurts," she whispered.

"Your head?"

She moaned and he rubbed the muscles at the back of her neck.

"He didn't see me there," she said.

John stilled. "No, he didn't." He knew she meant tonight, but he wondered if Jeremy had ever truly seen her.

"I was more Mama's daughter," she continued, while his fingers found and soothed the bunched muscles in her shoulders. "He relinquished me to her before I can remember. I always wanted him to notice me. We never got along, even though I tried to be good. I don't know why I feel so empty and alone now," she said so softly John had to strain to hear. "They're both dead and I never pleased either of them."

John thought she might cry then—he sure felt like it—but she didn't. She burrowed against his chest as if she wanted to crawl inside him, and in a way she had.

Margaret woke suddenly and alone, completely aware of everything that had happened the night before. She sat up. Her headache had dulled to a tender pain behind her eyes that reminded her not to move too fast. She dressed and went into the kitchen. The mess of food and dishes had been put away by her husband. He must have worked in the middle of the night to get to the mine by three o'clock. She wouldn't ever forget how kind he had been. He could have pushed himself on her in bed, but he hadn't. A shift of feeling occurred inside her and she felt a little more trust for the man.

She made some coffee and forced herself to eat some bread and honey to fortify herself for a grueling day. She drank two cups of the strong brew topped with milk and sugar before she walked to her father's room in the hotel he'd been living in. He had had few things. He'd been a simple man in his pleasures, she thought, just his cigar and his drink, his friends and his newspaper. She pulled out his nicest suit to bury him in. Then she searched through his wardrobe and his nightstand until she found a whiskey flask and some cigars. She shut the door on his room and went to check on Elizabeth.

The funeral was to be at four o'clock. Margaret had scheduled it then so John could come after working in the mine. She didn't go look at her father until three forty-five. He looked asleep. She was scared to touch him, but she gingerly slid the filled whiskey flask inside his coat. She lifted his hand to place the cigar under his fingers and the cold rigidity of his flesh dashed away her illusions of him sleeping. Unnerved by the absence of the soul, she turned away and saw John a few feet from her. His eyes were so dark, warm and alive. She wanted things from them, things she couldn't even name. She stared up at him even as he stepped to her side and took her arm. The warmth of his hand soaked through her dress and she followed him out of the room.

The slow tolling of the bell accompanied their walk in muddy earth behind the hearse to the cemetery. Elizabeth sobbed loudly the entire way. Margaret concentrated on the dancing black plumes of the glass-walled hearse. Her father would have loved to walk in his own funeral, she thought. He would have avoided her own dour countenance, patted Elizabeth on the head and then moved on, probably to stand near the tall strength of John Banning while the dirt sprayed down on the coffin and Elizabeth moaned. He would have looked around at the snow-covered Bodie hills, across the fledgling town in the middle of nowhere and up at the blue sky on this cloudless day, and he would have smiled because he loved it here. And when the mound of dirt was slapped with the back of a shovel he would have turned and walked away alone, prodding a sagebrush with his cane, his step lighter than ever she'd seen it.

"Margaret?"

She looked up from the grave. John was beside her, turned toward her, his hat in his hand. The wind lifted his honey hair off his forehead. Everyone else was walking away, heading back to town.

"Are you all right?" he asked.

"I don't think he's sorry," Margaret said. John looked astonished. "You don't understand. He was happy here."

John put his hat on. "I do understand. I'm just surprised that you do."

John made it home as soon as he could that night, but that wasn't until late, hours after supper. A shipment coming in at the saloon had postponed his plans for the evening, but he was sure his wife hadn't minded. He imagined her relief when she'd gotten his note. Or maybe she was still feeling empty and alone and was missing him. Whichever, he was still going to make love to her, even though he was exhausted from getting up at two-thirty every morning to work in the mine and now taking care of saloon business, too.

The house was dark. John lighted a lamp in the kitchen and threw a couple more logs on the dying fire in the stove. Margaret was sound asleep on her back in their bed. Her mouth was slightly open and her thick braid lay over her shoulder. John set the lamp on the dresser and stripped off every stitch of his clothing in the cold room. She didn't stir when he crawled in beside her, or when he unbuttoned her gown down below her breasts. She sighed and rolled a little toward him when he pulled her gown up to her waist. He didn't dare pull down the covers and look at her as he wanted, scared the cool air would wake her abruptly. And he couldn't put his cold hands on her, either. Carefully he folded back an edge of her gown and exposed a soft breast. He gently licked her small nipple and then blew on it. He watched the pink skin pucker and felt his body harden. He pressed himself into her warm, soft belly and choked on a groan.

She woke when he sucked her hardening nipple into his mouth. He felt the jerk of her body all along his naked length. He pushed her nipple out of his mouth with a flick of his tongue and met her eyes. He could see the gathering protests and kissed her mouth before she said anything. He wanted her tongue. He wanted her lips to move under his. How many nights before she welcomed him? His hand cupped the soft hair between her thighs.

"John—"

"Don't, Maggie. Don't say anything."

His mouth moved back to her breasts, which couldn't help responding to him. Between her thighs he rotated his palm, then kissed her mouth as he pushed a finger inside of her and found what he was looking for. Deep inside he felt moisture.

"Oh, Maggie," he breathed against her mouth.

She didn't understand why he sounded so relieved. Another of his fingers pushed deep inside her and she squirmed, but she couldn't get away from his hot mouth on her neck. His hand wouldn't stop moving. She strained her thighs together, hoping to stop the sensations that were growing in intensity, but the pressure made her feel his fingers more. She snapped her legs apart and his mouth opened on her cheek as his fingers went deeper and faster. She cried out and John moved over her and drove his hardness into her wet softness. He entered so easily that she understood that her body somehow readied itself for him. In and out, slowly, so slowly, again and again. Margaret's forehead beaded with perspiration. She stifled her moans, but once her hips followed him up as he withdrew.

"Oh, yeah," he encouraged in a ragged breath, poised on his hands above her.

But she didn't want to give in to this mind-robbing pleasure. If she did, her world would end. She turned her face away and dug her nails into the sheet beneath her as he went on and on.

"Maggie, kiss me." She wouldn't. "Put your arms around me," he asked later, but she didn't. Finally, he pulled out of her throbbing body and emptied himself on her belly. Kneeling between her thighs he reached over the bed for the towel. Margaret looked at him through lowered lids and studied his naked torso in the low lamplight. Her gaze moved down his wide, hairless chest, down a ridged, muscled stomach to the dark hair, much darker than on his head, that surrounded the still prominent shaft of his maleness. How strange we're made, she thought, and doubt grew in her mind of the wisdom of her mother's words about this act being unnatural. He wiped the wetness from them both as she watched. She looked up and met his eyes, and then a shock of embarrassment flooded her for the way she was staring while lying naked beneath him.

His eyes were dark and warm, and he didn't give her his usual engaging smile but leaned over her, his hands on either side of her face, and lowered his head. She opened her mouth beneath his and let herself feel his tongue, but she didn't respond at all, because she really didn't have the least idea that she could. He lay at her side and pulled the covers snugly up to their necks while she pushed her gown down to her knees. He went to sleep instantly. Margaret lay awake for a long time with a warm thudding in her temples and between her thighs.

Chapter Twelve

When John walked in the door after his shift the next day, with those brightly warm, dark eyes of his, Margaret knew what he wanted. She was frying pork chops and turned back to them as he shut the door and walked in. The very thought of the bed thing made her hot and irritable. Too many times throughout the day the image of him kneeling naked above her in the bed had coursed through her, leaving her with a hot, excited feeling.

He stood at the door and took off his hat and coat while she set their small kitchen table. She straightened as he walked to her. He bent to kiss her and she spun away. "You could say hello first!"

His brows rose. "Hello, my darling, sweet wife."

She glared at him. "We're not doing it tonight. I just thought I'd make that clear, so you can get your mind on other things."

He sighed. "I've been thinking about you and me all day. Even if I thought about something else, my body is too far gone." He looked down below his belt and Margaret's gaze unwittingly followed to see the growing bulge.

She snatched two plates off the shelf. "The more men get, the more they want." She was humiliated to talk like this, but determined to get things settled. "I'm not about to

ollow you into perversion just because you don't see the
mportance of restraining yourself.''

''Perversion!''

''Yes!''

''Just what is perverted about making love to my own
vife?'' His voice was loud.

Margaret slapped the plates on the table and looked to-
vard the stove. ''Your choice of place is perverted. Your
requency of demand is perverted!''

With one hand on his hip he rubbed his forehead.
'Maybe I'm too impatient with you, but hell if I'm per-
erted.'' He met her sea eyes, bright in her flushed face. ''I
hink you're scared because you're starting to like it, want
, probably even thinking about it during the day.''

Enraged by the baseness of his words and even more so
y the ugly truth in them, she strode up to him and stared
im right in the eyes. ''You are wrong. I think it's dirty and
isgusting and only serves the purpose of creating chil-
ren. And you know I don't want children! But I know a
ormal man can't abstain, so I'm willing to serve you on an
ifrequent basis.''

John gasped. ''Serve me! What? Once a year! And dirty?
irty! You think last night was dirty when I didn't hurt you
ne damn bit. Hell, Maggie, you were soaking wet. Was
aat dirty?''

''Yes! Dirty!'' she shouted.

A muscle twitched in his cheek as he stared, teeth
enched, at the woman standing before him with hands on
er hips.

''I'll show you what dirty is.'' He grabbed her around the
aist and tossed her over his shoulder. Margaret screamed
d kicked and pummeled and then went completely still
hen he walked out the back door, not through the bed-
om door. He hopped down the steps and carried her

around the house. There were people everywhere. The me
had just gotten off shift and filled the dirt road on their wa
home to family or to the saloons, gambling dens, resta
rants and lodging houses.

"John, put me down," she whispered furiously as me
stopped to stare and gape. He strode to a corner that wa
frequently crossed by wheels and feet and where the sno
was slushy with mud. Margaret's mouth opened in shoc
as he bent and placed his hand on her chest, pushing he
down in the freezing slush. Then he rolled her over. Afte
he was finished he stepped away from her. "Stand u
Margaret."

Slowly, shakily, she did. Her hand raised to her face an
wiped off a gob of mud.

"That is dirt," he said softly. "And now you are ve
dirty. You are filthy."

She didn't flinch from his gaze yet was aware of the ti
tering crowd around them. She jerked into motion an
strode past him. He stood shaking his head and watche
her march back to the house. A few male spectators move
closer.

"Havin' trouble with the missus?"

"You think you had trouble before, just wait!"

"Let me know how she takes to that. I might try it!"

"Nah, they always get back at you in some unde
handed way."

"Uh-oh, here she comes now."

John turned and saw Margaret marching back, lifting he
feet high through the half foot of snow that covered th
path back to him. She held out a huge frying pan. His fa
went blank as he waited. Steam and good smells rose fro
the pan. Pork chops, bread, applesauce and greens we
dumped on top of one another at his feet. The men that ha
stayed to watch *tsked* softly and some chuckled.

Margaret met John's eyes challengingly. A ghost of a smile tugged his lips up. She didn't want to amuse him and so she threw down the pan, too, straightening with worried regret when the edge of it glanced off his foot and he grimaced. She turned and walked down the street toward Elizabeth's house.

"Like she thinks I can't get my own dinner," John muttered, still wincing from the blow to his foot. The men around him laughed and walked on. "Witch," he whispered under his breath, watching his wife mix into the people on the sides of the street.

"What happened?" demanded Elizabeth, staring at her muddy wet sister standing in the open door.

"I slipped."

"Where is your coat? It's freezing out there."

"I noticed." Margaret stared back at her disheveled sister. Her hair was down and floating blond and soft around her face. Her robe rounded over her growing belly.

"Well, come in!" Elizabeth pushed Margaret to the hot stove in the parlor. "Stand right there. I'll get you something dry to wear." Margaret quickly stripped her outer clothes when Elizabeth came back, but retained her undergarments. She pulled on the white blouse, which was too big, and the brown wool shirt, which was too short.

"How'd you come to leave your house without your coat?"

"I didn't think."

Elizabeth stared at her. "Why? Were you having a fight with John?"

Margaret blinked. She pulled the blanket Elizabeth had handed her tightly over her shoulders.

"Danny always slams out of here without something when we argue. What were you and John arguing about?"

"I don't want to talk about it."

"Then I'll make you some tea. You can stay for dinner, too."

Margaret did stay. For the first time she let her sister cook for her. Margaret kept her company in the warm kitchen and Danny read the newspaper at their little square table. The cornbread Elizabeth made was tasty and the sliced roast beef with gravy was tender, even though Elizabeth served no vegetable.

"You've become quite a cook," Margaret complimented her.

Elizabeth beamed. Across the table, Danny laughed. "She makes this well, even if it's all she makes." Elizabeth punched him. Behavior that at one time was embarrassing and childish in Margaret's eyes suddenly appeared slightly enviable and friendly. While they did the dishes Elizabeth casually suggested that Margaret could spend the night. Margaret wrote a note for John, and Danny promised to drop it off on his way to the saloon.

"Does Danny still spend too much time at the saloon?" asked Margaret as the women sat bundled together on the large sofa in the parlor in front of the wood stove.

"Yes. He says it's a big, busy saloon. They have two bartenders besides the two of them, but they're going to have to hire another."

"I want him to sell."

Elizabeth stared at her. "Danny will never agree."

"Doesn't it bother you that they go right back there after Father was killed inside that place?"

"It was a ricocheting bullet that killed Father. It wasn't because he owned a saloon. He could have just been visiting there and still gotten shot."

"Yes, he certainly could have. And so could our husbands."

"Why, Margaret, you sound like you care."

"Of course I care! I don't want anybody to die. Did you hear that the boy who started this got put in jail? He's only eighteen. Younger than you. The sheriff said he'd imbibed generously of spirits. The saloons don't offer an ounce of good, Elizabeth. They're just traps for men who want to shirk their responsibilities. A few drinks and a man doesn't remember he has a family at home. His judgment is clouded and small frustrations, irritations, conflicts of the moment take on too much importance. So do small pleasures."

"How would you know?"

"I overheard enough of Father's conversations and I've seen Danny neglect you enough to form an opinion. And I, unfortunately and unintentionally, drank too much champagne myself one night."

Elizabeth grinned. "Yes, I remember. John walked you home. Did 'small pleasures' seem very important that night?"

Margaret reddened considerably. "I don't remember very well. And that's yet another problem with drink—memory loss. How are you and my niece?" she asked, changing the subject and looking at her sister's belly.

"Your nephew is fine," Elizabeth replied, giggling. "Even if I am beginning to look like a buffalo."

"You're not."

"He's moving now, but I'm too fat for anyone else to feel him from the outside. Do you want to see the baby clothes I've made?"

Margaret admired the extravagant gowns and embroidered blankets. Elizabeth never made anything simple. If she was going to sew, she was going to fill the garment with fripperies.

"Are you less nervous about having children?" Elizabeth asked.

Margaret's hand stilled over the christening gown. She shook her head.

"Hadn't you best get used to the idea?"

Margaret bit her tongue at her sister's knowing voice. She couldn't mention what John did to prevent a child.

"Is that why you two are fighting?" Elizabeth peered into her sister's face, trying to catch every nuance of expression, the only way anyone usually had to tell what Margaret was thinking. The tightening of her features told volumes. "Lord, I hope you're not denying him."

"Elizabeth, please..." Margaret ground the word out, clenching her hand on a little baby gown.

Elizabeth stared at her sister's averted face. "Mag, I know men can be a little, well, violent in their desires, but when you surrender it's like a little piece of heaven here on earth."

"Or hell in disguise," Margaret snapped, throwing the gown into the basket of tiny clothes.

"Oh, Mag, this is the problem, isn't it? Men have their needs and—"

Margaret whipped her head around to face her sister. "I think everyday is being a bit too needy!"

Elizabeth swallowed. "Well," she whispered, "it's like that at first when it's all so new and you're in—"

"Enough." Margaret held up her hand. Elizabeth opened her mouth. "Enough, Elizabeth."

Her sister shrugged and folded her baby clothes neatly into the basket. "Danny says we're going to be rich. He's been buying stocks in all the promising mines." She looked up at Margaret and smiled. "Has John invested in more than the stocks Daddy left you?"

"He'd better not be. I don't place much value in dreams of riches."

Elizabeth went to bed soon after and Margaret curled up on the sofa with several blankets. The sofa was too short and she was cold without the warmth of John's body lying beside her. She heard Danny come in late and the creak of the bed under his weight. Elizabeth moaned sleepily and minutes later Danny started talking. They'd left their door open to get the warmth from the fire and Margaret could hear him ask why she was in their house. So, John hadn't mentioned anything at the saloon. Margaret was glad he kept his tongue about their private life. But she cringed and pulled her pillow over her head when Elizabeth began a long, elaborate explanation of what she thought was wrong with her sister's marriage.

Margaret woke early and stiff on the sofa after sleeping a total of two hours. In the dawn she brushed the dried mud from her stiff dress and put it on. She left before she heard a stir from the bedroom.

John was home minutes after his shift was over. Margaret's heart jumped as he walked in. He hung his coat and doffed his hat. She turned back to the steaks she was frying.

"Enjoy yourself last night?" he asked.

Margaret thought of the short sofa she had slept on and shook her head without thinking.

"That's too bad. I had a pleasant, warm evening in the saloon."

They didn't speak again until halfway through the meal.

"Danny still is hardly home. I think you should hire someone else to help out at the saloon."

"That wouldn't get Danny home more. It would get me home more."

"Why? Elizabeth needs him home more than I need you!"

He shoved his unfinished dinner away from him. "I know this is no marriage of love for you, but you don't have to go out of your way to be unpleasant about it."

Margaret flushed with anger. "And I know this is no marriage of love for you, either, so don't pretend. And I meant that because of Elizabeth's condition, she needs her husband home more."

He leaned his elbows on the table. "I agree."

Margaret looked up into his face and got lost in his deep brown eyes. He had a gray tinge to the skin around his eyes that he hadn't had when he'd first come to Bodie.

"You do?" She pulled her gaze from him and stabbed a potato with her fork. "And you shouldn't be working two jobs. I don't understand how you can continue to endanger life and limb in that dark, dirty tunnel of a mine, seven days a week, twelve hours a day, for four dollars a day. If you won't sell the saloon and want so much to work to excess, why can't you quit the mine and start your own carpentry business? Have you even asked Danny if he'd be interested in something useful like that?"

John snorted. "You know Danny as well as I do, if not better. He loves that saloon. He's a good bartender and he's attentive to the customers even if he does drink too much. He's found his place."

"And what about Elizabeth and the baby? He's investing everything they have in mines that are not promising anything."

John nodded. "But that's not our business. If Elizabeth wants more control of the money she's going to have to take it. If she wants him home more, she'll have to get him there herself."

"How is she going to do that when he's usually sotted? She's never been very strong and always too nice for her own good. She needs our help—yours, especially. You can send Danny home. You can take over the books. You can put some money into Elizabeth's hands."

John threw down his napkin. "For God's sake! When will you let up? He'll just take any money right back from her and she'll willingly give it. She'll do anything for him! That's the kind of woman she is. And I'm not Danny's daddy. I'm not going to tell him what to do! They'll just have to pick up the pieces if this all falls apart for them. If she didn't have you taking care of her for so long, maybe she wouldn't still be running to you for help. Why don't you start worrying about your own marriage?"

Margaret stood and cleared the table.

"I'm not worried about a marriage I never wanted in the first place! I'm not pleased to be associated with a man that sells whiskey and in the same place where my father was killed. You sell something that brings out the baseness in people."

John leaned back in his chair and crossed his arms. "You mean lust?" he asked quietly.

Margaret turned away from him and started washing the dishes. "Not just."

"I'm sorry you find my attentions so disgusting. Tell me, if I was a simple carpenter, would you like being in bed with me?"

"No," she whispered.

"Then I see no advantage to selling the saloon. Besides, I like the saloon! It's full of friendly people who want a good conversation and some company, which is a lot more than I can get here!"

He left the kitchen and Margaret didn't just wash, she scrubbed the dishes. When she crawled into bed he was still awake. He lay on his back in the middle of the bed, arms under his head.

"Will you please move over?" she snapped.

He sat up, still in the middle of the bed. "Don't take that tone with me, not in bed. You can be a damn nag everyplace else, day and night, but in our bedroom you'll be nice."

Margaret stood beside the bed, her mouth gaping. "Don't curse," she finally managed. "And you started this by lying in the middle of the bed. You knew I'd have to ask you to move."

"Yeah, I started it. I want a goddamn fight." He jumped to his feet on the bed, bounced once and glared down at her. "We're gonna have this out."

Margaret swallowed and looked up at him in his long underwear. "What do you mean?"

He hopped down from the bed and pulled her by the arm into the kitchen. "Sit down." He lighted a lamp and joined her at the table in a chair across from him. "I've got the feeling that you're going to try and deny me as long as possible."

Margaret kept her face expressionless while she felt the blood draining out of her face and down her neck.

"And I don't break my back in that stinking mine for twelve straight hours and then make sure the saloon is running smoothly to come home to a cold wife."

"You should have thought about that before you married me. You knew I didn't want *that* part." She fisted her hands in her lap. "Did you think you'd change my mind?"

"Yes," he said quietly.

Margaret crossed her arms over her chest. "I can't approve of drink. I can't approve of your selling it. I think it leads men down a path of selfishness and violence. You don't know how women feel, sitting at home while their husbands spend their income on drink, gambling and loose women. And the example for the children—''

"Spare me the lecture. I'm making money, not spending it. I'm not beating you. And I'm too busy trying to woo my own wife to have any time left for other women. Now, I want to discuss sex.''

Margaret blanched. "I won't."

John stood and pulled a full whiskey bottle from behind a pewter platter on the shelf above the counter. He set it and a glass on the table.

"Don't you dare!" Margaret jumped out of her chair and grabbed for the bottle.

He pulled it out of her reach. "Sit down," he said softly, "or I'm going to start drinking. We're going to come to an agreement about some important things here and now, or I'm going to drink this whole damn bottle."

Margaret slowly sunk to her chair.

"What is your optimum frequency for conjugal relations?" he asked politely.

Margaret pursed her lips before answering. "Once a month," she said determinedly, knowing she could never ask for less, but even that answer astounded him.

He poured himself a drink. "Get serious."

Margaret glared at his glass and then into his eyes.

He leaned forward, cupping his glass in his hand. "My optimum is twice a day."

"That's impossible."

His brows lifted. He raised his glass and rested his elbow on the table. "Is it?"

"Once every two weeks!"

He shook his head. "Every day."

"Once a week," she said desperately.

"Every other day and that's as seldom as I'll accept."

Margaret jumped out of her chair, her eyes fastened on the glass he held. "That's too much!"

He put his glass down and leaned forward in his chair. "Look, I'm a married man. I have to come to you for what I need. Hell, I don't want to go anywhere else. You don't like drink and I can limit that. And I understand I can't toss you a coin and expect you to do whatever I want whenever and wherever. So I'm telling you what I want. We're not going to work out if I feel I have to fight to make love to you. I want an agreement."

"I don't want us—"

"Maggie, I don't want to leave you. I like you. I know that seems ridiculous to you, but give me a chance. You need me." She was trembling and looking away from him, her thick braid hanging over her breast. John wondered when she'd really let him know her. When would she confide in him and let him know what was behind her fears? "Do you accept every other day?"

"I don't know if I can," she whispered.

"Will you try?"

She turned slowly around, her eyes on the bottle she was itching to throw out the door.

"Will you tell me why you think you have to hate being with me?"

"Do you have no sensibilities at all?"

"None as tender as yours."

"I don't have to demean myself further by discussing this. Drink yourself to oblivion for all I care, but don't you ever dare touch me after you have whiskey on your lips. I'll fight you, whether it's your day or not."

John leaned back, his eyes hard and dark, not liking how she agreed without actually agreeing, thereby depriving him of feeling he'd made any inroads on her. "Is there anything you don't feel strongly about?'' She shook her head. Their eyes held a long time. ''Maybe that's why I like you.''

Margaret's eyes widened. ''What do you mean?''

He looked away and shrugged. ''Hell if I know.'' He poured his whiskey back into the bottle and corked it. ''I'll take it to the saloon tomorrow. Don't go dumping it out and wasting good money.'' She nodded stiffly. ''Go get in bed. I'm going to come collecting.''

She blushed and hurried into the bedroom. John threw another log on the fire in the stove and turned out the lamp on the table. In the dark kitchen he waited, leaning his hip against the hot stove until he had to jump away. It was a game he'd played with his brother many times years ago. John always won. He was filled with the same push to win now, to prove something, but this time with a silly woman. He longed suddenly for the comfort of his family in San Francisco, the way it used to be before his pa had died. What the hell was he doing here with a woman who didn't want him and working in a dark tunnel he was hating more everyday? The only thing he did like was the warm, friendly saloon that made him bundles of money. And the rare smile from his stubborn wife.

John's desire was nonexistent when he climbed into bed beside his stiff wife. He lay on his back staring at the ceiling just as she did.

After long silent moments Margaret realized he wasn't going to touch her. Confused, she turned her head on the pillow to face him. His eyes were open. ''What is it?'' she whispered. She was relieved yet unexpectedly disappointed and humiliated. ''I thought you...I don't understand you. Why did you really marry me?'' His head turned toward her. ''Was it for the saloon?'' He said nothing and she could see only dark holes where his eyes were.

"What answer would you like? That it was for the saloon? Or for you?"

He didn't expect her to answer, so he wasn't surprised by the long silence that followed.

"For me," she whispered many minutes later.

Chapter Thirteen

John tensed. Her breathy whisper clutched like a claw at his sides. Slowly he rolled to face her. Her eyes were downcast. "You're in luck then," he said lightly. He propped up on an elbow and rubbed his knee along her calf. Desire was spreading in his groin. "I wanted you. I won't lie, I wanted the saloon, too, but you I wanted much, much more. Your father refused to let me marry you without taking the saloon, too." His hand settled on her belly and the muscles beneath it contracted violently. He pressed gently against her. "I don't see how you can doubt that I want you."

"But that's just..." *Lust,* she finished to herself. "I don't understand," she whispered. "I'm plain."

He chuckled. "You're not."

His face nuzzled her neck and his hand cupped a breast. Already his touch had become less alien than it had felt the first time. Through her gown he kissed her nipples. Gently, he closed his lips around one. Margaret felt his mouth tug feeling up from between her thighs. He raised her gown to her waist and touched her soft hair.

"We have nothing in common. I hate Bodie. I hate the saloon. I hate this!"

He moved his fingers against her. Margaret clamped down on her bottom lip and arched her throat off the pillow. His open mouth and wet tongue caressed her neck while his hand continued to move.

"I like your cooking," he whispered. "I like your manners and morals, your face and form. And you do like this!"

"Please! Must you touch me like that?" She grabbed his arm with both of her hands and pushed him away. "You don't even really know me."

He looked down at her. "Margaret Ann Banning, you are blind. It's you who doesn't know me." He turned away from her and pulled the covers up to his neck.

Margaret was shocked. He wasn't going to finish. She felt like kicking him in the backside. Before this man she had known exactly who she was and what her place in the world was, and everyone else's place, for that matter. She hadn't been a woman to feel what could only be called lust. Now her face was flooded with heat and she wanted him to turn back around. She lay awake for hours.

When John came home the next day he kissed her cheek, her chin, got a quick one in on her lips before she pushed him away. He lifted the lid on a pot of boiling water. "How long until supper?"

"Almost half an hour. I wasn't sure what time you'd be home."

He nodded. "That gives us time. Get your coat."

"Why?"

"We're going to Bodie Pharmacy to get a soda."

Margaret looked askance.

"Now what's wrong? Is soda forbidden, too?"

"No. I just..."

He got her coat for her and helped her on with it. "Then let's go."

They walked side by side without touching through a layer of new-fallen snow that artistically covered the piles of garbage that had been thrown in the street. John took her elbow when they entered the pharmacy and helped her onto a stool at the soda counter.

"What do you want?" he asked her.

Margaret looked at the menu board hanging above the counter. There was chocolate, cherry, raspberry, lemon, sarsaparilla, ginger beer and more. "My," she said, turning to John.

"Don't tell me you've never had a soda."

"Oh, I had some ginger beer once at a party, but I've never been to a counter and seen such a selection."

"Why not?"

Margaret shrugged and bent a little forward to see what the patrons farther down the counter had ordered. The woman had something red in a tall glass and the gentleman with her had something brown. "Too frivolous, I suppose," she answered softly. "I'll have raspberry," she decided, feeling almost wicked. John ordered a coffee soda and then leaned his forearms on the counter and regarded his wife, who was busy watching the man prepare their drinks.

"I've seen Elizabeth in here a number of times," John commented when the waiter placed her tall soda in front of her. She didn't seem to be listening to him but focused round eyes on her tall glass. She opened her pink lips and secured them around the end of her straw. He watched the red liquid rise up her straw and her eyes close when the soda reached her mouth. She raised her mouth, looked down into her glass and swirled her straw around in the froth before she sucked again.

"Were you forbidden to come to a soda fountain?" he asked when she was half-finished.

"No. I never thought of going by myself and no one ever asked me to."

John barely tasted his drink, so busy was he wondering why the woman he had married was so different from her sisters.

They ate dinner as soon as they got home, and though Margaret complained she was too full she put away a nice-sized slab of roast beef and a small mound of mashed potatoes. He sat back and ate slowly, listening to her talk about the efforts of her and her church congregation to raise the funds to build a church. She was animated and her sea eyes sparkled while she told him that they had to have church services in the Odd Fellows Hall. He wondered if her happiness came from the soda he'd bought her or the fact that he couldn't make love to her tonight.

"So, will you come with me next Sunday?"

John shuddered. "Do I have to?"

Margaret leaned forward. "Of course not. Do you have to do anything I ask? You didn't seem to feel you had to close the saloon on Sundays when I asked, or shut down at ten o'clock and open at six in the morning instead of staying open all night. I've really had very little influence. It would just be important to me if you came," she said softly.

John sighed. "All right." He pushed back his chair and stood. "I'm going to the saloon before you ask me to build the damn church for you." He didn't like her odd little smile, as if she'd already been considering the idea. To wipe the thought right out of her mind he bent over and gave her a wet kiss.

A pattern for their nights evolved. On the days they couldn't make love according to their agreement, he came home for an early, hot meal and then left for the saloon. The other nights he took her by the hand after dinner and led her to the bedroom, where he kissed her and touched

er, just enough to get her breathing a little ragged and her
skin to heat, and then he'd turn away from her. He hoped
one day soon she'd tell him not to stop. If not, he was going to die an early death, but he wanted his wife to want
him, not endure him.

Sunday had come damn fast, John thought, trying to
match an order Danny had made with the delivery surrounding his feet in the cold workroom adjoining the saloon. Church service was at seven, half an hour away, and
order or no order he'd be there. He was not going to let
Margaret down when he was trying to gain her trust. He
sighed, crouched and pried open a case of champagne.
They were completely out of the drink. He stood, bent his
knees, grabbed the wood case and heaved it up in his arms,
which were tired from a full shift at the mine. He walked
next door into the bar, which at six-thirty was full, and set
the case down in front of the icebox with a hard crack.

Thomas Herzog hurried over. "Be careful," he admonished fiercely. John glowered. Did this man work for him
or the other way around? Thomas was sidestepping around
the case of champagne as if it were precious porcelain. John
opened one of the small doors in the cooler and shoved a
couple of bottles into the rack. Behind him he heard a
strangled intake of breath. "Gently, Mr. Banning!" John
turned and skewered his hired bartender with a narrowed
gaze. He hefted a couple more bottles into his hands, threw
them up in the air in front of the man, caught them and
pushed them into the rack with the others. He heard a crack
just as his hand was coming down.

He squinted at a bottle and pulled it out by the neck.
Holding it up to the light by thumb and forefinger, he
looked at it. "Did you hear that?" he asked Thomas. The
bartender nodded and stepped slowly forward, a white

towel in his hand. He'd just reached John's side when the glass bottle burst and the cork flew up into the ceiling. John still held the neck and stared at where there had once been a bottle of champagne. The saloon was quiet and John heard the drip of champagne off his face onto the floor. He licked his lips and sucked in a glass shard rolled in a pleasant alcohol base. He spit and threw the bottle neck to the floor.

"The damn bottle was defective!"

He reached for two he'd previously placed in the cooler. Thomas grabbed his arm and yelled "No!" as John yanked the bottle out. He elbowed Thomas away and set them on the bar. The explosions were almost instantaneous. John and Thomas stood stock-still, their chests well sprayed. Thomas slowly turned his head to his boss.

"Champagne bottles become very brittle when they get too cold," he said softly and slowly, as though he were talking to a small child. "They were not protected well enough for the temperature they traveled through outside and needed to be handled very delicately."

John turned to Thomas and pointed his finger at him. "From now on you can unpack the stuff." He looked down at himself. "Hell, I have to go listen to that minister now." A sprinkling of chuckles erupted across the room. Danny was smiling idiotically, but he dropped his grin and tried to frown when John looked his way.

"Better go change," he suggested loudly before bursting into laughter.

John pulled on his coat and stomped out to the rising waves of laughter in the room. He didn't frown long. He laughed as he touched his stiff hair; the champagne had frozen in it by the time he opened the back door of the house. Margaret was pulling on her gloves in the warm kitchen.

"I thought you were going to meet me there." Her pretty nose crinkled. "You smell like a distillery! And what did you do to your hair?"

"It's just pomade, and I met with a little accident. Maybe I could go next Sunday instead?" he asked hopefully.

"John! You promised! And maybe you'll have another accident next Sunday. And I don't like that perfumed oil in your hair. You have nice hair and that stuff ruins it."

John swore softly and threw off his coat. He picked up the pail of water from the floor and set it on the table. "As if I wanted to get sprayed with this stuff," he mumbled while he unbuttoned his shirt, his back to his wife.

"Hurry," she said.

John grunted in reply. He pulled off his undershirt and Margaret bit her lip as she watched him bend his broad, naked back over the pail. He splashed his face, dipped a rag and scrubbed at his hair and wiped his chest, belly and arms. Margaret turned away to stop herself from staring and fetched him clean garments. She handed him the undershirt, then pushed the white shirt onto his arm, enjoying the feel of helping him.

"So, you like my hair, hmm?" he asked, smiling.

She blushed. "It's all right."

They were only a few minutes late. Hymns were still being sung. They took two chairs together in the middle of the room. Margaret handed John a hymn book and then she jumped right into the chorus, knowing the words without opening her book. John stared at the words on the page and cleared his throat. He leaned a little closer to his wife and listened to her voice. He'd never heard her sing before and enjoyed the soft soprano she had. He looked around at the collection of people totaling about thirty, twenty of them women. He didn't know there were so many respectable-looking women in Bodie. Where did they all hide? One to the side of him was looking at him and John was sure he saw her sniff, smelling the champagne.

Next to him, Margaret caught a whiff of alcohol now and again when John moved in his seat. She didn't really care. At least he had come with her. She realized how lonely she'd felt even in this congregation of churchgoers, but with John by her side she felt as if she had a friend. She was a little alarmed by how accustomed she was becoming to his affection and his company. He sat very still beside her during the sermon and didn't fidget as she'd expected him to. She saw that next to the proper Mr. and Mrs. Hoyt, Mr. Baxter was nodding off. His wife kept elbowing him in the ribs. The woman looked very embarrassed and Margaret sat a little straighter. She glanced at John and all her contentment flooded away when she saw his drooped head, his chin on his chest, his shoulders rising and falling evenly. She refused to draw attention to him by poking him and making him jerk awake, so she sat out the sermon, once catching Mrs. Hoyt's righteous gaze on her sleeping husband. The hymn book slid down his thigh and Margaret caught it before it crashed to the floor. Then she stared straight ahead and listened to Reverend Hinkle's plea for everyone present to create a home for God here in this wild town.

John woke when the closing hymn was sung. His head snapped up and he looked quickly at his wife. He wasn't sure how much time had lapsed and if this was the same song he'd dropped off to. He noticed Margaret had his book so he gave up his hope that she hadn't noticed his transgression. At least she hadn't yanked on his ear the way his ma used to do when he had to go to church as a boy. He stood when she stood.

People were milling around, talking with one another, and John wanted to go home, crawl into bed and go back to sleep. He wasn't even interested in kissing. He groaned inwardly when Margaret looked at him and said, "There are some people I want you to meet."

He followed behind her, his hat in his hand, his eyes on her hips clad in gray wool as she approached the snobby Mrs. Hoyt. Why Margaret wanted to associate with the woman when she looked down her nose at them, John did not understand. Halfway there they were accosted by Jim Baxter and his wife.

"Ho! Banning, I thought that was you!"

A smile broke across John's face as he shook hands with the miner on the same shift as him.

"I pointed out to Lydia that I wasn't the only one sleeping through Hinkle's sermon. Irritates her, my dozing, but she doesn't know what a twelve-hour shift is like." He looked down at his red-faced wife.

"Yeah, I'm not sure if I'm forgiven or not," John said, glancing at Margaret. She cocked an eyebrow and he was kept in suspense. "I'd like you to meet my wife."

"Oh, we've known Mrs. Banning since she was Miss Warren. You'll have to join us for supper some evening."

"Yes, please do," added Lydia. "I'd love to have a fellow commiserator in being married to a miner," she said, smiling at Margaret.

Margaret, who'd never been on an intimate acquaintance with the Baxters, found she would like to be. "I would like that, too."

They talked a few more minutes, accepted a dinner invitation for the next week and then parted. Margaret looked around and saw the Hoyts talking with Reverend Hinkle. She started forward and then stopped. From behind, Mrs. Hoyt's black hair, wound tightly on her head, small hat and long black coat reminded her of her mother. And like her mother, Mrs. Hoyt found only disappointment and failings in people. She was no friend and Margaret didn't understand why she aspired to be liked by the woman. And neither did she understand why she'd wanted to be just like her when a woman like Lydia Baxter was much more pleasant. She turned around abruptly and almost smashed into John.

"Who do I meet now?" he asked.

Margaret averted her gaze. "Never mind. They don't deserve to meet you," she added softly. She walked toward the door. John stood in surprise for a moment before he took off after her.

The evening at the Baxters' was enjoyable for everyone. Lydia made roasted chicken and a chocolate cake. The men talked about mining and stocks and running the saloon. Margaret and Lydia talked about cooking and sewing and how there were too many saloons, too many unmarried men and too much snow in Bodie. Margaret was softly humming on the way home even though she was freezing. The stars were bright in the clear sky and the moon was big, illuminating the snowdrifts against the building walls.

"They are very nice people, aren't they?" Margaret asked as John opened the back door for them.

"Yeah," he said, smiling, thinking she sounded as if she'd met few people in her life. He felt really married having dinner with another couple, and now he wanted to end the day with her loving him as he loved her. Instead, he turned his back on her when they got into bed. He was too tired for reluctance. The past week of touching without consummation had taken its toll on him, without seeming to have the effect he'd wanted on his wife. She'd never asked for more.

Margaret lay still until she heard John's deep, even breathing. She plumped her pillow behind her and sat up in bed. Tonight had been a night he could touch her. She looked down at him and wondered why he hadn't. He was exhausted, of course, working two jobs and living on fewer than five hours of sleep a night, but she worried he was losing interest. Her heart pounded. She flushed as she realized she wanted him to pursue her. She wanted to pretend he did care about her. Sometimes when she almost believed it, she felt so comforted, so light and alive. But she wouldn't truly believe him unless he sold the saloon and still wanted her as his wife.

John came home at noon from the mine the next day, three hours early. He slammed the kitchen door behind him, dumped his lunch tin and hat on the table and pulled out a chair. Margaret came out of the bedroom still pinning her hat on. He was filthy and foul smelling, obviously not having washed at the mine. His face was blank as a board.

"Why are you early?"

John didn't like the way she asked. He also didn't like the hat she was sticking on her head. He realized he didn't like any hat on her head. "Are you going out?"

"I'm having lunch with Elizabeth. Did you quit?"

He nodded.

"Good."

"No, it's not good. I'll just stay in the saloon day and night now and get your temper up, but go ahead and go."

"I will." She had no desire to stay and subject herself to his surly mood when she had no idea what was wrong. "Will you be home for supper?"

He leaned back in his chair and stuck his filthy boots on her table with a shrug. His eyes were daring her to comment on his lack of manners. Lord, he was spoiling for a fight. She turned her back to him and pulled on her coat by the door.

"Margaret, stay."

She looked over her shoulder, her hand already on the doorknob. His feet were off the table. He'd left dirt on it. His eyes were beseeching her. Margaret felt their pull down low in her belly. She shook her head, refusing him, refusing her feelings. She pictured them in bed in two minutes if she stayed, and she was very scared of what she'd find out about herself there. The bleakness in his eyes before she turned from him haunted her. She pushed her feelings down, down, down and walked out of her little house.

Elizabeth complained throughout lunch. "You are not obese," Margaret reassured her for the third time.

Elizabeth picked up her fifth cookie. "Okay! I'm not obese, but I *am* fat. Danny hasn't made love to me in three weeks," she added in an agonized voice. "I fiddled with him until...you know, and he knows how that gets me, and he still didn't touch me."

Margaret carefully set down her teacup. She did not know.

"He thinks I'm repulsive."

"Oh, Elizabeth! I'm sure he's just busy at the saloon. And he's being considerate of you in your condition."

"I don't know if he's busy at the saloon, but I do know that's where he always is! And considerate of me! Obviously, you're not enjoying yourself with John or you wouldn't say that. I'm surprised. I thought he would be man enough to soften you."

"Elizabeth!"

"I don't know why I confide in you, because you don't understand anything." She began to cry. Margaret pulled out her handkerchief and handed it to her.

"Oh, Beth, I'm sorry. Don't cry. Think of the baby. It's best, I'm sure, for the child's sake that Danny isn't...isn't, you know."

Elizabeth blew her nose. "Oh, Mag, that's just more of Mama's talk. I don't believe it's going to hurt my baby if Danny touches me. Mama used anything she could as an excuse to keep Daddy away from her."

"That's not fair. You know how she suffered."

"I know how we all suffered living with her! And you try to be just like her! Why, for God's sake? She was the most miserable woman I've ever known."

"Well, she's dead now, so I'd think you could be more compassionate and generous with her memory."

Elizabeth was crying again. She got herself upset every-time Margaret had seen her in the past couple of weeks. If this was how she acted around Danny no wonder he pre-ferred the saloon, not that she approved. Elizabeth ate two more cookies while she sniffed loudly.

"I don't know what's wrong with me."

"You're pregnant. And you're cooped up in this house too much. Bodie in winter is worse than Bodie in summer. Now we have snowstorms instead of dust storms. And it doesn't seem like Christmas is only a few weeks away since we're not home in San Francisco. This will be our first Christmas without Mother and Father. Even Victoria won't be here." Margaret stood and cleared the table of their sandwich remains. She also removed the rest of the cook-ies. Margaret sat back down at the little table and poured her sister some more tea.

Elizabeth stared out the window at the light rain that had begun falling. "Ice," she muttered.

"Yes," sighed Margaret, thinking of the slippery path she'd have to walk home. "I hate Bodie," she added under her breath.

Elizabeth turned from the window and smiled, the tear tracks still on her face. Margaret stared at her for a moment. She wasn't used to this pregnant moodiness in her usually optimistic sister.

"New Year's Day we'll go for a sleigh ride. Would you like that?"

Elizabeth nodded, her smile crinkling her eyes. "I'm glad you stayed in Bodie."

Margaret looked at her sister severely. "It's just until that baby is born. Then I'm on the first stage back to civilization."

"Oh? And how does John feel about that?"

Margaret averted her eyes from her sister's grinning face. "We haven't discussed it in a while." She thought of him sitting at the kitchen table, looking at her in that needing way. She should go. She knew for a fact that Elizabeth would never have left Danny for lunch with her sister if he'd come home and asked her to stay.

"Come keep me company and I'll wash the dishes for you." Margaret led the way out of the parlor.

Elizabeth perched on the edge of a chair in the kitchen. "Stay for supper, Mag," she urged, rubbing her round belly. "John probably won't be home until late."

Margaret dunked the plates in the rinse water. "Why do you say that?"

"You haven't heard?"

Margaret glanced over her shoulder. "Obviously."

"There was a terrible accident at the Standard. Lawrence Cobb had his face blown off and another miner lost a hand."

Margaret slowly washed a teacup. "He didn't mention a word of it."

Elizabeth leaned forward. "You've spoken to him? He came home?"

"He was there when I left."

"Gosh, Danny ran off to the saloon to hear all about it. Of course, he would have been running off there anyway." Elizabeth wiggled her bottom back into the chair. "Since John was the one who carried the body out of the mine— at least that's what we heard—I thought he'd have a story to pass around with the drinks."

Margaret rubbed her forehead, still holding the teacup, which dripped warm water down her arm. "Maybe he didn't want to talk about it." She remembered how dirty he'd been. Something must have happened, since he hadn't washed up and changed at the mine the way he was required to. He'd been uncharacteristically angry, too.

"Maybe he wanted your womanly comforts." Elizabeth studied her sister's face while Margaret washed another dish. "How are you and John?" she asked intently.

"We're fine, thank you." Margaret dried her hands.

"Do you like being married, Mag?" Elizabeth stood and searched along the kitchen shelves for the rest of the cookies.

Margaret turned and watched her. "I don't know."

"Because of the bed part?" Elizabeth reached the end of the shelves. "Mag, where are the cookies?"

"I threw them out."

Elizabeth's mouth dropped open. She looked at her sister accusingly then ran to the door. Dirty snow and slush stretched endlessly beyond the steps; only footsteps, no cookies, marred the surface. Elizabeth shut the door on the frigid air and turned and eyed her sister. Margaret had her coat on and was pulling on her gloves.

"Thank you for lunch, Elizabeth."

"Don't be so polite. You made it. I suppose that gives you the right to remove the cookies from my presence."

Margaret wrapped her shawl around her neck and chin. "I've left you stew and bread for supper." She picked up her basket and looked at her sister's pouting face. "Oh, Elizabeth!" She reached into the basket and pulled out a cinnamon-sprinkled sugar cookie and handed it to her sister. Elizabeth's mouth pulled up in delight immediately.

"Be nice to John when you get home, *if* he's still home. Unless, of course, you don't give a hoot about him and plan to leave him in about three months." She took a small bite of her cookie. "A little loving makes up for a lot of bad things in life, Margaret," she added softly, following her sister through the kitchen and the parlor.

Margaret paused with her hand on the front doorknob and looked into her sister's very intent face. Elizabeth thought she was very wise, Margaret knew. She was uncomfortable being thought the fool. Would her dead mother be the only person who'd come close to approving of her? Elizabeth and Victoria, closer to their father, seemed so much happier with people, even if they weren't keeping the spiritual fires burning. "I don't know much of anything anymore, Elizabeth," she said. She opened the door and the cold blast of windy air chilled her. "I'll call on you tomorrow." She trudged home through the slush and ice.

Chapter Fourteen

John was sitting in the same chair as when Margaret had left. He'd washed and changed, and his honey hair shone and waved in the lamplight on the dim, gray afternoon. She felt his handsomeness in the depth of her stomach and the back of her throat as he quietly looked at her.

"You're back."

"Yes." Margaret slowly unpinned her hat and hung it on the hook by the door. She removed her coat and gloves while his dark eyes lingered on her. She noticed his gray sweater had large holes in the elbows, and she thought of the thick red sweater she'd almost finished for him. One stockinged foot was resting on a chair seat before him, his bent leg molded closely by tight, faded denims, almost white at the knee.

"Are you all right?" she asked.

"You heard." He picked up a mug and drank.

She walked a step toward him in the warm kitchen. "What are you drinking?"

His eyes stung her face. "Whiskey."

Her mouth tightened at the expected answer.

John sprang to his feet and thrust the mug under her nose. "It's coffee! Old, reheated coffee."

Margaret stepped back and raised her chin. "I simply asked."

"Nothing is simple with you," he rasped. "I saw your eyes light up with temperance zeal." He shouldered past her and threw the mug into the basin. Margaret flinched at the crack.

"That wasn't necessary," she said.

Without facing her he combed his fingers through his hair. "Maybe I should go to the saloon," he muttered. "God knows, everyone would like a first-hand account."

Margaret stiffened. Elizabeth's words chimed in her head about John wanting comfort and her stomach flip-flopped. "Are you hungry? I could fix you a sandwich."

John shoved his hands deep into his tight pockets and turned to her. "No, I don't want a sandwich."

That wanting light was in his eyes and Margaret's hands went clammy. "Something else? Some cookies?"

"I'm not hungry."

"Well, I'll start on supper. You'll be hungry soon."

The light in his eyes went out. He stared at her and she looked helplessly back, knowing she had pushed him away and unaccountably sorry for it. He strode out of the room.

"Where are you going?"

"To put on my boots!" he shouted from the bedroom.

Margaret followed. "Why?"

"Because I'm going out."

"Don't." She filled the bedroom door.

John looked up from where he sat on the bed lacing his boots. "Give me one good reason for staying."

"It's raining out."

His mouth twitched. He looked down at his feet in intense concentration, then pulled the laces tight on the right boot. "You couldn't have given a better one. How did you know I was scared of rain?" She was quiet and he slowly ied the laces. "We both know you'd rather I drink than make love to you," he said quietly.

Margaret couldn't deny the truth of his words. Anything was better than being wide open and naked with him, losing control, feeling too much. Yet what a hypocrite she'd be if she wanted him to go to the saloon she hated. She didn't really want that. "I don't see why a hot meal wouldn't suffice."

"I'm sure you don't." He wearily leaned down to his left boot.

"We'll talk about it," she said with feigned confidence, moving out of the door and taking a step nearer to him. Talking always helped her sisters.

His hands stilled on the laces and his gaze flicked to her face. "I can talk at the saloon."

Margaret swallowed. "But I don't want you to go there." Her sweaty fingers tightened on the rust wool skirts of her dress. She looked down at his boots briefly before she met his eyes. "I can't let you go there for the solace you should find in your own home." She raised her hand to the first tiny black button at her throat. Her heart pounded with excitement and fear.

His eyes widened, then his face went blank. "So, the lamb will sacrifice herself to the wolf to keep him from the hellfire of the whiskey mill?"

His caustic, bitter tone scraped along her raw nerves. She held her fingers to the second button, where they trembled. "Isn't this what you want?" she asked in a humiliated whisper.

"I don't want a damn martyr!" His eyes snapped with black fire. Margaret stared at him, wondering what in the world to do next. John turned his face from her and gritted his teeth. When he abruptly stood up, Margaret flinched. He took a step around her in the tiny room and then stopped. He cursed, turned and grabbed her, yanking her close. "I do want..."

His mouth came down hard on her parted lips while his fingers dug into her tightly pinned hair. Margaret pulled on his wrists, trying to ease the hurtful pressure of his hands. He was consuming her mouth, yanking out pins as his mouth skittered across her face, tasting cheek, eye, forehead, ear. "I want it down," he rasped against her mouth. "Help me."

Margaret tried, but as she shakily removed pins he attacked the long row of buttons on her dress. He'd undone only a few when he grasped the edges and ripped the garment down, popping buttons.

"Stop it!" Margaret backed away from him, her hair falling around her shoulders and her bodice gaping open. She didn't recognize him in this frenzy, and she stared at him with eyes wide and limbs shaking.

John took a deep breath, then another, deeper one. He looked away from her and lifted his hands to his hips. Little black buttons littered the floor and winked up at him. He kicked one so it skimmed across the wood floor and hit the far wall. He glanced at his wife. She held her bodice together with both hands and her breath was still coming quick. She met his gaze.

"I'm sorry," he said, waiting.

Margaret licked her lips. "Why do you have to be so...so violent?"

He took a deep breath, shook his head and kicked another button. "I am sorry." He couldn't answer her any better. He didn't know what was driving him. He felt he needed her more than he wanted her. Since this morning's accident he'd felt he was about to explode with violent emotion. He took a step toward her.

Margaret held up her hand. "I'll do it." She sat on the bed and looked in the dressing table mirror to take out the remaining hairpins while John shifted from foot to foot beside her. She smelled a scent unusual to her bedroom, like raw meat and blood. Feeling John's eyes on her, she slowly brushed her hair. She took a deep breath and stood and removed all her clothes except for her chemise and drawers. The pungent scent assaulted her again when she folded her garments neatly on top of the dresser. She turned her face towards the foot of the bed, trying to identify the smell. Down on the floor in the narrow space between bed and wall was a pile of clothes. She stepped closer, momentarily forgetting the man staring at her, and walked toward the pile.

His gray flannel shirt lay on top. The soft fabric was ripped, as though it had been removed the same way as her bodice. The rank odor must come from the reddish brown stain that covered a great deal of the shirt. "Blood?" she whispered, already knowing. She couldn't stop staring at that stain. Elizabeth's words came back with new force. John had carried the body. Was this the blood of the man whose face had been blown off? She pressed a hand to her stomach and looked around at her husband's tight face.

"I suppose you're now too faint to continue our previous activities."

Margaret just stared at him, still seeing his soiled clothes, remembering the bright, spreading stain across her father's chest and the bloody linens after her mother's stillbirths and miscarriages and the horrible, painful finality of all that escaping blood.

The air went out of John under her stricken gaze and he sat on the bed. "Someone went to get his wife. She was here by the time I got Larry to the surface. With her two kids. Little boys." He raised a trembling hand to his brow

and held his head with his elbow braced on his knee. ''
don't know why they had to see their pa like that,'' he sai
hoarsely.

Pain unfurled in Margaret's stomach. She took a ste
forward and then another until she stood in front of him
but he didn't look up.

''And the woman sobbed so loud. I couldn't hear any
thing else. But the little boys didn't make a sound. The
were just pale, with glazed eyes. I wanted to push then
away.'' He shuddered, lifted his head and looked at his wif
with her hair down and in her white undergarments
Grasping her hips, he dug his fingers into her soft flesh
pulling her legs into his knees.

When he looked into her eyes, Margaret saw so muc
pain in his that she flinched. He shook her gently, his eye
beseeching her, as if she were his salvation.

''I felt just like them,'' he whispered, ''when my dadd
lay on the ground after he fell off the ladder.'' John sucke
in his breath and turned his face away, shutting his eyes.
tear squeezed out from beneath one of his tightly close
eyes and Margaret began to tremble with the need to com
fort him. She placed her hands on his shoulders, squeeze
gently and lifted them to caress his neck, the neck of
strong man who cared so much. He turned back to her an
circled her wrists with his fingers, holding her tight. ''It wa
my fault he died,'' he confessed. ''I threw him the hamme
instead of walking four steps over and handing it to him.
was mad at him, mad for a petty reason. He leaned out to
far and fell off.'' John couldn't stop the tears that slippe
from his eyes, though they came silently. He tugged Ma
garet's hands down to his hips and opened his legs so tha
she came between his thighs and sank to her knees on th
floor in front of him. He bowed his head against hers. ''I'
do anything to bring him back,'' he whispered. The tea

dripped off his face and fell on Margaret's chest, wetting her skin and dotting her chemise. "I loved that man. He taught me so much, and to think I have to live the rest of my life knowing that I killed him, that I took him away from everything he loved, took him away from me, is just about too much to bear."

Margaret pressed herself against him, wrapped her arms around his back and squeezed. She soaked in his pain. She had such a perfect place for it. Her own hurts in life fit perfectly side by side with his. He hugged her back tightly, absolution found. He gasped with the release of talking of it, crying over it.

Margaret felt her heart expanding to give him more room. Slowly, he pulled away from her, enough to look into her face. Gently, he traced her cheek with a finger and then pressed his mouth to hers. His hand cupped the back of her neck under her soft, thick hair. He read her face with his lips, touching every feature with a lightness that made her quiver. When he slipped his tongue into her mouth she accepted him. When he sought hers she gave it for the first time and he moaned deeply as he sucked gently on her flesh, hugging her belly and breasts into his body. He pulled away and Margaret saw a want and need in his eyes that went beyond simple lust. He grasped her chemise and she closed her eyes and lifted her arms in surrender as he pulled it over her head. One of his hands smoothed her back, pressing her close to him. He sighed. "You feel so good." He ran his hands over her urgently but softly, as if he couldn't get enough of her warm, healthy body. "Get under the covers. It's cold."

He unlaced and pulled off his boots and then joined her under the blankets. He pushed off her drawers immediately. Margaret didn't fight his hands, which seemed to touch her everywhere. She sensed his need to feel her, as if checking to see she was whole, to dull the sight of death. When he rolled over her she slid her hands under his shirt, which he'd pulled out of his trousers, and wrapped her arms around his hot smooth back and parted her legs. He cradled his face in the hair between her neck and shoulder. "You smell so good, so clean."

Satisfaction bloomed within her that she could help take away the pain. She hugged him more tightly, something like love making her want to give him everything.

He kissed her breasts, brushing his cheek and tongue against the tight nipples until she arched repeatedly beneath him. John shuddered. "Oh God, I need you." He unbuttoned his pants with one hand. When he entered her body Margaret sank her teeth into her bottom lip at the sweet pleasure. He moved and she hung on to him tightly.

"Oh, Maggie, Maggie, Maggie," he chanted while he moved ceaselessly on her and in her. His body was burning; her hands and arms felt scorched where they wrapped around him. She began to perspire and her lower body felt like melting wax. She licked her parched lips, not wanting him to stop. She was aching in the place where he moved inside of her, and she couldn't lie still. The ache quickly grew deeper and sharper. Her nails dug into his back and she lifted her hips. His wet mouth was on her neck, his wool sweater abraded her swollen nipples, the buttons of his denims pushed into her soft skin as his straining thighs pressed hers farther apart, and then he surged incredibly deep and tight against her and the ache she felt exploded into spasms of searing pleasure.

When she opened her eyes she looked into his and sensed that nothing would ever be quite the same. She'd given and he had taken. She'd received something she hadn't necessarily wanted, but the exchange had been made. His gaze probed hers. She heard her shallow breathing echoing his.

Her body was still steeped with pleasure and she felt she'd met a stranger within herself. He smiled at her gently, looking satisfied and sleepy. When he rolled off her, she missed him immediately but stayed still, staring up at the ceiling, wondering about this strange pleasure that had left her limp and complacent and feeling full of well-being. She didn't even feel ashamed, just a little sleepy and confused.

She turned her face to look at John. He lay on his back, his eyes closed, his breath even and deep. This man was her husband. The fact was still hard to comprehend, but she felt she knew him a little better now after his painful disclosure. She lifted her hand and softly poked her forefinger into the skin of his lower abdomen. He was real. She glanced up and found him watching her. Her cheeks flamed with heat. She'd been very bold to touch him like that.

He sat up and pulled off his sweater and unbuttoned and removed his shirt. He threw them on the floor and skimmed down his pants. The bed bounced as he shimmied out of the garment. Margaret clutched the sheet to her breasts. His torso was beautiful, all light golden like a statue.

"What are you doing?"

"I'm taking off my socks." He faced her completely naked, the quilt riding low on his waist. They stared at each other.

"We're finished until the day after tomorrow."

"Don't start a fight, Maggie."

"But we have an agreement."

"What about the times I missed?"

"You can't save up times."

"I can and did."

His eyes were too dark, too deep for her to think when looking at them. She glanced away, gathering her wits. "You are so greedy," she grumbled. His hand curved around the back of her neck and pulled her halfway to his descending mouth. He gave her light, unhurried kisses and moved his body close to hers. His naked hip touched hers and the kiss suddenly became hotter. Margaret fell to the pillows beneath him, hot need engulfing her. This was lust she thought

John kissed her until she was hot and limp beneath him. He took the hand that lay at her side and held it to his hip. She didn't pull away until he tried to place her hand on something she wasn't ready for. John took her hand again but placed it on his chest. Their eyes locked as she kept her hand against his hot skin. She traced a small circle over his breast and pressed her fingertips deep. Moaning, he lowered his mouth to hers. She responded so sweetly to his lips and tongue, her own tongue caressing his with a will of its own, that John moaned again. He slid down her, kissing her neck, her collarbone, then her breasts. Her hands combed through his hair, dipped down to his neck and then back up to press into his scalp. He suckled her, filled with exaltation, for this was making love. Finally, finally, she wanted him, she touched him. When he pushed into her she arched her lovely white neck off the bed. She came faster and harder this time, her hands gripping his slowly thrusting hips. She cried out, and the call sent him over the edge.

He didn't roll from her this time but held her still until she drifted to sleep. Then he left the bed and dressed. He was starving.

Margaret woke up with a gasp when he sat back on the bed with a steaming bowl of stew and a hunk of bread. She flushed when he smiled at her. She was naked, body and soul naked after what she'd experienced. She pulled the sheet to her chin and inched up on the pillow.

"Good stew." He held out a spoonful for her. She shook her head. He shrugged and ate it himself. He offered her some bread and she refused again. He slurped and swallowed and *mmmed* his appreciation. Margaret's stomach growled loudly. He gave her a measured look and again held the full spoon close to her lips.

Margaret's jaw clamped tight and her eyes narrowed, but the aroma of spicy gravy made saliva pool in her mouth.

"What's a little stew after what you've already taken from me?" John asked.

Margaret looked into his teasing eyes and he glanced down at his hand, his grin suddenly self-conscious. "And given me," he added softly. When he looked up again his eyes were serious.

Margaret shyly accepted the spoonful and several more, her hands clutching the sheet in her lap, her eyes avoiding his.

He set the empty bowl on the floor by the bed, the spoon clanking against the side of the bowl. "I feel good." He leaned back against his pillow.

Margaret looked longingly at her clothes across the room. John followed her gaze and fetched them for her, minus the corset. She pulled on the chemise so swiftly that John didn't see so much as a breast. As she wiggled into her drawers under the blankets she felt the gush of his seed. The room tilted crazily for a second. She sat up carefully.

"You didn't...didn't...I could have a baby now, couldn't I?"

"Yes."

Margaret wiped the back of her hand across her suddenly sweaty forehead.

"Is that so terrible?"

"I don't want to think about it." She crawled to the end of the bed, got off and put on her clothes.

John watched her whip her hair back up on her head and leave the room without looking at him. She's just scared, he told himself ten times, trying to batten down the anger

that was roused in him. She needed to be reassured, he told
himself, but what in the hell did he know about childbirth? She would be sure to point out his ignorance. But he
didn't want to prevent babies anymore. Coming into her
body had felt wonderful, and as she'd taken his tears, he
wanted her to take his seed. She was making noise in the
kitchen with her pots and pans. He got up and looked in on
her. She was scrubbing the range, furiously.

"Tell me," he asked, leaning a shoulder against the
doorjamb and hitching his thumbs in his pockets. "Is it just
my child you don't want or—"

"No! It has nothing to do with you." She leaned both
palms on the range.

"That's where you're wrong. It has everything to do with
me. You're talking about not ever giving me a family."

"Yes."

John pushed away from the doorjamb, pulled his thumbs
out of his pockets and walked slowly toward her. "Why?
Because you plan on walking out of this marriage?"

She quickly shook her head and then just as quickly
nodded. "I think that would be best." She saw a deep shaft
of hurt in his dark eyes before he looked away from her.

"Are you going to pretend I never existed when you go
back to San Francisco? Or will you be the divorced woman
from Bodie?"

"I don't plan on telling anybody," she answered quietly.

John stared at the wall, trying to understand this, but he
couldn't. "Why?" he asked, turning back to her. She
looked as upset as he felt. "After what happened..." He
trailed off, looking toward the bedroom. He felt un-
manned. She'd acted as though she felt a great deal for him,
yet she wanted to leave him. "How long did you plan to act
this farce out?"

"I told you before we married I wanted a temporary marriage," she responded, her back to him.

"How long?" He ground the words out.

"Until Elizabeth's baby is about a month old."

"Four more months. And what do you expect? Nights of passion in the bedroom when I know you're going to walk out on me?"

Margaret forced herself to face him and felt again what they'd created when she'd so willingly embraced him. He was all over her, like a cobweb, and it was impossible to see all the fine strands that wrapped and clung to her. "You know I didn't want anything to do with that part of marriage." She knew as she spoke that every time he touched her now she'd go up in fire and cling to him. Her body trembled at seeing the hard, angry hurt in his eyes, but she stood straight to hide her fear.

And what if he had already got her with child? Terror filled her at the thought of a child growing inside her, but she couldn't talk about it. Who would help her? She'd have to go back to San Francisco and find a good doctor. Her mother had never let a medical doctor attend her and maybe she would have had a better chance with one. But how did you stop them from dying inside of you? She wouldn't be able to live through that.

"You're right," John said abruptly. "You had it all laid out, the terms clearly stated. I'm the fool who fell on my face. I'm the idiot who was sure I could change your mind. But I don't have to stick around for any more of this." He turned and strode into the bedroom.

Margaret stood and watched him throw some of his clothes into a pile on the bed. He brought out his canvas bag and stuffed his belongings inside. Margaret's terror solidified to a hard black sphere inside her chest. Her breath was shallow and quiet as she gripped her rag in both hands and watched him walk out of the bedroom with his bag. He put on his hat and coat in the kitchen, then paused before he opened the door. He looked at her, his cap pulled low over his eyes so she could only see the bottom half of the dark brown ovals.

"I want you to be happy. I wanted to help make you happy."

"Why me?" she whispered. "Almost any woman of your choosing would love you." Like I think I do, she admitted to herself.

"What if I sold the saloon?" he asked tightly.

Margaret's heart crawled into her throat. "Would you?"

"What if I did?"

She twisted her hands, her eyes beseeching his. "I don't know," she whispered. "I still wouldn't want a child, but..." *Lord, do you care about me that much?*

John turned abruptly, closing the door behind him. Margaret listened to his boots tromp down the steps while the black sphere inside her grew and grew until she gasped. She dropped her rag into her bucket of soapy water and leaned with her hands on the range. "Oh, Lord, what have I done?" she asked aloud. "I think I love him, but I don't want to be a proper wife." Though it was late afternoon, Margaret went back to bed and slept until the next morning.

Chapter Fifteen

Margaret didn't know that love could feel so awful. Christmas Eve morn dawned cold, clear and still. She groaned as she threw off the covers. She could make noise. She was alone. John had slept elsewhere, eaten elsewhere, bathed and dressed elsewhere since their last confrontation more than three weeks ago. The house was too quiet without him. She missed his teasing smiles, his candy surprises, his warm length in bed, the interest in his eyes when she talked and his happy whistle. Frequently and reluctantly, she remembered the pleasure he'd given and taken in their bed and she ached with a dull throb. Why had it felt so divine? Why had her heart never felt so close to another? She hated her aloneness, but she had made a terrible wife, with her dread of childbirth and her reluctance for the intimacies of marriage. And a terrible wife for John, especially, since she hated the saloon and hated Bodie. He was better off without her. Why couldn't he see that? Why did he have to be so angry with her? The thought of him hating her made her sad and lonelier still.

Elizabeth had been prying mercilessly everyday into the state of her sister's marriage. Danny had told her John was living at a hotel, doing well in the saloon and never coming home to her, but Margaret remained mum and would tell her sister nothing, no matter how provoking the questions. She had promised Elizabeth she'd attend the Christmas Eve dinner at the new Grand Central Hotel with her and Danny. She couldn't see staying home alone on Christmas Eve, and Elizabeth had assured her that John would be busy at the saloon.

The day passed quickly. Margaret worked at the Odd Fellows Hall with the other Methodist women, accepting and passing out presents for the town's children. They had three Christmas trees set up and decorated to add gaiety to the room, but Margaret still felt gray inside.

Evening descended quickly. She donned a deep plum dress, her favorite color. Dressing in a color besides gray or brown made her feel almost festive. She pushed two golden citrine earrings through her ears and fastened her mother's locket around her neck. The gold heart had a clip of hair from both her mother's and grandmother's head. Margaret hoped to give it to a niece someday.

She put her finest pair of shoes in a small basket to change into at the hotel. After meeting Elizabeth and Danny at their home, she tromped with them through snowy streets to the hotel. In the front lobby they shed their coats and old boots and smoothed their hair.

"The gown looks lovely on you," Margaret complimented her sister. Elizabeth was wearing a burgundy velvet altered by Margaret to fit her expanding waistline.

Elizabeth beamed and lifted her blond head higher. Danny ushered them down the hall and into the dining room. A string quartet was warming up in the hall and Margaret's nerves tingled in anticipation of the music. Coal oil lamps were profuse and high and flooded the large room with bright light. The new gold-tinted flowered paper on the wall gleamed. Long tables were pushed together and guests were crowded up and down the room, the ladies smiling and gracefully accepting the chairs pulled out for them. Margaret followed Elizabeth's slight waddle down the row of occupied chairs to two empty ones on their side. Danny pulled out one chair for Elizabeth and took the other one for himself. The nearest empty chair was directly across the table and next to John Banning.

Margaret gaped at her husband, his elbow planted on the table, a champagne glass in his hand, his eyes dark and watchful as he met hers. He slowly stood and nodded. Elizabeth turned to Margaret, who still stood behind her. "You'll have to go around, Mag."

Margaret curbed a rude retort and didn't miss the twinkle in her sister's eyes. Elizabeth had known John would be here and had unfairly let her think he'd be at the saloon. What an untrustworthy brat! She made her way around the table, the roomful of laughter sounding tinny. John pulled out her chair and she nodded curtly, her nerves thrumming with wild anxiety at being so near him. He looked so handsome in his white pleated shirt and mother-of-pearl buttons. His coat and trousers were black and his hair shone richly in the lamplight. He pulled in his chair beside her.

"Hello, wife."

His warm, sweet champagne breath fanned her ear and she shivered. He touched one of her earrings with the tip of his forefinger. "Pretty." Her jaw tightened. "I've never seen you so colorful," he continued in a mild voice.

"It is Christmas."

"Yes, a brief spell of light in a time of darkness."

She glanced up from her white china plate and became lost in his gaze. Could she help it if the dark nut brown of his eyes was beautiful? He looked at her with irrepressible good humor. "This being Christmas, and we being the civilized folk we are, I know we can get along for one evening. We're just another husband and wife come to dine and dance.'' He filled her champagne glass.

"I won't drink it," she said stiffly.

"Of course not, but you won't have to constantly refuse the offers." He nodded toward an eager-to-impress waiter who stepped quickly up and down the table with his sweating bottle of liquor wrapped in a white cloth.

Margaret gave a slight nod of her head. "I see." She felt John staring at her. She wanted to tell him she didn't dance, either, which was true. At least, she didn't think she remembered how. She hadn't danced since she was fourteen. She was honest enough to admit that saying as much would only begin a disagreement. At least that would be something to keep him at a distance so she could calm herself.

"I like you in purple," he said, placing his hand on the back of her chair and leaning back to look at her from head to skirts.

"It's plum." She glanced at his face and was irritated to see he was amused.

"The color that I like best is the sea green of your eyes."

She felt her face heat. "Stop it," she whispered, glancing around, but everyone was absorbed in joviality, good company and fine liquor.

"However, the red in your face is a nice color, too."

She rounded on him then, her mouth pursed. He snatched his glass up and clinked it with hers, smiling broadly. "Cheers, Maggie." He took a good swallow and winked at her over the rim. "Go on, try to subdue me," he whispered merrily against her ear. "Your commanding ways are so exciting. And I know you won't enjoy yourself unless you try to restrain me."

"That's not so."

He cocked an eyebrow. "Maybe I'm wrong. Maybe you enjoy yourself by suppressing your own enjoyment." His hold on her gaze broke when the man next to him nudged him with a platter of oysters. The corners of his lips turned down and he offered the food to Margaret. She shook her head, grasped the platter and passed it on. He flashed her a smile. "We have one thing in common, hey?"

Margaret could not repress a small smile. "Our mutual dislike of oysters is hardly enough to base a marriage on."

"But at least we don't have to watch each other gulp down the slimy things." He shuddered.

"And us born in San Francisco. You'd think we'd have a taste for them." They had no problems with any of the other food offered. Margaret spread the caviar on a warm piece of sourdough bread and dropped a dollop of horse-radish on her slice of rare roast beef. She tried the ham studded with cloves, the yams whipped with brown sugar and the carrots with melted butter. While they ate the music swelled around them and voices broke into "Deck the Halls." When dessert came she absolutely refused.

"I can't," she whispered. "I'll truly burst with one more bite."

John looked down at her stomach, compressed beneath her dress by a cruel corset. "If that thing wasn't laced so tight... Must be what keeps you so thin."

"I didn't realize you objected."

John's grin was lazily sensuous. He picked up his wine-glass. "Yes, I'd like to see a fat Margaret."

"Fat?" exclaimed Elizabeth across the table. "She's never even been slightly plump a day in her life. She takes after Daddy. Maybe if she was in my condition..." Elizabeth frowned, looking at her hands, which had grown pudgy in the last month.

Margaret jerked her face from her sister when she felt John squeeze her knee. She looked at him and pushed his hand off her. He held his fork up, a moderate-sized piece

of mince pie cradled on the tines. She shook her head. He
wiggled it under her nose and the spicy scent was not wasted
on her.

"Just a taste," he coaxed.

She went cross-eyed watching the fork come closer.
When she could no longer see the pie, her gaze flicked up
to meet his eyes. He pricked her bottom lip with the tines.
"Come on. It's very good." She was held by his ardent,
teasing eyes. He dragged the tines along her flesh. "Open."
Her heart pounded, the room faded. There were only his
eyes, his lovely, dark eyes, and the ungovernable quirk of
his sensuous mouth. She didn't realize she'd opened her
mouth until he scraped the pie off against the back of her
top teeth. Sweet spice burst in her mouth. His eyes were
warm, and Margaret felt a hot flush of perspiration dot her
upper lip and forehead. She turned her gaze from him. No
one was paying them any mind. She was probably the only
sober one in the crowd. She glanced back at the man beside her, who was calmly finishing off his pie. Had she
imagined the intimacy of the moment? Had he simply been
making merry in the festive atmosphere?

She couldn't have been happier to adjourn to the parlor
of the hotel shortly after while the dining room was cleared
for dancing. The crowd exuberantly sang the words to the
carols the quartet played. John stood behind the chair she
sat in and squeezed her shoulder from time to time. It took
her two minutes to settle her tripping nerves each time he
touched her. She suspected he was barely aware he was even
touching her. His voice, husky and low, fell around her. She
held on to it apart from the others while she silently
mouthed the words herself.

The hall was ready for dancing, but Margaret would have
preferred to go home. She refused John the first dance. He
didn't seem bothered and danced with a merchant's wife

instead. He danced with Elizabeth and Mrs. Miller and Mrs. Baxter, and a blonde and a brunette, before finally he came back to her side. This time he didn't ask but took her arm and swung her into a waltz. Margaret stumbled over her feet. He raised his brows inquiringly.

"It's been a long time," she said.

He pulled her a little closer so her thigh banged against his. His hand tightened over hers and he whirled her around and around. His eyes locked with hers, his lips in a gentle smile. The music and the laughter filled her head and she grew warm where their bodies met. She was his wife, he could hold her closer than the others. She didn't pull away when their loins bumped, though his smile curved wider. The steady steps of the dance pumped heat through her until she was warm everywhere. She tightened her fingers on his shoulder to steady herself.

"Where did you learn to dance?" she asked.

"My mama."

"You do it well."

His smile flashed. "Why, a compliment from my wife!"

She flushed hotly. "Am I so stingy with them?"

John inclined his head. "But then, maybe I don't deserve them," he said, his cockiness gone.

Margaret didn't want to talk anymore. She kept her gaze confined to his lips, chin and neck and followed his lead around and around, relaxing into his arms and the music. The room of people slipped away, then the years, and she was fourteen again, wearing a white dress and dancing with Thomas Markham, away from her mother's prying eyes for the first time. Such promise and gaiety had seemed possible for her then. It had been years since she'd worn a white dress. Matronly colors were all her mother had bought her, and all she'd purchased for herself. For a moment she wished she was wearing white. She lifted her gaze to John's face and stared into his eyes. She felt young and close to carefree when locked in his admiring gaze. The dance ended and the appreciative applause brought the crowded room back into focus for Margaret. A beefy, red-faced man clapped her husband on the back. "Is this your lovely wife?"

John introduced her to Barnaby O'Brien, who almost immediately asked John for permission to dance with her. Margaret looked to John for refusal, but he very amiably abandoned her to the man, never looking at her tense face. The next dance was an exuberant polka, which Margaret tripped through the first few bars of before she remembered the steps. Mr. O'Brien was a big stepper with hot breath reeking of onions, oysters and whiskey. His hand was damp and squeezed hers convulsively. He chuckled when she banged into him and whirled her faster. Margaret expended every ounce of her energy just keeping on her feet without making contact with his body. When the dance ended he bowed over her hand and then tried to pull her along for the next one. Margaret yanked her hand from his, not caring a whit for her manners, and escaped to the side of the dance floor. She searched for John, her hands kneading each other in front of her. She found the dark brown eyes not two yards away, focused directly and intently on her. He was sipping liquor. He raised his glass and looked at her over it while he swallowed. She squared her jaw and made her way toward him, refusing two invitations to dance in the short distance.

"I'd like to go home now," she said upon reaching him.

John shrugged and shook his head, pointing with his glass toward the dance floor. "It doesn't appear that Danny and Elizabeth will be ready any time soon."

Margaret glanced to where her sister and Danny were waltzing, smiles on their faces. At first she was confused, and then sudden understanding followed by hot shame coursed through her. Humiliation that he didn't care to escort her home kept her staring at the dancing couples instead of turning to the man at her side. Far worse was that she'd let him know she'd expected his escort when they hadn't come together. Jagged anger at herself ripped through her. How could she have been so bold, so spoiled, to have expected anything from him when they were at such odds? Did she expect him to be a husband to her only when it was convenient for her? How selfish she must appear to him.

She took a small breath and chanced a brief glance at him. He looked unconcerned, practically unaware of her presence as he watched the dancing, his foot tapping to the music.

"I believe you're right," Margaret said lightly. "They do seem to be having a wonderful time." Her hands were trembling and she buried them in the folds of her dress. "Well, Merry Christmas, John," she said softly. Her gaze ricocheted off his face to the dancers and then the door that she began walking toward.

John turned his head, following her with his eyes. He hadn't missed the wounded vulnerability in her beautiful eyes. He'd wanted to rebuff her—she'd rejected him plenty—but seeing the effect of his words on her sensitive face made him instantly contrite. And she'd tried so well to hide it. He went after her, regretting that his pride had fouled this evening. He'd known she hadn't wanted to dance with Big Barnaby and had watched the stumbling, graceless progress of the couple around the floor, thinking she'd really appreciate him after that. And then she expected him to take her home when he didn't want her to go home. He caught her arm as she entered the lobby. She spun toward him, her eyes wide with surprise.

"Stay," he asked.

Margaret's forehead furrowed with confusion.

"We'll dance again," he said, tugging on her wrist.

Margaret looked past him to the dancers. Her gaze flicked from woman to woman, all dressed in their fancy things and smiling, drinking wine and champagne and looking very happy. She shook her head and pulled her hand free.

"Why not?" he asked sharply.

Margaret retrieved her boots from a pile of boots and sat down on a sofa. "I'm tired," she answered, sounding weary, but she also realized something. She was different from most other women, and not in a good way. There was something wrong with her. She was beginning to see that. All these years she'd thought, been told to think, that the problem was with everyone else. Others were too crude, too immoral, too slovenly, too stupid. But these people seemed quite happy with themselves and one another. Before, she had felt so superior, insulated by her righteousness, kept company by it. Now, when she was the one who couldn't measure up, who was lacking, she felt incredibly sad and lonely, and yes, tired.

"Well, I'll walk you home then," John snapped, and searched for his boots. He had to dig them out of a pile in the corner. He sat on a sofa across from her and yanked off his dress shoes.

Margaret, her boots on, her shoes in the basket, sat straight and looked at him. "That's not necessary."

"It's late." He tied his boots and stood.

She stood, as well. She didn't know how to dissuade him; he looked very determined. "Very well." She pulled on her cloak, hood and gloves.

They walked home quickly and quietly in the cold night. He opened the door for her but didn't come in. Margaret lighted the lamp while he waited on the back steps.

"Would you like some coffee?" she asked.

"No, thank you. I'd better be going."

"Back to the dance?"

John shoved his hands into his pockets and shrugged.

"Thank you for walking me home."

He nodded and began to turn away.

"I'm making Christmas dinner tomorrow. Danny and Elizabeth and the Miller family will be here. Would you like to come?"

He faced her, studied her. He shook his head. "The saloon will be busy with the mines shut down for the day. We'll have our hands full, especially when Danny is over here."

"Then you have to come in now so I can give you your present."

His feet did not move. "You didn't need to buy me a present."

"I wanted to."

"I don't have any presents for you," he said quickly, regretting the hasty words when he saw how they pulled her head up. "Look." He climbed the steps and leaned his hand against the doorframe. "This marriage is a sham. You want it in name only. Don't go doing nice little things for me as though I were your loving husband. Stop pretending."

Margaret clenched her hands. He was right, but it felt so awful to have him leave her here at the door. She wanted something she didn't understand, things she wouldn't dare name, and she knew deep, deep down inside that she could get them from John Banning if she dared. She watched him take a step back and begin to turn. Yet she was confused, too, for he ran hot and cold with her. "And what about you? You did your share of pretending tonight, acting the attentive husband. And you *will* accept my gift.''

He trotted down the rest of the stairs, turned and saluted her from the snow-covered ground. ''Whatever you say.'' He walked away and heard the door close and lock behind him. He sighed, rolled his shoulders and glanced up at the stars. His breath fogged out in front of him. Women. Margaret. She wanted him. She didn't want him. Tonight had been fun, dancing with her, holding her, flirting with her while looking into those beautiful eyes. But he didn't need the torture of being alone with her.

He shuddered. The cold felt good and clean and drove out the warm feelings in his body. He stepped briskly back down the street to his saloon. He hoped Keith and Thomas and the new man, Joe, had been able to handle the crowd tonight. His attendance at the party had been a last-minute idea. He'd received a letter from his mother today that had made him want the company of his wife. He knew no better distraction than her difficult personality.

He'd written home when he thought he still had a marriage. If he'd only waited a little longer he never would have had to mention Margaret. She'd have been a part of his life, a brief part, that his family never knew of. Instead, he'd had to announce it. His mother wanted to meet her. He shook his head. No chance. Margaret would return to San Francisco and maybe he never would. He hadn't missed the fact that Pat had not written and therefore had not forgiven him for his part in Pa's death. John's gut tightened to think that Pat still blamed him. He swore softly and bent to gather up a handful of snow, patted a ball out of it and threw it at a post on the porch of the Bon Ton Lodging House. The slap and spray of wet snow was gratifying and John scooped up more. His mother had written that his brother needed him, that the business was not doing well with only hired help. But Pat didn't need the help of a brother he hated.

John opened The Fortune doors and walked through the lobby, where cigars and bottled spirits were sold, to the double doors of the saloon. He stood a moment surveying the noise and the crowd under glowing lights, and then Keith saw him and waved him over. John forcibly pushed thoughts of Margaret and family aside and walked behind the bar.

Chapter Sixteen

Margaret made a feast for Christmas dinner. The four Miller children made enough noise to muddle her thoughts of John.

"John bought me a beautiful cradle for Christmas, Mag. You have to come over and see it."

Margaret set down the warm bowl of beaten, sweetened yams and stared at Elizabeth. "He did?"

"It's beautiful, isn't it, Danny? He painted it white with red stenciled hearts. What did he give you?"

"He hasn't finished it yet." Margaret turned from the company and hurried back to the kitchen for the turkey. Her cheeks burned. She couldn't meet anyone's eyes when she returned, sure she'd see their pitying knowledge of her falsehood. Danny, Elizabeth and the children were ready to fork up their food as Margaret set the last bowl on the table. She sat and cleared her throat. "I'll say grace." She made it long. "God bless those that are not here," she summed up, "Victoria and George, Aunt Diane and Aunt Matilda and especially Mother and Father, may they rest in your eternal arms. Amen."

"You let the food get cold just like Mama did," Elizabeth accused, handing the bread basket to Danny.

Danny, sitting at the head of the table, sliced the turkey with the ivory-handled carving knife John had given her. Margaret got lost for a moment in memories of her wedding night while she watched the knife slice through the meat.

After her company had eaten as much as they could, she packed a basket of food for John. She covered the basket with a cloth and laid the tissue-wrapped sweater she'd knitted and the sealskin gloves she'd purchased on top. Another dishcloth finished it off. Danny took the basket to the saloon shortly after dinner, eager to see how deluged with business The Fortune was. The women cleared up while Mr. Miller sat in the parlor, which Margaret had opened up for the holiday. The children played at his feet except for Ann Miller's eldest girl, who helped the women. "He's just waiting for me to finish up here and take the children back home so he can go see how business is doing at the saloon, too," Ann confided over hot, soapy water.

"Men!" Elizabeth exclaimed, laughing.

"You don't mind?" Margaret demanded, shoving a serving bowl inside the cupboard, looking from one to the other. There was a wistfulness in her sister's eyes, but Ann replied blithely.

"Just you wait until you have children, Margaret. A husband is one more to wait on and not as easy to distract, absolutely no help and a persistent critic. If it wasn't for saloons I'd take to the bottle myself."

Margaret stared at her with mouth open.

"You can hand me the greasy dishes now," Ann Miller said.

Margaret handed her a pan.

* * *

A week plodded by in numbing cold and Margaret never saw John. He sent her a brief note thanking her for the gifts. She burned the scrap of paper.

"He's very busy," Elizabeth told her. "The Fortune is doing well. You should be pleased."

"I'm delighted he's glutting the township with alcohol."

"He's putting the food on your table."

"No wonder my appetite is so pitiful."

"You never did eat much. I used to think you were so stingy with yourself to make everyone else feel like pigs."

Margaret set her teacup down on the table. "Oh, really? What changed your mind?"

"I now know you can't stand to enjoy yourself. That's why your husband moved out to a hotel."

"That was his choice, Elizabeth."

The younger woman rolled her eyes. "Please!"

"Well, maybe I did want him to leave! It was for the best. We're incompatible. I make a terrible wife, Elizabeth," she confessed softly.

Elizabeth stared at her sister. She'd never heard her admit she was terrible at anything. "How are you terrible?"

Margaret averted her eyes. "I'm scared of the..." She waved her hand toward the bedroom. "It's so intimate. I feel like I'm giving up my soul. And I'm so frightened of getting with child and having it die inside of me, like what happened so often to Mama. I start to think about it and I want to run away from him." She looked at Elizabeth to see how she had taken her big sister's first shared confidences. Elizabeth was rubbing her big belly with fearful eyes. Margaret flushed with self-recrimination for her inappropriate words. She did not enjoy seeing Elizabeth worried about her baby's birth. "Do you want another piece of cake?" Margaret asked, hastily lifting the plate.

Elizabeth accepted the offered sweet, quickly recovering her happy self. "Come to The Fortune tonight, Mag. It's New Year's Eve," she said quickly as her sister's mouth dropped open. "They're letting ladies in. It's perfectly respectable. A few of the high-class saloons are doing it just tonight to celebrate the New Year. Some of the saloons do it every night—the respectable ones I'm speaking of. They're some of the warmest places in town and some folks don't have much wood. Even children can come."

"I wouldn't—"

"They'll serve us tea and sandwiches."

"I don't—"

"What are you scared of? The Fortune's a first-class establishment. No floozies allowed."

"I will not do my socializing in a saloon."

Elizabeth banged her cup and saucer down on the table. "You don't do any socializing at all! You're the unfriendliest person I've ever known. You could at least go to keep me company! You're so selfish! You're getting more and more like Mother everyday. How you can want to be like that witch, I'll never understand!"

"Don't call her names! Good Lord, she was your mother!"

"Well, I certainly wouldn't call her names when she was alive or I might have gotten locked in the wardrobe like you did. Now she can't get me. Don't look so shocked. Did you really think Victoria and I didn't know that she sometimes did that to you? Oh, we made sure we looked real pretty and smiled real sweet whenever we entered a room with her in it."

"You don't understand. She had a hard life, what with losing all those babies and—"

"Maybe, but I saw how she tried to make everyone else's life miserable. That woman couldn't bear for anyone to be happy. I asked Daddy why he ever married her. He said she was the prettiest girl in Brooklyn when she was sixteen and he thought he was in heaven when he ate her cooking. And here you are, probably the best cook in Bodie, with the cleanest house, and you're a miserable woman, Margaret Ann Warren!"

"It's Banning."

"Is it? You certainly fooled me."

"I don't see your husband home much more than mine, Elizabeth," Margaret snapped, instantly regretting the cut.

Elizabeth flushed a dark red. "At least I *want* mine home! At least I know how to love. And if I hadn't had to get pregnant, I would be out there with him."

Margaret didn't doubt for one second that her sister would be serving drinks behind the bar alongside her husband if she could fit back there, but she did doubt her own sense in letting this quarrel go on. She rubbed her temple with her forefinger. "All right, I'll go with you New Year's Eve, strictly to keep you company. Will that make you feel better?"

Elizabeth sniffed, her pretty little nose in the air. She glanced at her frowning, worried sister and lowered her chin. "Yes, it would."

Margaret wore black. She grasped a basket of sewing in one gloved hand. The lights, the warmth, the noise as they entered almost shoved her back out the double doors. Elizabeth pushed firmly in the small of her back. Margaret's gaze swiveled to the right side of the room where she'd seen her father die. Nothing about death clung to the crowded round tables now.

"Let's get a seat while there are still some left." Elizabeth led them to where a group of women clustered at tables around the wood stove. Plates with sandwiches and cakes were on every table. Children sat in their best clean clothes, close to the stove. Margaret sat next to a woman nursing her baby. She followed the babe's eyes, which were fascinated by something above. Margaret also stared when she looked up at the beautiful cut glass chandelier, which threw prisms of light around the room from the profusion of wall and ceiling lamps.

"Nice, huh?" Elizabeth nudged her in the side, her voice full of excitement at being out of the house.

Margaret nodded and slowly lowered her eyes to the long mahogany bar directly across from her. John. A man was talking to him, gesturing animatedly, but John was staring at her. She executed a tight wave and he bobbed a stiff nod. She looked away and stared at the teapot but saw only his crisp white shirt, black vest and black arm garter and his thick honey hair, free of oily tonic.

"If you want tea so much you just have to lift the pot," Elizabeth said, reaching for the handle. She poured them each a cup. The tea was hot and strong, and the ham sandwiches were delicious. Margaret ate three without counting. Her nerves had played out and she couldn't curb herself.

The nursing baby was five months old. Margaret had asked. He was a beautiful bald child with big brown eyes. Something stirred inside Margaret as she watched the child beat its mother's breast with his fist. Dee, the mother, was impressed with the saloon. Her husband brought her a glass of sherry and Margaret hid her disapproval by pulling out the piece of quilt she was working on. The women at the table admired the green, white and blue piece of art.

"It's a baby quilt. For my little niece or nephew here," she said, inclining her head toward Elizabeth.

"I'm lucky to have such a sister." Elizabeth beamed. "You should see the baby clothes she's made."

The fortifying food and tea kept Margaret's hand nimble. Her eyes strayed frequently to where her husband worked one end of the bar. Danny worked the middle and a man Margaret didn't know worked on the other end, taking up Danny's slack when he visited the ladies and replenished their refreshments. She never saw her husband take a drink of anything but water or coffee. Close to midnight, when the pitch in the room was increasing, he came over. Margaret felt hot and cold simultaneously as he leaned down at her side. The chatter of the women at her table increased in inanity as they squabbled over the best way to bake bread in a Bodie oven.

"This is a surprise," he said so softly near her ear that she knew none of the women could hear him.

"Elizabeth wanted my company."

"Obliging of you."

She couldn't tell if he mocked or complimented her, so she simply nodded.

"You look like you've come to a wake."

She glanced up at him then. His eyes were amused and she allowed herself a small smile. "If I wore plum it might look as if I were enjoying myself."

His answering smile was appreciative and sensual. "And are you?"

If she said no she'd be lying, but she couldn't say yes. "I'm making do."

He nodded. "It's a pleasure seeing you," he said formally, and walked back to the bar.

"A little courtship with our handsome saloon owner?" teased Dee. The other women all grinned at her.

Margaret glanced around the table and flushed with embarrassment.

"My sister is married to him," announced Elizabeth. There was a collective gasp at the table. Margaret stabbed the needle into the quilt.

"I thought he lived in a hotel," Dee said, puzzled.

Margaret looked up expressionlessly. "Sometimes he does."

"Newlyweds, are ya?" asked a robust woman across the table. Margaret nodded. "Sometimes it takes a while to adjust to marriage. My Joe and me fought days on end. Five children later I'm too worn-out to fight with him."

"I think the good Lord gave us babies just to keep us occupied," another woman said.

"He could have waited a bit longer," complained Elizabeth.

"You won't feel that way when the babe gets here," said Dee. "This little one is my first. When I held him in my arms I felt blessed. There were moments when I thought I wouldn't live to see him. The doctor had to almost sit on my belly to push him out!"

Margaret's stitches went crooked before she steadied her hand. She'd seen a midwife do just that to her mother when she was thirteen. The women continued to discuss babes and birthing and child rearing until the revelry gained momentum close to midnight. Danny poured the women champagne and passed bottles of it among the men. The crowd had grown and billowed around the room. A noisemaker was slapped into Margaret's hand by another woman.

"Where is that husband of mine?" exclaimed the robust woman. "I want my first kiss of the New Year."

Elizabeth's eyes widened. "Oh, Mag, we've got to go to the bar!" She yanked on Margaret's hand until her sister dropped her sewing. At the bar Elizabeth released her sister's hand, pushed her toward the end of the bar and wove her way through the crowd to find her own husband. Margaret lost sight of her sister's blond head in the press of men and looked down at the noisemaker she held. People were spinning them already in the seconds left. The buzzing noise and gleeful shouts filled the room. Margaret looked up. John was across the bar handing out champagne bottles. This was ridiculous, she thought. She didn't want a New Year's kiss, but she stood there and stared at him until she caught his eye.

His brows rose in question. She felt her face go stern and stiff. Someone grabbed another bottle out of his hand and his eyes didn't budge from her face. Only seconds were left until midnight. Men were crowded at the bar, separating the two of them. The countdown resounded in her ears. She took a step forward, then another. Her slim shoulder slipped between the men at the bar. A few corks popped prematurely. Margaret stood on the brass foot rail, her hands gripping the bar, and John hefted himself up on the counter, his hips braced against the polished mahogany, his palms flat on the shiny surface. *"Happy New Year!"* broke out all over the room at the stroke of midnight. She leaned forward and their mouths met hard and quick. They pulled back briefly.

"Happy New Year," he murmured, then surged forward and took her mouth again, this time more demonstratively, with his tongue thrusting through her lips. Margaret grabbed his shoulders when his force almost pushed her away. His mouth continued reckless and ardent on hers while someone slapped him on the back and grabbed another bottle of champagne from behind the bar.

Margaret was gasping when he levered himself back to the floor behind the bar. Their eyes held, his alight with

ire she'd ignited. Her heart pumped madly. A man slith-
red between her and the bar, then another. She leaned to
ne side not to lose sight of John's dark eyes. One more
nan came to the bar and John looked away to serve them,
napping the connection. Margaret stepped back and stared
t the backs of heads of men she didn't know. She wanted
o push them all away; she wanted to extend her arm over
he bar and touch John's shoulder again. Instead, she gave
er head a little shake and turned away. How could she
ave felt more connected to him in a few moments than she
ver had with anyone else in her life? Elizabeth waved to
er, holding a glass of champagne, her big round belly
naking men scatter in front of her. Margaret sighed.

"Elizabeth, you already drank a glass at the table before
nidnight."

"I like it."

"I'm taking you home. You look exhausted."

The blonde tilted her head and drained the glass. "Now
'll sleep well. You don't know how uncomfortable it is be-
ng so huge." They pulled on their wraps back at the table
nd said goodbye to the couple of women still sitting there.
'Did you kiss John?" Elizabeth asked as they wound their
vay through the crowd to the door.

"Yes."

"Why, Margaret, I'm proud of you."

"You're a silly girl, Elizabeth."

"We can't all be as serious as you." The piano player
tarted banging the keys again and Elizabeth grabbed
Margaret's arm. "Let's stay a little longer."

Margaret arched one chestnut brow. "We could. And we
ould sleep late. I'll just have to cancel the morning's sleigh
ide."

Elizabeth gasped. "Never mind. We'll go."

Margaret held her sister's arm as they walked outside and down the plank walk. Margaret searched for ice, while Elizabeth chattered about whether she wanted a boy or a girl.

"As if you have a choice," muttered Margaret. "Just be happy if it's healthy."

"Oh, don't be a wet rag."

"Careful, these are steps here."

"I'm so fat I can't even see them." Elizabeth thought that was funny and laughed and laughed. When she settled down she bent her head to her sister's shoulder. "Thanks for coming, Mag."

"You're welcome." Margaret tightened her arm around her sister's waist and wondered why this didn't feel like enough anymore.

Margaret awoke to the clatter of someone in her kitchen. She sat up, her heart stroking hot blood into her head. A familiar whistle trailed into the bedroom. The intruder was not a criminal. Margaret swung her legs out of the bed and wrapped a quilt around her. She walked quietly to the doorway of the kitchen. John dropped a thick slice of butter into a frying pan. He turned his head to her as the sizzle of hot fat filled the silence.

"What are you doing?" She pushed back a strand of hair that had escaped her braid.

His eyes twinkled and he smiled roguishly, looking from the top of her head to her thick, gray woolen socks. He held up a bowl in his right hand. "Making pancakes."

"In the middle of the night?"

"It's about three in the morning." He shrugged. "I'm hungry. The saloon didn't have the fixings for what I wanted."

"Oh."

He spooned in the thick batter under Margaret's watchful eyes. He looked sober. She didn't smell any alcohol fumes emanating from him, but the pan of warming syrup on the stove filled her nose with its sweet scent.

"Do you want some?" he asked, his gaze sliding back to her.

"I don't usually eat this early." She walked to the window to avoid looking at his mouth, which reminded her of that ungoverned kiss. Such a beautiful mouth. "It's snowing."

"Lightly."

She turned around to view him from behind. She realized with a jolt what he was wearing. "You're wearing my sweater!"

"Mmm-hmm." He flipped the cakes.

The red sweater fit perfectly over his broad shoulders and long back. "Do you like it?" she couldn't help asking.

He nodded. "But not as much as I like who made it." He looked at her then and Margaret thought the floorboards beneath her were going to collapse. She watched him get two plates and two forks and stack two pancakes on each plate. He poured the warm syrup over the cakes. "Come sit down." He set the plates down on the kitchen table and poured more batter into the pan.

Margaret took a seat and wrapped the quilt tightly under her arms. He sat across from her. "Dig in." The cakes were light and melted in her mouth along with the sweet syrup.

"Very good." He gave her two more. "I didn't think I could eat so much at three in the morning," she said after finishing her seconds.

"I think there's probably a lot you don't know about yourself."

"Really?" She pushed her sticky plate away from her. "I don't think I know much about you, either."

"What do you want to know?" He leaned back against his chair and waited.

Margaret shrugged.

"You don't even know what you want to know." He got up and poured more batter into the pan then stood with arms crossed over his chest and his feet spread, looking down at her.

"I'm not one to ask personal questions."

"Then I guess you'll never know me personally." He turned his back on her and inspected his pancakes.

Margaret was examining the crescent whites of her thumbnails when he sat back down at the table with his stacked plate and glass of milk. She looked up as he took a long draft. "How come you didn't drink any alcohol tonight?"

He put his glass down. "I don't when I'm working."

She licked her lips. The crust over her repressed curiosity had just been flaked off. Now every question she'd ever had about him was oozing to the surface. "Why did you come to Bodie?"

He pushed his half-eaten pancakes away. "To get away from my family."

"You don't like them?"

John prepared himself for the inquisition. "I had to get away from everything that reminded me of my father. My brother and I couldn't work together since he understandably blamed me for Pa's death." He kept his face expressionless as she studied him.

"He hasn't forgiven you yet?"

John shrugged. He didn't mention that yesterday he'd received a short note from his brother. *Come back*, was all it had said. John felt torn between anger at the terse com mand, relief that his brother wanted him back and wonder as to whether Pat had forgiven him or just needed his help.

"Will you ever go back to San Francisco?" she asked softly.

He shrugged again.

"No wonder I don't know much about you. You don't answer questions!"

"Try again."

"What were you and your father fighting about?"

"My mother." He leaned forward and touched his glass, running his thumb and forefinger up and down it. Margaret's brows rose, commanding him to elaborate. "She'd made arrangements for me to escort the daughter of one of her friends to the theater. This was not the first time, or the first girl she had convinced I wanted to marry."

"You didn't like this girl?"

John shrugged. "She was pretty. She was also putty in my mother's hands. But the point was I didn't need my mother to pick my women." John watched Margaret digest all his words.

"Will you ever forgive your mother?"

"I already have."

"Do you like Bodie so much more than home?"

"I came out here to do something different. And I have. And you've been a wonderful distraction." He smiled in an attempt to inject some lightness into the conversation.

Margaret was dependably serious. "Distraction from what?" she asked, sitting straighter.

His eyes flicked away from her impatiently. "From what I've already told you. From the accident," he added quietly.

"What happens when I'm not such a distraction?"

A smile cracked and grew wide across his face. "You'll never be mush in my hands. You'll always be kicking up the dust about something."

Their eyes held until Margaret turned away from his warmly appreciative gaze. She heard the scrape of his chair as he got up and she listened to the tread of his footsteps as he walked to the counter. Hearing a few intimate details of his family somehow made the feelings she tried so hard to curb for this man bloom and flourish. Every detail of his life that made her know him more was like another drop of water on a dying plant. She clenched her teeth to clamp down the love she felt for this man, but it had been smoldering for too long. She didn't remember when exactly it had begun. When he came back to the table he sat in the chair next to her and tugged on her braid so she turned her head. She followed his eyes to his lap, where a flat package sat wrapped in tissue paper and ribbon. Her heart pumped faster. She raised inquiring eyes.

"Since I've accepted your Christmas gift, it seems only fair you should accept mine."

"I never declined it!" She blushed at exposing her eagerness for the gift.

He chuckled and handed her the present. She slowly tore off the paper and opened the box of elegant writing paper and envelopes.

"It's beautiful. Thank you," she said sincerely, trying to dampen her smile as she met his eyes.

John was astounded that she was so pleased with a box of writing paper. Hardly the romantic gift from a husband. "You must not get many presents," he remarked gruffly.

Margaret tensed with the box in her hands. "I am rather childishly excited about it."

"I'm not criticising you," he said softly. He touched her cheek and her eyes flew to his. "I have another one for you, but first..." He leaned toward her, his left hand grasping the arm of her chair while his right hand curved around her neck.

A thank-you kiss was only fair, she told herself. She parted her lips and was left wanting when he brushed his mouth across her cheek, then her eyes, closing them, and her nose. Her hands tightened on the box she held as she waited an eternity for his mouth to come to hers. When it did it was as soft as a rose petal and much too brief. She leaned forward for more substance and he came back to her, his tongue twining into her mouth, tangling with her own. The restless yearning she'd been mastering the past week broke free and rose up quick and strong. She opened her mouth wide to receive him.

He broke away and tugged the box out of her clenched fingers and threw it on the table. Her eyes flew open. His face was flushed, his eyes very bright and turbulent. He yanked her chair around so their knees rubbed together.

"John?"

"I'm feeling a little crazy," he said hoarsely. "One more kiss and then I'll get out of here. Only you kiss me this time." He grabbed the quilt where it lay snug under her arms and pulled her forward.

"I did kiss you!"

He rubbed his lips back and forth against hers. "Put your tongue in my mouth," he whispered. Margaret flinched, but her hands came up to his chest. "Just once," he coaxed. "I want so much more, but I'll settle for that."

Her hands slipped up to round on his shoulders. "Then you'll go?"

"If you want."

Her fingers dug into his shirt and the muscle beneath. She sat up straight and planted her mouth on his. She pushed her tongue into his hot mouth. John sucked hard and Margaret whimpered. Immediately, he gentled and slipped his hands beneath the quilt to hold her slim back. Margaret's hands slipped around his neck, and her knees strained against his, the ache between her thighs overwhelming her reticence.

John squeezed her shoulders and then rode up her arms and removed her hands from his neck. He pulled his face from hers. Margaret closed her eyes and measured her irregular breathing. John didn't try to hide his fast, panting breath. He arched his hips on the chair and shoved his hand into his pants pocket. He pulled out a gold ring set with a diamond. Margaret gasped.

"Do you want it?" he asked roughly.

She reached to touch it and his fingers closed around it.

"Do you want it? Do you really want to be my wife?"

His voice was harsh and Margaret stared into his piercing eyes. She realized he was asking for a wife in all ways and forever. She wanted to protest, but the ring was beautiful, and she was honored and flattered and downright beguiled. She felt as if she were hanging on a swinging door and outside was John and so much brightness and so many terrifying unknowns. Inside was darkness and aloneness, but so safe and predictable. She had to make a choice soon. She nodded. His fingers opened and again she reached for the ring. He moved it away.

"I'll put it on you." He held her hand and slid it over her finger. The metal was warm from his body. He lifted her hand to his mouth and kissed the ring, the tip of her finger, her palm. Margaret's eyes were riveted on his lips. She shivered down to her toes. He lifted his head and stared deep into her eyes. Her fingers curled tight around his. His arms wrapped around her and he hugged her hard.

"Oh," she moaned, feeling cherished for the first time in her life. The casing around her heart was weakened throughout with tiny cracks. Her legs separated and her pelvis came up hard against his knees, hot forbidden pleasure ricocheting through her trembling body.

His mouth came back to her lips and her tongue naturally slipped into him. He pulled her onto his lap and groaned deeply as her body pressed into his groin. "Oh, Maggie, Maggie, Maggie, I love you." Her arms cinched tight around his neck and he stood, lifting her with him and holding her tightly.

Chapter Seventeen

John laid her on the bed while kissing her. The quilt had fallen from her body in the kitchen and the sheets were icy through her flannel gown, but her husband's body was hot. He lay on her, one arm beneath her shoulders, the other beneath her bottom, pressing her into him. She felt no revulsion, no reluctance. Instead, her arms couldn't hold him tightly enough. From his mouth and his hands and his hard body she sought heat, and connection, and things she couldn't say to herself. Her pulse roared in her ears and she tore her mouth from his. "Oh, John, do you really?" she asked, her hips lifting against his.

His body stilled on hers and he lifted his head. "I do," he whispered. "I do love you." He unfastened his trousers and pulled up her gown. Margaret parted her thighs, her hands on his tense shoulders, her eyes on his face as he looked down at their nakedness.

Her tremors began as he slowly entered her. Margaret dug her fingers into his wool sweater and threw back her head. She couldn't control her strangled cries, and her lower body surged with pleasure. She arched and shuddered while he swore softly and continued to look down at her.

John thrust deep and hard and Margaret cried out. She sensed he was as insane as she'd been seconds ago and she wrapped her arms around him and crooned as pleasure gushed within her again, only this time she was not as impatient. She lifted her hips to him and for him and felt the surge in his body as his strokes quickened. As he was about to finish, she lowered her hands to his hips. She almost cried out for him to stop, but waited. John gave a pained groan and collapsed on her. Margaret shivered with what she'd just let happen.

John rolled slowly to her side and she felt his eyes on her. She pulled the covers up to her neck before glancing at her husband.

His eyes were warm, admiring.

She looked away, embarrassed at how wantonly she'd responded to him.

"You feeling ashamed?"

"Yes."

"Oh, Maggie. We're lucky we like each other so much that way. The pleasure between us is a blessing." He got out of bed and removed every stitch of his clothes. Seconds later she felt his warm body ride all along her back and legs. She took a deep breath and allowed herself to enjoy the heat while his words circled in her mind. She wanted to cast them out, but she was too honest to deny there might be some truth in them.

And he had said he loved her. Oh, that made her warm on the inside, matching the heat from his body until Margaret thought she could never be cold again—until she remembered that she might be pregnant.

John woke late to the winter sun trying to peak under the curtains. He stretched and turned, running his palm down the sheet where he wished his wife's body lay. He sighed and then groaned. God, it felt good to be back here in her bed, in her house, in her arms last night. He threw off the blankets and jumped out of bed and dressed in the previous night's clothes. His others were at the hotel. After he poured water in the bowl he looked over his shoulder before dousing Margaret's comb to straighten his hair. He was drying off his face after a good scrubbing when he sensed her presence.

She stood in the doorway, her eyes huge and very green in the morning light. He smiled, ready for any mood under the earth's big sky. And he was surprised when she smiled back, no doubt tremulously, but still a smile.

"I have some warm bread and hot stew ready."

"Sounds good." *God, you're beautiful.*

"Danny sent a boy to fetch you to the saloon, but I told him you were feeling unwell and needed to sleep."

"That's fine." *Feelin' like a wife, are you?*

"And I wanted to know if you'd like to join Elizabeth and me on a sleigh ride after you eat."

John hung the towel up and walked to where she stood. "Yeah, I'd like that."

Danny came, too. They glided down Main Street under a blue sky. John sat with Margaret behind her sister and Danny. Margaret was subdued while Elizabeth giggled in accompaniment to the bells on the harness and bounced like a child in her seat. John noticed Margaret studying the touches her sister and brother-in-law graced each other with, but he couldn't read his wife's expression. They rode up Green Street to Bodie Bluff to see the view of the surrounding mountains and Mono Lake.

"Oh, look!" cried Elizabeth.

Margaret stood in the sleigh. "It is spectacular," she said breathlessly, staring at the blue expanse of lake circled by white mountains.

Danny wrapped an arm around Elizabeth's back and she cradled her head on his shoulder. Slowly, Margaret sat back down and avoided looking in front of her as Danny kissed his wife.

"Maybe I should take over the reins if you two are going to keep this up much longer," John said loudly.

Danny broke from his wife and flashed a grin behind him. They sped down the hill to the edges of town and up and down every street until all their cheeks were bright red. John never touched Margaret, though they were subjected to hand holding and kisses and squeezes by the couple in front of him. Margaret couldn't look at him, scared he'd see how much she wanted him to touch her lightly and lovingly, and she didn't like wanting his touch so much.

They braked in front of the livery stable and the men stood, groaning with cold, and then stiffly climbed down. John held his hands up to Margaret. The contact of his new seal gloves over her coat and clothes was unsatisfying. He met her eyes and she trembled. Suddenly something hit her hard on the shoulder and she spun around to see snow falling off her coat and Elizabeth grinning at her. Margaret didn't understand until she watched Danny scoop a handful of snow, pat it and throw it at his giggling wife. John chuckled behind her and got a snowball in the chest from Elizabeth. One whizzed past Margaret's ear and she jumped. Elizabeth shrieked as she received big white snowballs from both men at once.

Margaret looked down at the snow at her feet. Living in San Francisco all her life, she'd hardly had the chance to touch snow, but that wasn't stopping the others. She bent and gingerly poked her gloved fingers through the thin top crust and into the soft snow. She dug out a handful and watched it sift through her fingers before she began to pat it into a ball. She made the snow as perfectly round as she could and turned to the others, who were oblivious of her as they lambasted one another. Margaret took aim and fired her ball at John. The snow hit him in the neck.

"Whoa!" He turned on her and Margaret took a step back. "The lady's in!" he yelled. All three threw at Margaret at once, getting even her head as she bent to retaliate with more snow. As she tried to make her ball round, John caught her with a huge misshapen ball and knocked her little one out of her hands. Then suddenly the attack swung to Danny and he was hit until snow sprinkled every part of his body. They threw furiously, laughing and shouting loudly until Elizabeth was gasping for breath. John took the last snowball in the face. He straightened, glaring furiously at Margaret.

"You bent over," she cried, taking a step back.

He wiped the snow from his face. "Just you wait, Mrs. Banning."

Margaret grabbed more snow, fashioned a quick ball and launched it at him. He took a step toward her after the snow fell from his chest. She threw another one and another and stopped bothering to make balls but just threw loose snow, which fell in a fountain over his head where he stood an arm's length from her. He still glared at her. He was thoroughly dusted with snow. Margaret brushed her hands off and tilted her head. "That will do."

A smile cracked his face, then completely stole away his fierce expression as laughter broke from him.

"Thank you for the ride, Mag!" Elizabeth said, coming up and taking her sister's arm.

"Coming to the saloon?" asked Danny.

John looked at his wife. Her eyes were still playful. "Soon," he answered. "I'm going to walk my wife home." They were quiet on the walk but shared a smile when they

ooked at each other. He pushed open their door and went
ight to the stove and built up a fire.

"I'll make some coffee."

"I can't stay. I have to go relieve Keith."

"Oh." She stood next to him in front of the stove and
pulled off her gloves.

He turned to face her. Her cheeks were flushed apple red
from the cold wind. Her eyes were a sea in sunshine. Lost
n their sparkling depths he drew closer. His mouth descended the last inch and her lips softened beneath his
touch. She raised her hand to clasp his cheek as he kissed
her over and over, tasting the shape of her lips, bumping his
cold nose against her colder one.

The fun in the cold air and now the coziness of the private, warm room encouraged Margaret to open wide to the
experience of the moment. Her emotions were unblocked
and unmastered and she ached to love her husband, to have
his love in the physical way he had shown her. The kiss
turned wet and urgent and he drew her close.

She moaned, feeling breathless and reckless and crazy.
Raising her hands to his neck she pressed close, wanting
him so much, so desperately. She wanted more than the bed
part, she wanted him, John Banning. She felt so alive, so
unlike herself. A strange, wild woman possessed her, and
the scariness of not knowing herself made her cling tightly
to him.

"I'll be back late, love," John whispered against her
mouth.

She cried out softly at the endearment.

"God, I love you . . . love kissing you . . . love being with
you," he rasped.

She nodded her head. "Yes," she whispered. *Crazy. I'm
totally crazy. I've lost my mind,* she thought. *No, I'm in
love, but I can't say it. It will disappear like a soap bubble.*

This thing between them was so strong, getting stronger every day. Her compulsion to be with her husband in every way was on the verge of surpassing all her fears.

He pulled away, smiling recklessly as he straightened his hat. "See you later, Mrs. Banning."

Margaret nodded and smiled shyly, hugging her arms close.

Before the latch had clicked into place she had stopped nodding and started shaking her head. "None of this was ever supposed to happen." She sank down into a chair and wondered what to do with her day. She had no direction anymore. What did a woman do when everything she'd been taught to believe fell apart? When the man she foolishly loved had married her to get a saloon? Margaret looked around her well-scrubbed kitchen. She sewed, that's what she did. She pulled out her basket containing the baby quilt.

John made The Fortune's bank deposit and had to unpack a load of hard liquor at the saloon. He stayed until late checking the saloon's inventory of wood, lamp oil, liqueurs, cigars, wines and beer and wrote up an order for more beer from the local Bodie Brewery. Keith and Thomas showed up for their midnight shift and John cleaned the mirror behind the bar and polished the mahogany wood counter and the brass trimmings. He ran his hand slowly over the smooth, polished wood, thinking of his wife, her welcoming acceptance of him. He didn't think she'd be leaving him. He smiled and then remembered how she'd looked a little confused and scared when he'd gone to the saloon this morning. He felt a brief trepidation that maybe she'd packed up and left as soon as he'd left the house. But she wouldn't leave Elizabeth, not yet. He hung the cloth he'd been using under the worktable and said good-night to Keith and Thomas.

She was still home. John crawled into bed without waking her. He laid his head on the pillow and debated which his body wanted more, love or sleep. His spine sank into the mattress. Effort was required just to roll over and pull her warm body close before his eyes sank shut.

In morning's dawn John awoke, stretched and sighed and nestled his face deep into silky hair. His hand tightened on a breast and his elbow rubbed against her belly. He lifted his head and looked to the window. It was late. That was not a surprise, but Margaret's presence in bed this late was. He rubbed her leg with his and rolled her to her back. Her eyes flickered open as he kissed her still mouth. John whispered against her lips while looking into her eyes. "Where's my breakfast, wife?"

Her brow furrowed and she looked past him to the light room. "Oh!" She tried to sit up and John held her with a strong hand on the ribs below her breasts.

"I can live without breakfast, but not without you." His mouth came back to hers, eager and determined. Margaret's arms twined around his neck.

The pounding on the back door broke them apart. "Mr. Banning!" called a young voice.

"Damn!" He looked at his wife, all willing and sweet. "Damn, *damn!* I guess Keith doesn't want to work much past his shift." He kissed her hard and quick and pulled out of her arms, hopping into his trousers on the way to the door. Beyond the door he flung open was a covering of new snow that was still falling from a white sky.

A boy of about eleven shivering on the doorstep announced, "Mr. Kincaid says he needs help shoveling snow."

"I believe it." John chuckled, surveying at least three feet of the white stuff. "Well, what do you want more, the best breakfast you've ever eaten or a coin?"

The boy squeezed his gloveless hands together. "I'll take the breakfast."

"Come on in, then." He turned to the bedroom and Margaret stood in the doorway in a gray dressing gown.

"What would you like?" she asked, moving into the room. "Pancakes, eggs and sausage, or biscuits and jam?"

The boy wet his lips and stared at her, trying to decide, while John ran into the bedroom to dress.

"Hell, Maggie, make 'em all! It's freezing out there," he yelled from the bedroom.

"All?" she repeated. The boy's eyes danced. "Very well. You can fill the stove with wood." Margaret pulled out eggs and flour and milk while John rushed back through.

"I'll shovel our place first," John said, pulling on muffler, coat and gloves and banging out the door. He whipped the shovel off the back stoop and cleared the snow down the steps and made a path to the road. He was ready for some hot food by then, but replaced the shovel and trotted down a crunchy path to the saloon. Thirty minutes later his nose and lips were going numb, probably were as blue as Thomas's, who shoveled alongside him, but his back was drenched with sweat. He heaved the last shovelful of snow and he and Thomas stomped into the saloon. Keith, warm behind the bar, poured them a cup of coffee.

"Thanks. Stay a bit longer while I thaw out?" Keith nodded and John took his coffee to the wood stove and removed his heavy coat and gloves. He had just sat down when the kid he'd had Margaret feed walked in with a big basket. He heaved it onto the bar. "From your missus," he said, and trotted back out. Keith pulled back the cloths and steam billowed up. He took a deep sniff and groaned. John jumped up and came to inspect.

"There's enough for five of us!" he announced. They dished themselves up heaping servings on the plates she'd included and tossed a sausage to Keith's mutt. John pushed a plate of eggs and biscuits to a regular customer sitting too close not to be affected by the sight and smell of home cooking.

"Marriage has its compensations," Keith said after a burp.

"I'm going to have to thank her real nice for this," John said, pouring himself another cup of coffee.

"Buy her another doodad or earbob or something else useless?"

John lowered his brows. "That's not what I'd had in mind."

Keith grinned. "Thinkin' you'll thank her how you'd like to be thanked?"

John raised his mug. His smile was amused. "Yeah. Maybe not quite fair, huh?"

Keith shrugged. "It's gonna be a cold night. Who's to say what a woman would rather have?"

John looked out the window at the still steady fall of snowflakes. "Damn wind is picking up, too. I'll be lucky if I can tunnel my way home."

Chapter Eighteen

"I hate this place!" Margaret muttered as she gripped the basket she held in one hand and the umbrella she used as a walking stick in the other and fought her way through the wind up Green Street. She turned down Fuller Street on her way to bring Elizabeth and Danny breakfast. Her sister had about enough patience to make oatmeal in the morning. This would be a welcome surprise, but she wondered if she was going to make it there without falling or freezing. She rapped on her sister's door with her umbrella.

Danny, with tousled hair and disheveled clothes, opened the door. "God, I'm glad you're here!" He pulled her inside and shut the door behind her. "Her pains started about an hour ago."

The basket slipped from Margaret's hand and dropped to the floor. "But it's too early!"

Danny shrugged and tried to smile. "Only a month. Maybe it will be easier now."

Margaret shook her head slowly, but Danny pushed her toward the bedroom.

"Oh, Mag, am I glad to see you!" Elizabeth was sitting against every pillow in the house. "It's really not bad, yet."

Margaret said nothing. The breakfast she'd eaten congealed into a rock in her stomach. "Is there anything I can get you?"

"Mag! You look like I'm at death's door instead of just having a baby. And yes, I'd like some coffee."

Margaret tried to smile. "That I didn't bring. I'll go make some."

"And I'm going for the doctor," added Danny.

"It's early yet, I don't—"

"He's coming over, Beth!"

Margaret studied her brother-in-law as he came into the kitchen and wolfed down some of the breakfast she'd brought. He didn't put food on a plate, just scooped some scrambled eggs up with a biscuit and popped a couple of sausages into his mouth. "How long for the coffee?"

"A few minutes."

He nodded and wiped his greasy hands on a dishcloth. "I can't wait. I'll be back with the doc."

Margaret nodded. She thought it her duty to reassure him, but by the time she had opened her mouth to do just that, he was out of the kitchen. She could think of nothing to say that she believed any way.

When the doctor arrived, he closed himself in the bedroom with Elizabeth while Danny stared at blowing snow out the front room's window and Margaret sipped her coffee in the kitchen. She heard Elizabeth laugh and she wondered how the girl could be so cheerful at a time like this. She dumped her coffee out; she was awake, nervous and trembling enough. The bedroom door opened and she hurried over.

"She's got a way to go," the doctor was telling Danny. "I'll check back in a couple of hours. Try to get her to rest. She's going to need her strength later."

Margaret wouldn't give Elizabeth any coffee. "It's not going to help you rest," she argued with her sister. Danny drank three cups and jittered from the bedroom to the front room to the kitchen and back to Elizabeth, who chatted between regular, mild contractions. Margaret forced herself to eat a biscuit from breakfast. Midday, Danny announced he was going to tell John what was going on. He came back two hours later, well-fortified, from the smell of him. Margaret couldn't find it in herself to disapprove. She wouldn't have minded some way to dull the thrum of fear that had taken residence in her chest.

At twilight Elizabeth sat up straight in her bed. "They're getting stronger," she called out.

Margaret patted her thigh through the blankets and lighted a lamp, dispelling the dark lavender light. Maybe God had heard her prayers. "This is good. We want that baby to come, don't we?"

An hour later Elizabeth groaned and reached for her sister's arm, her fingers digging in. "I'm wet," she moaned.

With her free arm, Margaret drew back the blankets and saw the wet, pink-tinged sheets. "Your water broke." Elizabeth looked at her in confusion. Margaret wet her lips. "What do you know about birth?"

"Nothing. You were the one who always helped Mama."

"I'll explain it all—after I send Danny for the doctor."

"It will be soon, then?"

"I hope so."

Five more hours strained away. Elizabeth grew weary, but the doctor made her walk around the room on Margaret's arm.

"Can I have some water?"

"I'll get you some," Margaret responded. She perched Elizabeth on the bed and went to the kitchen. The doctor followed her.

"She lost the plug hours ago, but she's not opening up."

Margaret lifted a clean glass off the shelf. "I know that."

"She's also tired and has yet to do any real work."

Margaret stiffened. "She was too excited in the beginning. She wore herself out."

The doctor adjusted his tie. "These first ones take a long time."

Margaret walked past him back to the bedroom. Danny had said her pains started at five that morning. She'd been in labor for seventeen hours. Mother had labored as long with her sixth only to birth a dead babe.

The doctor caught up with her before she reached the bedroom. "I have a pneumonia patient to see. I'll be back within the hour."

Margaret grasped his arm. "Don't go," she whispered furiously.

"I have to," he said, removing his arm. "I'll be back very soon, I promise."

Danny left with him.

John came by at midnight. "How are things going?" he asked uncomfortably.

"Not well."

John put his arm around her shoulders. "You look tired."

She twisted away. "I am."

"Is there anything I can do for you?" He ran a finger down her cheek.

Margaret stepped back and pushed his hand away. "No."

"I'll stay."

"That's not necessary." She returned to Elizabeth's side while John built up the fire in the front room. The adjoining door to the bedroom was open for the warmth and he heard the doctor ordering Elizabeth to walk and her whine of refusal. Then Margaret's voice came low and insistent and he heard shuffling steps. He sat on the sofa wondering how he would be reacting if it was Margaret trying to birth his babe. He knew he wouldn't be sitting in a saloon, his head inches from the table, practically unconscious the way Danny was. He would be in that bedroom with his wife. John fell asleep imagining Margaret big with his child and delivering it easily into the world. He woke with a start in the dim lamplight. He pulled out his watch. Three o'clock. He knocked on the doorjamb of the open bedroom door, making sure he stood out of view of the bed. Margaret came to him, her face pale and stiff.

"Any news I can take back to Danny?"

"Tell him he'd better never touch my sister again." She turned her back on him.

John sighed. He didn't have to tell Danny anything. The man was stretched out over two tables when John got back to the saloon. The Fortune was crowded with the men getting off their shift and endless toasts were made to the unconscious father-to-be.

Morning dawned clear and cold. The baby was no closer to coming than it had been the afternoon before. Margaret pushed aside the bedroom window curtain and saw the drifts of snow against the buildings. Men and women were busy shoveling and tunneling. She pressed two finger pads to the glass, which dripped with condensation, then lifted the fingers to her forehead, anointing herself with the icy wet in the warm room. She lifted her eyes to the clear skies of heaven. All night she'd been praying and was now closer to despair than she'd ever been in her life. She mashed her forehead and nose against the glass and tried to make her mind go blank. Behind her, her sister slept a light, troubled sleep. The doctor snored in a chair beside the bed.

Margaret sat in the chair on the other side. Elizabeth's eyes fluttered open. Her gaze was clear and she smiled tiredly. "Hi. Where's Danny?"

"He's asleep. Shall I get him?"

Elizabeth closed her eyes, a small smile lingering on her face. "Don't fib, Mag. I know he spent the night at the saloon. And yes, go get the clod." Margaret stood. "Brush my hair first?"

John was pouring coffee for a slumped Danny at the bar when Margaret pushed open the saloon door. John saw her immediately and righted the coffeepot. Danny's gaze lifted slowly from his third cup of the strong brew to the woman cloaked and pale a few feet in front of the door. Condemnation filled her huge eyes, making Danny wince.

"She wants you."

"The baby?"

Margaret shook her head, turned and left. Danny glanced up at John. "Something must be wrong."

"Maybe," John agreed, looking at the door that still swung slightly after his wife. He knew the contempt he'd seen in her face had less to do with the drink Danny had imbibed than with Danny's maleness and what that had done to her sister. In that moment, he knew his chances of ever having a child were as slim as they could get.

Danny trudged home and found his wife sitting propped up in front of pillows. She smiled at him, but she looked haggard. He felt her eyes on his stubbly face and rubbed his cheek. "I look bad," he stated. They grinned at each other. Then his eyes dropped to her rounded belly. "It didn't come."

She shook her head. "The contractions have stopped. The doctor is going to give me something that's supposed to get them going again."

Danny nodded. "I won't leave you again."

Elizabeth grasped his hand.

In the kitchen Margaret watched the doctor pull the ergot out of his bag. "I don't like this," she said in a strained whisper.

The man tensed. "Do you have a better idea?"

"If I did, do you think I wouldn't have mentioned it?"

He faced her, his hand gripping the bottle of ergot. "If I used forceps I would probably lacerate her horribly. She's not dilated fully. Since the child is dead I could do a craniotomy, but frankly I've never done—''

Margaret held up her hand. "I'd never let you do that anyway." Elizabeth would never forgive her if she let the doctor destroy the child's head so he could pull it out, but maybe her sister's life was worth the hatred she'd have to bear. She rubbed her throbbing temples. "Maybe we could just wait," she whispered.

"For what? A miracle? The ergot will stimulate the uterus and cause strong contractions, painful ones, so we'll have to give her laudanum, as well. I've used the drug many times before and never had a problem."

Margaret clasped her hands and pressed them to her lips. She'd never seen her mother's body give up the way Elizabeth's had. "All right, give it to her."

The drug took effect quickly. The contractions started again hard and fast. Danny held one of Elizabeth's hands and Margaret the other.

The force of the contractions expelled the child as they hoped, but also caused the hard head of the stillborn babe to severely lacerate Elizabeth's cervix and perineum.

"It's here, it's here," shouted Danny, shaking Elizabeth's hand. Margaret scooped up the baby, washed and covered it. Elizabeth's contractions continued, and soon the placenta was expelled. The pains persisted, however, while her body bled from her wounds. Over Elizabeth's blond head, dark with sweat, Margaret met the doctor's bleak eyes. He was gray around the mouth.

Margaret wanted to change the bloody sheets, but Elizabeth refused to loosen her grip on her sister's hand. "Baby?" she whispered. She looked from Margaret's unsmiling face to Danny's relieved one. She whimpered and tried to sit up but was too weak.

"You can have more," Margaret said, squeezing her sister's hand.

Danny jumped up from his chair and went to the cradle at the foot of the bed. Elizabeth watched her husband become very still and tense, then realized she didn't hear any crying. She shut her eyes, turned her head against the pillow and moaned. Margaret felt her heart shrivel.

By afternoon Elizabeth trembled with fever. "Help me, Mag," she said softly, just as she had when she'd fallen down the stairs at five years of age and Margaret was the first one there. Margaret slid her free arm around Elizabeth's neck, hugging her sister close, her lips brushing the soft damp hair.

By evening Elizabeth had stopped speaking, only rolling her head toward whoever was talking.

"She's going to die," cried Danny, holding her hand, now limp, between his. Elizabeth's eyes were glazed as she rolled her head toward Danny.

"Be quiet!" snapped Margaret.

He looked at her. "She's dying. Can't you see?" His voice rose hysterically. Margaret whipped her arm across the bed and slapped his face. The contact felt good, the venom vitalizing, and she drew her arm back again, but the doctor grabbed her hand and forced her into her chair. She looked down at her sister. Elizabeth's eyes were closed and Danny began to weep.

No amount of cold compresses ceaselessly applied to Elizabeth's body deterred the steadily climbing fever, but Margaret continued to dunk the cloths in cold water.

John came and stood in the doorway for a long time, watching. The mourning atmosphere in the room scared him. He'd never been in a house where childbirth was taking place. No wonder Margaret was scared to have a baby. He was about to turn away when he saw something bundled in the little cradle he'd bought for Elizabeth. He took a step forward into the dim room, wondering why the baby didn't move. The doctor took his arm and stopped him from getting closer. "Stillborn," the doctor whispered. John looked at Margaret, oblivious of his presence. He turned away and lighted a lamp in the front room, then made biscuits and gravy for a late supper. Only he and the doctor ate any of it. They washed it down with a pint of beer John had brought to the house.

Elizabeth's fever never abated. Margaret, on her knees at the side of the bed, listened as her sister's last breath escaped her lips. Her hands had been clasped for hours, her elbows on the bed. Now she shut her eyes and searched for a feeling besides black despair.

Danny was twitching in an uncomfortable sleep in a chair across the bed from her. "She's gone," Margaret said.

Danny jerked awake and glanced at Margaret. "I was just dreaming about her." He dropped his face to his hands and cried. The doctor and John came in. Margaret stood. "Get him out of here," she told John.

"She's his wife, Maggie," he said softly.

Margaret looked from her husband to her brother-in-law to her sister. The sudden rise of emotion within her body expanded her lungs. "If it wasn't for him—"

John strode across the room and clamped a hand over her mouth, stepping in front of her as a barrier between her and Danny. "You will respect his grief," he said in a low voice, audible only to her, "or I'll take you out of here."

She struggled against him, hatred welling up and overflowing her at his strength, his maleness. John lifted her and carried her from the room. As soon as he released her she stepped away from him. Her eyes were bloodshot from two nights without sleep, her face was gray and her hair was fuzzing out of her coif.

"I'll take you home."

She looked toward the bedroom. "I have to...to...do something."

John shook his head. "You have to rest. Let Mr.
Ward—"

"No!" She wouldn't let the undertaker dress her sister's
body. The very thought made her ill.

John held up a hand. "All right, but not now. Leave
Fanny alone."

She shut her eyes, trying to think, and swayed on her
feet. "This isn't fair," she whispered. "I have to... I must
have done something wrong. She shouldn't have... Not
Elizabeth." She heard John come close and she backed
away, her eyes snapping open. "I'll just sit for a while on
the sofa."

"No. We'll go home." He got her coat and pushed her
arms down the sleeves. Margaret tried to button it herself,
but she took so long that John brushed her hands away and
did it for her. He led her through the streets to their house
with his arm around her waist and she followed as if she
were blind, deaf and dumb.

At home he poured her a glass of milk and cut her a slice
of bread and a slab of cheese.

"I'm not hungry," she said from her chair.

"But you'll eat." He sat down next to her and she stared
straight ahead. He picked up the cheese-covered bread and
held it to her mouth. "Open. Bite. Chew. That's it."

She ate half of it and then reached for the glass of milk
and drained it. She shook her head when he lifted the food
again.

He carried her to the bed and stripped her of her coat,
dress, corset and shoes. She was asleep when he finished
covering her.

Margaret awoke in early morning darkness, her husband's body hot against her back. She scrambled out of the
blankets, fighting the dimness of the room, the blackness
of what had happened.

Lamplight flared and the bed bounced as Margaret got up. Through blurry vision John watched Margaret walk to the dresser in white petticoats and camisole and lift his watch. Her forehead wrinkled and she met his eyes.

"Why did you let me sleep so long? She's still..." She flung the watch down on the small table. John winced.

"Danny took care of her."

"What do you mean? By himself? Did you let that undertaker touch my sister?"

John pushed himself up to face this unrecognizable woman, so different from the woman he'd been loving just days ago.

"He did it alone."

Margaret gasped. "That's impossible. He was drunk and falling apart."

John patted a place beside him on the bed. She shook her head. He crossed his arms over his chest. "I think you underestimate him, and his love for Elizabeth."

"I estimate it at very little. He felt free to go off and drink his days and nights away in that saloon. *Your* saloon."

"I don't think his drinking is quite the issue here."

"Oh, no?" Margaret strode into her previous bedroom, threw open her wardrobe and pulled out clean clothes. John followed her. She faced him with her arms full. "I bet you she'd still be alive if he wasn't such a drunk."

John flinched. "How can you say such a thing? From what the doctor told me, nothing went right with her labor and then she got a fever."

"And I blame you for not selling that vile saloon," she said bitterly.

John blinked and shook his head. He leaned against the doorjamb and watched her button up a black dress. "I'm sorry Elizabeth died," he said softly. "Don't blame me for it." She didn't bother to look at him but sat in a chair and pulled her shoes on. John felt as though he were at the ocean, standing in the water as the outgoing tide pulled the sandy ground away below his feet. With a rushing in his ears he felt a previously unimaginable emotional distance spreading between him and his wife. He had to bring her back. He had to make her let go of the anger. "Why don't you cry?" he asked softly. She stood and twitched her skirts around her feet.

"Are you suggesting that I didn't love my sister?"

He shook his head and briefly covered his eyes with his palms. "I know you did. You loved her very much. And it's so unfair that she died. I just think maybe you'd feel better if you sat down and used my shoulder to cry on."

Margaret did not respond. She walked to the room that had been her father's and pulled out a big, heavy valise. As she hefted it through the kitchen John's eyes went wide. He followed her to their room. "What are you doing?"

"I'm packing."

Cold fury erupted in his stomach and flowed outward along every vein. He watched her place neatly folded clothes in the bottom of the bag. When she pulled the dresses out of the wardrobe and brought them into the bedroom, he snapped and grabbed her arm.

"You're leaving me?" The words sounded incredibly stupid even to his own ears.

"I never made a secret of it." She tried to pull away, but couldn't.

"You accepted my ring, Margaret. You can't just walk out on me. I know Elizabeth's death is terrible, but I didn't cause it. You don't have to leave me."

"I'll give you the ring back!"

"I don't want the ring. I want my wife!"

Again, she tried to tug away. When she couldn't she shoved her face close to his. "I don't want to be your wife! I don't want you pawing me and controlling me! I especially don't want to be a barkeep's wife, who only married me for a saloon. And I don't want the chance of having your baby. I don't want anything to do with you."

John dropped her arm. His mouth was tight. "It's not that you're running from your own guilt? For agreeing to give Elizabeth the drug that ripped her apart?"

She jerked as if struck, her eyes going wide for a split second before they narrowed. "Well, you're one who knows about guilt and running away from it, aren't you?"

His mouth opened and closed. "Give me back the ring," he said in a monotone.

"Gladly." She tugged on the gold band but couldn't get it over her knuckle. She tried again. "I'll send it to you!" She snapped her bag closed and dragged it to the kitchen, where she put on her coat, then she slammed out the door.

The stage to San Francisco left at five. Margaret slipped and stumbled down to the ticket office. They'd have to dig through snow and ice to bury Elizabeth. She couldn't be there for that. She knew she would split apart and become crazed if she had to watch her young, happy, lively sister lowered into the ground while the ugly barren hills looked down in their mocking, cursed mineral richness.

Chapter Nineteen

Margaret was always the first one up in Victoria's home. She started the fire in the kitchen stove and made the coffee strong, the way John liked it. She spread a thick piece of bread with butter and honey and sat at the dining table chewing quietly. The dawn bloomed beyond the window and in the silence of the sleeping house she allowed herself to wonder where John was as the morning sun rose. Was he in the house she'd left? Asleep in a hotel bed? Was he already at the saloon? She imagined him in all those places and then, finishing her bread, she shoved thoughts of John Banning out of her mind.

For four months now she'd lived with her sister and George. Her usefulness had been negligible, something she'd not counted on. Victoria already had a housekeeper and a cook. What she did need was someone to talk with about childbirth and babies, since she was pregnant. For all Margaret's experience with childbirth, she knew nothing of babies. And since her experiences with delivery were filled with pain, Margaret had only warnings and admonitions on that topic. Victoria did not want to hear about her mother or Elizabeth, and Margaret would have found it difficult to speak of them if asked. Elizabeth's death was a nightmare she had yet to wake up from.

Margaret spent her days sewing and embroidering and quilting and crocheting. She made a wardrobe of baby clothes and with every stitch she wondered what had become of the tiny little garments she'd sewn for Elizabeth's child.

Every Sunday she went to church, but she couldn't sing. She visited her maiden aunts, Matilda and Diane, and felt stifled and odd sitting in their crowded little parlor.

A measure of happiness was found tending the small flower garden behind the house, where she often sat to sew. She entertained herself with ideas on how she'd expand the flower beds and extend the rows if the yard was hers.

In the evening she'd dine with Victoria and George at the elegantly set dining table and listen to them share their day. George always had at least one amusing event to relate about the grocery and sometimes a frustrating one. Victoria was interested in his business and knew everyone he spoke of. She walked to the grocery everyday with a lunch to share with him. Over dinner she told him about what she had done in the house, what she had bought or read. Margaret might share what piece of sewing she had started or just finished, or what flower had bloomed that day, and her sister and brother-in-law always listened very politely. But Margaret knew their interest was feigned, just as she knew their talk at the table was more formal than when she was not present. She sometimes heard them laughing and even arguing behind closed doors. This was simply the way it was. Since Margaret had always only wanted to be a part of her sisters' lives, not have her own, she didn't understand why she felt so empty, so light and meaningless, like a dried petal on the wind.

Margaret took the last sip of her cooled coffee as the cook came in the back door. The housekeeper would arrive immediately after breakfast. Margaret usually listened as her sister gave the day's instructions to the woman. She had always seen Victoria as sloppy, but now Margaret discovered her sister was very good at directing from a comfortable chair.

George came in with the morning newspaper and took his seat at the head of the table. He poured himself some coffee after saying good-morning to Margaret. "Looks like it's going to be a nice day."

"Indeed it does."

That was the usual extent of their conversation. Margaret watched her brother-in-law snap his paper open and lower his dark brown eyes and bend his head. Margaret listened to the sounds from the kitchen—the crack of eggs against the pan, the sizzle as the globs hit the heat. She closed her eyes and heard the thud of a heavy utensil on a wood table. A spoon beat against a bowl. More sizzling, this time furious. Bacon. She heard the menu before she smelled it. Fried eggs and bacon and pancakes. The cook carried out a big platter of the food and George heaped his plate. Margaret watched him eat. On George the amount of food he ate thickened his chest, his stomach, his arms. John had eaten just as much, but where had it all gone? Her husband's body had been sculpted muscle under soft, smooth skin. Margaret blinked and took a large gulp of cool coffee and rebuked herself, not so much for thinking of the man's body, but for thinking of him as if he no longer lived. She watched George break the yolk of an egg while she tried to stop thinking of the man she'd cast out of her life.

"There's plenty more."

Margaret jerked her eyes to George's face. He smiled, quickly, easily, and gestured to the platter.

"I'm sorry for staring. I was just...thinking." She felt her face go hot. He nodded and returned to his paper.

Margaret picked up a piece of bacon and nibbled at it. George downed the rest of his coffee and slapped the paper on the table. He wiped his mouth with the linen napkin and nodded again at Margaret. Victoria came down the stairs and met him in the foyer. Margaret heard the rustle of their clothing as they embraced and their words of farewell. The breaking of a wagon outside the house on the quiet street interrupted the purr of their loving words. The front door opened.

"My goodness!" Margaret heard her sister exclaim.

"What did you buy?" demanded George.

Margaret walked to the window and saw a freight wagon below, piled with crates and bundles, some under canvas. Her sister disclaimed any knowledge of the contents and Margaret watched the driver swing down and stride up the steps to the house.

"Margaret," called her sister. Margaret walked to where they stood in the open door. The driver was dirt covered and weary eyed. Her sister held out an envelope. "He says it's furniture. The contents of a house. For you. Also, he claims to have been delayed." Margaret met her sister's probing eyes and reached for the envelope. Her fingers went numb and her stomach twisted as she methodically ripped it open.

"Where are we going to put it all?" worried Victoria.

Margaret pulled out a check for $2,675 and a short note dated from January. *Here's your half. I've deducted two hundred dollars for the ring.* Margaret stuffed it all back in the envelope and met her sister's gaze expressionlessly. "From John," she said blandly. Her fingers formed a fist around the paper.

"Where is John?" asked Victoria, one brow arching.

"What are we going to do with it?" Margaret asked, avoiding her sister's question.

"Yes, what are we?" mocked the driver, looking from one person to the next.

George shook himself. "To the store warehouse! Plenty of room there. Temporarily." He looked intently at his wife who smiled reassuringly. "Follow me," he told the driver.

"Why don't you just ride alongside me?"

George looked askance at Victoria, then down at his fine wool suit, then shrugged. "Why not? Excellent idea." He forced a smile and avoided looking at his sister-in-law before he followed the driver down to the dusty wagon.

Margaret turned back inside and went up to her room. "I'll be up soon," Victoria called after her. "I just need some breakfast first." Margaret put the check and the note in her dressing table drawer and sat down in front of the mirror. She stared soberly at her reflection, the large eyes, the pale, thin face, the unsmiling mouth. She'd lost weight in the last few months and her clothes were loose. Her gaze flicked down to the gold ring still on her finger. She pulled it almost all the way off and then pushed it back on. What madness had kept her from sending it back? She couldn't think of it. Instead, she thought of the date of that too short note. The amount of money he'd sent meant that he'd probably sold his share of the saloon and the house—and almost immediately after she had left. Margaret was bewildered by his leaving the saloon. Why? Was it less important to him than she'd thought? Was he still in Bodie? Was he here in San Francisco? She ran the nails of one well-manicured hand along the table edge. Why wasn't he demanding a divorce?

Victoria knocked as she pushed open the door. "So?" She pulled up a gold velvet chair and sat across from her sister. "Where is he?"

"I don't know."

"What did his letter say?"

"It was more a note than a letter."

Victoria sighed loudly. "I thought I saw a check."

"So you did."

"Well?" Victoria grimaced. The baby always kicked hard immediately after she ate. "Why did he send you money and what are you going to do with it?"

"I don't know." Victoria's glare was so impatient that Margaret continued. "I imagine he feels he owes me half of what he has. After all, it was marrying me that got him the saloon. And I suppose with the money I should find a place of my own to live."

"That's not necessary. You're welcome to stay here."

"Forever?"

Their eyes met. "Of course."

"I think you'd best discuss that with your husband, Victoria. I believe he feels I'm here only temporarily, just like that wagon of furniture."

Victoria waved her hand. "Don't worry about him. I'm not going to have my sister go off and live by herself when she has family perfectly capable of taking her in. Besides, I'll need your help with the baby. George will be thankful you're here then, or he'd never have me to himself again." She looked around the room her sister occupied. "You like your room, don't you?"

"It's a very nice room."

"You're free to change it or decorate it as you want. Maybe you'd like some of the things from Bodie in here."

"There's more than one roomful of furniture in that wagon."

"Well, sell the rest."

Margaret stiffened. "Sell Mother's things?"

Victoria rolled her eyes and saw a large brown spider dangling from the ceiling to the left of Margaret. She stood and pushed her chair right under the bug. "I have no sen-

imental fondness for Mother's things. I had little enough
ondness for Mother herself! Besides, George and I have all
ew things and I'm very pleased with them. I don't need a
unch of old furniture cluttering up my home.''

"What are you doing?" Margaret jumped up as Victo-
ia removed a slipper and stepped up on the chair. "Victo-
ia, get down!" Her sister calmly smashed the spider under
er slipper.

"Yuck," she said, staring at the brown smudge on the
eiling. "I'll have to have Mrs. Hoseman clean that up."

Margaret, her face red, grabbed her sister's arm and
elped her off the chair. "Don't ever do that again! What
f you'd fallen? Have you no thought for your condi-
ion?''

Victoria's eyes widened. "I was perfectly all right." She
lanced down at Margaret's hands still painfully gripping
er arm.

Slowly, Margaret released her. "Have a care, Victoria. I
on't want to witness another tragedy."

Victoria gazed at her sister apprehensively. "You worry
ar too much. The baby and I will be just fine." She averted
er eyes from her sister's worried ones. "I'm going to go
ress."

Two weeks later Victoria's belly dropped perceptibly.
'Thank goodness," Margaret exclaimed, staring below her
ister's midriff when she and George entered the dining
oom for dinner. "Elizabeth never..." she trailed off. "This
s a very good sign."

When Victoria tried to leave the house the next day to
ake a stroll and shop, Margaret ran out the door after her.
'Where are you going?''

"I thought I'd look in the millinery."

Margaret shook her head. "You could have that bab
any minute! You must stay home!"

"I'll return directly if I feel the slightest twinge."

"You could be too far away at that point. Come i
now!" Victoria remained where she was. "How can yo
take a risk like this?"

The younger woman swung around, her little purs
swinging from her wrist, and stomped back up the steps t
the house, waddled past Margaret and threw her purse o
the receiving table in the foyer.

Victoria remained in the house for the next week, excep
for sitting in the small garden behind the house.

"I know to be cooped up is hard for you, but you mus
think first of the baby and your condition," Margaret saic
bringing Victoria another cup of warm herb tea.

Victoria glanced at her sister and ignored the tea on th
little table by her arm. "Is this how you took care of Eliz
abeth?"

Margaret stared at a rosebush in front of them. "No.
left Elizabeth to her own devices. I was preoccupied at th
time."

"Oh? And you think that's why she died?" Victoria'
tone was sarcastic and Margaret faced her.

"I don't know. I just don't want it to happen again. An
I frightening you?"

"Yes." Victoria pushed herself out of the chair, shakin
her head at Margaret's extended arm. She paused in th
double doors to the house. "You may drink my tea, Mar
garet. I believe you are the one most in need of it."

Victoria had no appetite for lunch the following day. A
four o'clock her pains began and Margaret sent the house
keeper for George and the doctor. They were at the hous
in twenty minutes.

Margaret got Victoria up to her room, removed her outer clothes and put her to bed.

"It's not bad yet," Victoria whispered, her hand smoothing her belly over her chemise.

"Then try to rest. You'll need your strength."

"I'm sitting in bed, isn't that enough?"

Margaret's face was pale. She straightened the quilt over her sister.

"Margaret, stop fussing. You're making me nervous."

Margaret perched on the edge of the bed. She clasped her clammy hands in her lap and listened to her heart pound while she waited for the doctor.

"I wonder if it's a boy or a girl! I can't wait!"

"Victoria, lie down."

"It feels like a giant tree has fallen on me when I lie down. I'm much more comfortable sitting up." She puffed the pillow behind her back and spread her knees, resting her forearms on them and leaning forward when a contraction hit her. Margaret had never seen anything so undignified, but staying flat had not kept her mother alive and walking hadn't helped Elizabeth, so why not this?

The doctor came and timed her contractions.

"Where is George?" asked Victoria.

"He's downstairs, dear," the doctor told her. "Let's not give him a long wait."

Margaret thought Victoria was doing admirably well. She continued to lean into each pain and as soon as it passed she'd breathe with relief. "I can't wait," she said over and over.

Four hours later the contractions became more intense and Victoria grabbed Margaret's hand, squeezing with each shuddering pain. Her water broke and she began to moan as pain rippled through her. She looked to Margaret for reassurance, but Margaret was grim-faced and trembling.

"It's hurting now," Victoria whispered.

Margaret jerked her head in a little nod and Victoria collapsed against the pillows.

"Can't you do something?" demanded Margaret of the doctor. "Shouldn't you check to see if everything is okay?"

"I did that." He pulled out his watch. "Fifteen minutes ago."

"Well, do it again!"

"I don't need you to tell me how to deliver a baby."

"Someone needs to tell you to stop scribbling your memoirs and tend to my sister."

"Your sister is doing fine. The labor is proceeding along a normal course."

Victoria shuddered forward again with another pain. Her hair was falling in her sweaty face. "Margaret, stop fighting with the doctor and come hold my hand."

Margaret hurried over and the doctor returned to his writing. Victoria squeezed tight around her sister's fingers, which were squeezing just as tightly. She relaxed as the contraction passed. "I want George," she moaned.

"You don't want him to see you like this."

"I want George. Get him."

"Doctor, come check her!"

The man sighed and put down his tablet. He flicked the sheet back. "Well, well."

"What's wrong?" demanded Margaret.

Victoria looked at her sister's pale, strained face. "What's wrong?" she echoed weakly.

"I can feel a hairy little head up there a ways. Just relax, you're doing fine."

Victoria looked again at her sister, who was wiping her own sweaty face. "I want my husband," she pleaded with the doctor. "Please."

The doctor looked at the sisters and then strode to the bedroom door, threw it open and bellowed, "George!"

Another pain hit and Margaret grasped her sister's hand. Victoria pulled away. "Don't touch me! Get away!"

Astonished, Margaret sat and stared at her sister while George's heavy footsteps sounded up the stairs.

"Stop staring at me!"

"What's wrong?" George's voice rasped from the doorway.

"Oh, George, get her out of here," Victoria pleaded.

"Everything is fine with your wife and the baby, it's your sister-in-law that..."

George walked to the side of the bed and turned to Margaret. "I think you'd best go downstairs. Have a glass of sherry."

Margaret shook her head. "I can't leave," she whispered.

Victoria grabbed her husband's hand and buried her face in the wool cloth of his coat sleeve. George smoothed back his wife's hair, then went around the bed and pulled Margaret to her feet.

"No! Victoria, I just want to help you!" George gripped her shoulders and forcibly walked her out of the room and shut the door on her back. Margaret stared at the white door. She felt as if a giant wind were blowing her backward. She pressed her hands to the wood door, her fingers curling, the nails digging as her sister's cry came through. The hallway was dark and she couldn't see. She dropped her forehead against the door. "Please, God," she begged, "don't let them die." She prayed ceaselessly. Her hands and feet went numb as she stood motionless for hours in blackness and fear.

A jubilant shout made her tense. A baby cried. Margaret opened her eyes and still she saw nothing. Her hand dropped to the doorknob and she twisted it uselessly. "Victoria?" she called.

When George opened the door Margaret squinted against the light. She stumbled and George caught her under the arm.

"Mag, it's a boy." Victoria smiled from the bed. She held a swaddled bundle to her breast. Margaret walked slowly forward, unaware she was being supported by George the entire way. Victoria's hair had been brushed and braided back. Her gown was a fresh one. George led her around a pile of soiled sheets. The room smelled of his pipe tobacco. Margaret glanced up at her brother-in-law's flushed, smiling face. The doctor was packing up his things.

"He's fallen asleep!" Victoria laughed. "Oh, isn't he marvelous, Mag? We've named him Jeremy George."

Margaret touched his cheek. "Can I hold him?" she whispered.

"Of course." Victoria handed him over, her earlier animosity gone.

The soft weight of the sleeping babe made Margaret's stomach tighten. She wanted to press him close, close to her own breast. She ached inside and wanted—

"Give him back now," Victoria said, her hands reaching up. George stepped close and sat on the edge of the bed as Margaret returned the infant. She stood looking from one pleased face to the other as the parents stared down in joy at the child. They didn't noticed when Margaret left.

Margaret made her way down the hall to her own room, the pain radiating from her stomach down her limbs. She glanced at the sky outside her window and realized it was near dawn. So long she'd stood in that hall. She pulled out her chamber pot and set it on her bed. Removing the lid, she stared down into the clean, white porcelain interior. She lowered her sweating head to be sick, but nothing would come up. The lid slipped out of her hand to the bed.

This pain had to go somewhere, but there was no place left in her body to push the feelings. This was the way it would always be. Margaret, the aunt who'd steal greedy moments with her nieces and nephews while their rightful parents had the full joy of them. But that had been her choice. She just hadn't realized she'd be shoved outside the door. She hadn't counted on husbands being such a help to their wives. Who'd have thought George would have known how to braid a woman's hair? Would John? Would John have pounded up the stairs to be with her?

The answer was positively yes. Margaret shuddered. She'd given up so much to have so little. A tear fell from her face and splashed into the chamber pot, and she stuck her finger in the wetness with gentle amazement. With a low moan she picked up the porcelain pot and hugged it to her belly as she trembled. Her eyes burned and tears slipped down her face.

She slid the pot back under her bed, took off all her clothes, removed all the pins in her hair and crawled naked under the blankets and sheets. She wrapped her arms around a fat pillow and buried her face in its plumpness. Not comfortable, she drew another one between her knees. Her weight loss had made her limbs bony and sharp. She closed her eyes, blocked the tears and tried to force sleep. But two minutes later she gasped with the strength needed to rule her body. She choked on the tears running down her throat. She gripped the pillows tighter and couldn't help but wish they were John's warm body.

At first the tears hurt, as though they were being squeezed out of rock, but as they continued to fall, Margaret felt the pain in her heart instead. She cried for all the stillborn babies she'd seen, and for Elizabeth and her mother. Finally, she cried for herself, and John. She cried because she was scared to have a baby and yet wanted one just as much.

She fell asleep just as the sun rose full in her window. The baby across the hall cried out and was quickly comforted.

Chapter Twenty

Margaret worked fast. After less than an hour's sleep, she'd drunk her morning coffee and searched the newspaper until she'd found an ad for Banning Carpentry. She shoveled down some toast and eggs and then flung open her wardrobe and searched its contents. Nothing was suitable. She had gray, black, brown, one plum, one drab olive and one rust. Outside it was spring, and her heart was a bud barely peeking at the sun.

"Of course," Victoria said when Margaret asked to alter one of her sister's dresses. She searched her sister's wardrobe and pulled out a bright, new leaf green. The baby was sleeping beside his mother and Margaret touched his cheek before she tiptoed out.

She took all morning to alter the dress. Her fingers hurt from moving quickly and relentlessly. She put the dress on and sat in front of the mirror. Her eyes looked less bloodshot and snapped with green. She pinched her cheeks and twisted her hair up in a loose style. She pulled a few curls down around her temples and forehead and curled them more with a wet finger and thumb.

The walk to Banning Carpentry dulled the pounding of her heart until she saw the swinging sign above the shop entrance. Her hands began to perspire within her gloves.

She walked stiffly forward. The door was locked. Anxiety
dropped away and keen, shredding disappointment tore
through her. She cupped her hands to the glass and peered
inside at the dark interior of long tables and wooden floor.
She backed away and wet her lips. Going back to Victoria's was unthinkable. She should have come earlier. Already it was noon, and they were probably building a house
somewhere or eating lunch. She looked up and down the
street, hoping to see John's rolling stride coming toward
her. There were plenty of men and women about, but no
John Banning. She noticed a narrow stairway to her left
and remembered with a flash that John used to live with his
mother and father above the shop. Her heart leapt to her
throat as she forced herself to climb the stairs. Halfway up
she heard voices. Three-quarters of the way to the door she
recognized John's voice.

"I was up late," he yelled.

"Patrick is counting on you," snapped a woman's voice.

"I'm doing my work. I just do it when I damn well feel
like it!"

Margaret studied the clean white door in front of her.
The brass knocker and knob shone even in the dimness of
the stairwell.

"No! You'd rather waste your life away than get serious
about anything. Wasn't Bodie enough of an adventure?"

Margaret's hand stilled, the raised knocker held tight in
her fingers. She waited.

"Maybe not."

Margaret bit her bottom lip. She rapped the knocker
twice and clasped her hands in front of her. Quick, hard
footsteps came close on the other side. The door was flung
open. Margaret's stomach dropped to her knees and she
stared. John's eyes went round and he froze with one hand
on the door. The light from the apartment washed across

Margaret and flooded the stairwell. Her eyes slipped from John's messy hair and unshaven face to his untucked, thin-with-washing, white cotton shirt, brown corduroy pants and stocking feet. Her eyes flicked back to his face and saw that he was still looking down her own person. There was a chilling blankness in his gaze when their eyes met again.

She licked her lips. "Hello."

"Who is it?" A dark-headed woman came up beside him.

John looked down at his mother, back to Margaret, and cleared his throat. "My wife."

"Oh!" John's mother stepped in front of her son and held out her hand. "Come in, dear. Margaret, isn't it? Sit down. We'll have some tea and get acquainted." She pulled Margaret in.

"I don't think she came to have a chat with you, Mother."

"Don't be rude, John." She ushered Margaret to a chair.

The room was light and airy, with white lace curtains at all windows and lace dripping over sofas, chairs and tables. The wallpaper was ivory with large pink cabbage roses that matched the pink, dull red and gold upholstered furniture. The carpet was more pink, mixed with gold and green.

"Thank you, Mrs. Banning." Margaret took the chair and looked beyond the bright, dark eyes of the mother to the dark eyes of the man. He was not pleased, and Margaret began to tremble. He took a seat on the sofa across from her. The room was entirely feminine, but John looked at his ease, a foot crooked over his knee, while he stared and stared at her as if she were a bug.

"I'll have coffee," he said over his shoulder in the direction his mother had gone. He turned his dark, fathomless

eyes back to Margaret, whose straight back was one foo
from the lace drape of her chair. "You've lost weight."

"Yes," she responded quietly, now feeling self-con
scious, scrawny and ugly. He said nothing else.

"How have you been?" she asked politely, wondering
where all her jubilant, determined feelings had gone.

He shrugged. "Okay."

"Have you been back long?"

"About as long as your furniture."

She flushed. "I only got that a couple weeks ago. Some
thing about snow blocking roads and a sick freighter. You
sold the house, then?"

He nodded. "Danny sold off some stocks and bought m
share of the saloon." He looked at her expectantly, wait
ing for her to protest his selling the saloon to Danny. Sh
said nothing, but he wasn't sure if it was because at tha
moment his mother came in carrying a tray.

She poured the tea into a delicate white-and-gold cup an
handed Margaret a rich, dark brew, then placed a mug be
fore John. "It's so nice to meet you, Margaret. John ha
told us so little about you," she said, pouring her own cup.

John rolled his eyes and lifted his cup. He choked an
shuddered. "It's ice-cold!" He looked accusingly at hi
mother.

"Well, imagine that! And to think it was scalding hot thi
morning when Patrick came by to get you."

John banged the mug down on the table. He fixed hi
eyes on Margaret until she shook so terribly she had to pu
her cup and saucer down before the tea sloshed over he
dress. She realized then that her feelings hadn't gone any
where. They were right here in her shaking, perspiring
body.

"So, Margaret, John did tell us that you've been living
with your sister since January. What are your plans?"

Margaret dragged her gaze from John's unreadable features and looked at his mother. "I'm not sure," she said hoarsely.

"Mother," John cut in, not taking his eyes from Margaret, "don't you have some shopping to do?"

"None at all, John."

He turned his head and met his mother's curious, excited eyes. "Please."

She smiled, a curving of her cupid's bow mouth, then stood and stepped behind John, rested her hand briefly, caressingly, on his shoulder. "I need to get us something special for supper to celebrate Margaret's arrival. I'll stop by and invite Patrick and Amy. How wonderful to have everyone all together!"

The silence in the wake of her exit stretched until Margaret cracked. "Your mother seems very nice."

He snorted. "She wants me settled and responsible. She wants grandchildren."

"You don't want to give them to her?"

He watched her. "Why are you here?"

Margaret laughed nervously and shuddered inwardly at the inane sound. She cleared her throat. "I came to see you."

"I didn't suppose for a minute that you'd come to meet my charming mother."

Margaret swallowed. "I wanted to see how you were."

He raised his hands, palms out, on either side of his face. "You've seen."

"How long has it been since you've shaved?"

He flashed her a smile while his eyes remained virulent. "Now that's the Margaret I remember."

She looked down at her clenched hands. That wasn't the Margaret she wanted to be. Why was it so hard to say any of the things she had thought and felt while in her sister's home? "How is Danny?" she asked, striving for a neutral subject.

"He's fine, which you'd have known if you'd ever taken the time to send him a message."

She hadn't done that. She'd been thinking only about herself, her own grief. He must hate her. "You don't want me to stay, do you?"

He rested his arms over the back of the sofa and turned his head to look out a window. "I want you to get to the reason behind this polite little visit."

Margaret looked at his broad chest, his outflung arms stretching the shirt taut. His jaw was hard, his eyes narrowed as he waited. She opened her mouth but couldn't force the words out. Thinking maybe she could show him, she pulled off the gloves so he could see the ring she still wore. As she had hoped, he turned and his eyes fastened on the gold band.

"It's fine with me if you want to keep pretending you're married so no one else bothers you. I'll give you your divorce anyway. I want to be free to marry someone else."

Margaret sucked in her breath and held it. She looked down at her hands and waited for the pain of his words to finish barreling through her. Tears pressed and she squeezed them back. She had to bend her head so he wouldn't see that one was slipping down her face. She never cried, but since Jeremy was born she couldn't seem to stop. "I didn't come here for a divorce," she whispered. Humiliated, she stood, one glove falling, several tears splashing on the tea table. John stared at her, trying to see her face, but her head was bent and she held her hand up, her forefinger rubbing her temple. She walked quickly around the table and hurried to the door.

"Wait! Your glove." He retrieved the item and saw wet drops on the table. "Margaret!"

By the time he turned, she was already gone. He heard the tap of her heels down the stairs and ran to the door. The stairwell was dark and empty. He ran down, slipping in his stocking feet, and shot out into the sunlight of the sidewalk. He looked both ways for a slim woman in a bright green dress.

"Damn!" He threw the glove on the ground and stuck a hand on his hip, rubbing his forehead with the other hand. A man in a brown wool suit passed by and trod on the kid glove. "Hey!" John glared at him and the man looked behind him, puzzled, and hurried on. John swiped up the glove and slapped it against his other hand. He turned.

She stood against the wall right next to the stairwell. He'd run past her. The skin around her eyes was red and puffy. Her lashes were soaked, but her cheeks were dry. She clenched a white lacy handkerchief in one hand. Her eyes were huge; it was obvious that they'd seen everything. He advanced. Margaret pressed against the wall. When he was two feet away she slipped back into the stairwell.

"I couldn't leave without saying what I'd come to say," she said nervously, hitting a step with the back of her boot.

"Say it."

Margaret stepped up and back onto the first step and then the next when he kept approaching in his bullish style. His lips were tight and she couldn't read his eyes in the dimness. Halfway up she stuck out her hand and pressed her palm below his shoulder.

"Stop." His body was warm and hard and she waited a second before she pulled her hand away, slowly bringing it to her side. He had stopped and his eyes were focused where she had touched him.

"I missed you," she said breathlessly. She clasped her hands together and squeezed. "I came to see if we could be husband and wife again." He looked up at her. Slowly, he stepped to the next step, the one just below her. She remained where she was and endured his study of her face. Suddenly he stepped around her and Margaret exhaled in loud surprise. She turned and watched him trudge up the steps and disappear into the apartment above. He left the door open and the light cut a wedge into the hall. She looked down to the rush of noise below, then followed John and stood in the doorway. He leaned against the back of the sofa, arms crossed, ankles crossed, and staring at his socks.

"Why?" he asked quietly.

He didn't believe her, Margaret realized. He didn't trust her.

"I'm still the same man." He looked up at her. "In spite of your green dress and different hairstyle, you're the same woman. And we don't suit. I still like saloons and pints of ale and bedroom pleasure."

She closed the door. Her face felt hot, her neck itched and prickling heat spread across her back and chest. "I can't imagine being with anyone else."

His eyes widened and then he looked away. "Of course not. You don't want to be with anyone. Not really." He turned back to her. "Does your sister want you to leave? I gave you enough money. You could start your own boardinghouse and boss everyone around."

She walked halfway toward where he lounged, so deceptively casual. "I don't want you so you can take care of me."

"Then what about me do you want?" he roared, coming off the couch and stomping over to stand directly in front of her. "Just what did you miss? What exactly did you like about being my wife? You left me after I'd given you everything I had!"

For a split second Margaret saw right through his shouting and his flushed, furious face to the wound she'd created when she walked out on him. And then his face closed and her own anger boiled over.

"My sister had just died! She died just like my mama did. What I feared most, the very most, happened, and I couldn't stand for you to be near me with your...your love! It was Danny's love that killed Elizabeth. But you weren't very understanding then, were you? I'd lost someone I loved so much and I couldn't bear to feel anything else! I didn't want to feel anything, because then I'd have to feel everything." She looked away across the room to a blue-and-white vase filled with a profusion of pink flowers. They were lovely. If she stared very hard at them she could pretend none of this was happening.

"So what changed your mind?"

Margaret choked. She clenched her eyes shut, but hot tears gushed anyway. She wouldn't look at him. She could feel him waiting, but she felt as if she'd contracted a fever, and she shivered with hot and then cold and thought how nice it would be to faint. She faced him.

"I've been lonely," she whispered. "And then Victoria had a beautiful little baby. They're such proud parents. And...and..." She looked away. "I kept thinking about you, and thinking and thinking, and I had to come to you because I'd rather die birthing your child than die not loving you. I hope and pray that any child I have will be born alive and healthy, but...I'm willing to take the chance that maybe it won't."

She looked up at him. His eyes were leveled somewhere below her chest. His face was still blank, his arms crossed, and she trembled and the tears kept coming. Finally, he looked up and his eyes were red.

"If you ever leave me again—"

"I won't. I won't." She lifted her drenched handkerchief and wiped her cheeks. "I'll go with you anywhere and stay forever.'' Her eyes flicked away. ''I'd prefer to stay in San Francisco, though.'' She looked back at him. His brows were arched. ''And I'd prefer to have a house of our own.''

''But if I insist we move back to Bodie and bring my mother with us?''

''I'll go.''

He chuckled. ''And nag me all the way!''

''Nooo!''

He smiled at her and gently traced the path of one big tear down her cheek. ''I'll build you a house of our own here in San Francisco. But right this minute the nearest bed is the one here in my room.'' It was a challenge and their gazes held.

''Lead the way,'' she said softly.

John repressed a groan and caught her trembling hand. His room was neat and sparse. His mother's presence showed in the ruffled gold curtains and the quilted green-and-gold bedspread. The only furniture was a washstand, a chest, a wardrobe and a bed. He closed the door behind them without taking his eyes off her as she walked to the middle of the room and surveyed it.

Slowly, he approached her. ''It's been so long,'' he whispered.

''Yes.'' She smiled and placed her hands on his shoulders and smoothed them down his arms, back up and then down his chest, feeling the exquisite pleasure of his warm body. He bent to kiss her and she opened her mouth greedily. John couldn't stop kissing her, groaning into her sweet, willing mouth. He pulled her hips tight against his and she sighed. His kiss grew ravaging and his force bent Margaret back and away until their lips parted.

''Come back,'' he moaned, slipping his hands up her back, pulling her into his chest. Her hot breath brushed his jaw as she turned her head and buried her face in his neck, her arms holding him, hugging him in passion, deeply and fully. Lightly, she pressed a kiss to his hot neck, then a trail of them along the taut tendons there as he lifted his head and trembled in imposed restraint. Gently, she brushed aside the collar of his shirt and pressed her lips to his collarbone. She unbuttoned his shirt. John bent his head and watched as she caressed him with soft lips. Loosely, he held her hips, letting her pace their lovemaking, understanding she needed him to slow down but feeling each press of lips and slide of hand as torture when he wanted to grab and delve and grind. Margaret pushed the shirt off his chest and over his shoulders. Letting it hang softly from his upper arms, she smoothed a hand down him from a brown nipple to the tight muscles at his navel to the waistband of his pants. Swallowing, she raised her gaze to his.

"You're beautiful," she whispered. "From the first moment I saw you in Bodie I thought so." His body tensed under her hand. "And I'm so glad you sold the saloon, but I'd be here even if you hadn't." Her eyes searched his, dropped to his curved mouth, down his golden, smooth chest, his ridged belly. His hands squeezed her waist. This was her man, her husband, friend and lover. He would be the father of her children, her provider, her warmth and comfort for many, many years ahead. Her eyes filled with tears and she wrapped her arms around his neck, brought her face to his, wetting his cheek. "Oh, John, I lo—"

The door flew open and hit the wall. The entwined couple jerked. Cradling Margaret, John turned slightly. Margaret peeped over his shoulder and saw a man with round blue eyes that immediately narrowed. His hair was honey colored, his skin paler than John's.

"I thought maybe you were still in bed. I see I wasn't far wrong."

John grinned. "This is my big brother, Patrick," he said, pulling a scarlet-faced Margaret around with him. "And this is my wife, Margaret."

John's brother flinched. His tight features flooded with color. "Oh! Well, good. I'm sorry about... Just excuse me. I won't count on your help today, then." He suddenly smiled. "Good! Maybe you'll be worth something now."

"Get out of here!"

Patrick, still smiling, reached for the knob. His chuckle carried through the door after he closed it.

Margaret backed out of John's arms as the latch clicked.

John pulled his shirt off his arms, threw it to the floor and pinned her with his eyes. "Now, where were we?"

"Can't you lock the door?"

He shook his head. "There's no lock."

"What about your mother? She might do the same—"

John shook his head. "She wants grandchildren, remember?" Margaret blushed and turned away from his warm eyes. "Come here, Maggie."

She had to take four steps to reach him. She twined her arms around his neck and came flush against his naked chest. "Love me some more," he whispered against her eyelids as his lips roamed over her face. She squeezed him more tightly and opened her mouth. They kissed until they both trembled.

When Margaret pulled away she lifted her hands to her hair and took the pins out one by one, setting them on the table next to the bed. Her gaze ranged down her husband, who stood silently watching. Passion thudded thick and heavy through her limbs. She turned when her hair was down, lifted the long length away from her neck and offered John the hooks on the back of her dress. She could hear his breath coming hard and strained as she quickly undressed. She glanced at him and his hot gaze flicked from er naked body to her eyes. He stepped forward and crushed her against him, cupping her bare bottom.

"I'm so skinny," she whispered. "Do you think me ugly?"

John pulled back to look down into her eyes. "Ugly? Good Lord, woman." He looked down her body and grinned. "You're beautiful. You're pink and white and kinda dark rose right here," he said, touching between her thighs and making her squirm. "And you're soft," he said, brushing her hip. "And hard," he said, touching a puckered nipple with the back of his fingers. "You're woman," he murmured against her neck. "My woman," he rasped, wrapping his arms around her.

Margaret was awash in him and herself. With his words and his touches he was filling all the empty, dark places in her soul with loving light. He pressed her into his hardness, bruising her soft flesh with pant buttons and ridged masculinity. She dropped her hand to his waistband and set her fingers to the first button. John stiffened and pulled his mouth from her lips and his hand from her bottom. He clasped her hand and pulled it to his lips. "You don't have to prove anything." He searched her eyes, trying to impart his care.

Margaret smiled sensuously and he stared. She kissed the knuckle of the hand that held hers. "But I do," she whispered.

He shook his head. "No."

She pulled her hand free and loosed the second button. He covered her hand with his and stilled her movement. "I don't want you to feel ashamed."

She stared down at their hands. Calmly she pulled her other arm from his shoulder and removed his hand from hers, placed it on her hip, then undid the third button.

John's gaze jumped from her downcast face to her moving hand. "Is this shameful?" she asked. He jerked, his gaze flying above her head as she burrowed into his drawers and enclosed his length in her warm hand.

"No," he groaned.

Margaret continued to touch, to feel, to let herself experience his maleness until he held her hips painfully tight and panted softly in her ear. He yanked her hands away and held them by the wrist at her shoulders, pulling her close and searching her upturned face. "Maggie?"

Margaret smiled. He was trembling with passion, and yet his eyes had never been so worried.

"I'm not ashamed. I'm in love."

John groaned and wrapped his arms around her. Her hair was sweet smelling, her neck warm and soft, her nipples tickled his chest. He pushed her to the bed and she pulled him over her. She shoved his pants down and he made them one with an impatient thrust.

Afterward, hearts pounding, legs entwined, he lay at her side.

"Don't ever leave me again," he demanded in a harsh whisper.

She met his eyes. "Never."

"I love you, Margaret Banning."

She closed her eyes briefly. There was almost too much feeling in his voice for her to absorb. She opened her eyes and rolled to her side to face him. She placed her hand over his heart. "Don't ever stop," she whispered.

He pushed himself up onto an elbow and brushed her hair off her face. He placed his hand over her heart. "I won't ever stop." His hand slid lower, and cupped her breast, which had lost some of its fullness with her loss of weight. "I want to do it again, Maggie."

Her eyes sparkled. "So do I."

Chapter Twenty-one

John ran down the street, dodging carriages and wagons, took a sharp turn around a corner and ran up the front steps to the recently completed home he'd built for Margaret and himself. He dashed through the front hall and pounded up the stairs. Their bedroom door was open and he swung around the frame. No one. He froze just inside the room, staring at the bed, still made.

He'd left the building site as soon as the maid Victoria had sent to him had said Margaret's time had come. He'd run all the way. Nothing could have happened yet, he assured himself as he turned from the room. For nine months he'd believed everything would be just fine with this birth and this baby. Now, the time here, he expected the worst. He went down the stairs wondering if Margaret was at her sister's. No one had bothered to mention that part of the plan.

Halfway down the stairs he heard women's voices, then Victoria rounded the foot of the stairs.

"I thought I heard someone running through the house," she said, smiling. "Margaret's in the garden still. She's being very stubborn about going up to her room."

John followed Victoria to the back of the house, his gut tensing in worried anger that his wife was being difficult at a time like this.

"Hello, John," she greeted when he walked out the back door. "Don't frown so. I'm just going to finish cutting these roses to take upstairs with me."

"Where's the doctor?"

Margaret suddenly bent forward. "Not here yet," she whispered.

John swore loudly and strode over to his wife and lifted her off her feet. "You're going upstairs, now."

"My flowers," she cried.

"Victoria, bring those!" he barked over his shoulder.

Margaret wrapped her wrists behind John's neck and gazed at his tense jawline as he carried her to the stairs. "I love you," she whispered.

John paused, one foot on the first step, and squeezed her tightly against him, his forehead dipping down to her chin. Then he started up the steps. He set her down by the side of the bed and unhooked her dress. She pushed him away when he tried to take it off her.

"Go," she said gently.

"No, Maggie, no," he pleaded. "Let me help."

She shook her head. "Go downstairs and wait for the doctor. I'll be fine. Victoria is here."

John turned and saw the other woman standing inside the bedroom door. The flowers, a huge bouquet of pink and white, were in a vase on a small table directly across from the bed. He walked toward the door and looked back at his wife, who was bent over again. He started to retrace his steps, but felt a hand on his arm. He looked down at Victoria.

"You need to do what she asks," she said firmly.

John shuddered. He turned to the door again, but then grabbed Victoria's hand. "You'll let me know if... You won't leave me down there unknowing if she..."

"I'll let you know. Go down and wait for the doctor."

John walked slowly down the stairs. He stood just behind the front door and stared at the beveled glass, drumming his fingertips on the solid wood of the door. He flung the door open at the first rap of the knocker and saw only a woman. "Yes?" he demanded, looking beyond her. He saw no one who looked like a doctor approaching the house. The woman in front of him said something, but he didn't hear her and impatiently he looked back at her. "What?"

There was a hint of a smile quirking up one side of her mouth. "I'm Dr. Bloomfield. I believe your wife is expecting me."

John stepped back and looked the trim woman up and down. She was holding a black bag. Her eyes were very dark, almost black, and definitely amused as they regarded him. He thought of a few things to say but restrained himself, since they all sounded stupid in his head.

"May I come in?"

He realized how long he'd kept her standing and he jumped back. "Of course!" He closed the door after her. "They're upstairs in the bedroom at the front of the house." He led her to the stairs and then moved away so she could pass, as if an invisible wall prevented him from putting a foot on the steps. "Dr. Bloomfield," he called softly, when the woman had taken a few steps up. She turned, her white blouse a beacon in the dim hall. "You'll let me know if I can do anything? Or if things don't go well?" he added in almost a whisper.

Dr. Bloomfield turned fully around and faced the anxious husband. "I certainly will, Mr. Banning."

John tried every seat in the downstairs portion of the house before he finally settled in a white-painted wooden rocker in Margaret's flower garden. Watching the roses she loved bob in the breeze he thought back to when he'd first seen her in the dining room of the Bodie house. It seemed like yesterday. He traced every step of their relationship until this moment as he waited, while the fog moved in and covered the blue sky.

He had to give Dr. Bloomfield credit. She or Victoria came down every half hour and told him that everything was fine. Not that he believed them, but the reports kept him from barging into the bedroom to find out what was happening. Margaret had never mentioned that she'd engaged a lady doctor. But then, she'd spoken very little of this day at all. Was that reticence designed to keep him calm or her calm? He suspected she did it for the both of them. She'd have had to explain too much to him that he didn't understand about this part of being a woman. It was his job to wait, to serve if needed, to bless what she delivered into this world.

Joining him in his vigil was his brother, Patrick, who came at sunset. His wife, Amy, went upstairs. John's mother came, too, bearing boxes of wrapped gifts. The men made supper and the women bustled in and out of the kitchen, filling a tray with sandwiches and hot tea to take upstairs with them, where Margaret was comforted and encouraged and surrounded.

Shortly after eleven o'clock at night, thirteen hours and twelve minutes after Margaret felt her first pain, she delivered a pink baby girl.

John's fingers tightened on the handle of his coffee mug as he heard a door upstairs flung open so hard it hit the wall, and then feet came pounding fast down the stairs.

"It's a girl!" announced Amy, her fair cheeks flushed, her blue eyes sparkling.

John nodded, unable to speak, and rose stiffly. His brother jumped up, pulled the coffee mug out of John's hand and shook his brother's hand. "Congratulations!"

John nodded again. "Can I...?" He looked toward the stairs.

"Yes!" Amy grabbed his arm and pulled him along beside her.

As John arrived at the bedroom door, all the women were filing out of the room, smiling. His mother gave him a quick, hard hug. He walked slowly into the room and saw his wife holding a white-wrapped bundle, looking down at it enraptured. She was whispering. The floor creaked beneath John's feet and she looked up, smiling.

"She's so beautiful," she said.

Yes, she is, John thought, looking at the woman in his bed. He sat gingerly on the edge and peeked at the little face, whose eyes opened suddenly, startling a gasp out of him, which provoked a giggle from his wife.

"Are you all right?" he asked softly.

"I'm wonderful—as long as I don't move too much," she said, smiling again.

"Can I hold her?" Margaret handed him the bundle. The baby's eyes were closed again. She was unexpectedly warm, a light weight in his arms. John stood, feeling like a giant holding the most precious treasure in the world in his arms.

Margaret burrowed back into the pillows, her body feeling heavy and tired. She watched her husband rock their healthy baby. She closed her eyes and thanked God for the blessings in her life.

"What should we name her?" asked John.

Margaret's eyes fluttered open. "Don't rock her so fast," she murmured sleepily.

"That's a nice name!" John grinned at her. He sat back on the bed, reluctant to give up this prize. He stared down at the sleeping face with perfect little lips and nose and ears. "I love you, Maggie," he whispered, looking up at his wife. He thought she was asleep, but then her lips moved.

"Good."

* * * * *

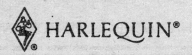

⬧ HARLEQUIN®

THE TAGGARTS OF TEXAS!

Harlequin's Ruth Jean Dale brings you
THE TAGGARTS OF TEXAS!

Those Taggart men—strong, sexy and hard to resist...

You've met Jesse James Taggart in FIREWORKS!
Harlequin Romance #3205 (July 1992)

Now meet Trey Smith—he's THE RED-BLOODED YANKEE!
Harlequin Temptation #413 (October 1992)

Then there's Daniel Boone Taggart in SHOWDOWN!
Harlequin Romance #3242 (January 1993)

And finally the Taggarts who started it all—in LEGEND!
Harlequin Historical #168 (April 1993)

Read all the Taggart romances!
Meet all the Taggart men!

Available wherever Harlequin books are sold.

WELCOME TO

The quintessential small town, where everyone
knows everybody else!

Finally, books that capture the pleasure
of tuning in to your favorite TV show!

Join your friends at Tyler in the eighth book, BACHELOR'S PUZZLE by Ginger
Chambers, available in October.

*What do Tyler's librarian and a cosmopolitan architect have in common? What
does the coroner's office have to reveal?*

GREAT READING...GREAT SAVINGS...
AND A FABULOUS FREE GIFT!

Each book set in Tyler is a self-contained love story; together, the twelve novels
stitch the fabric of the community. You can't miss the Tyler books on the shelves
because the covers honor the old American tradition of quilting; each cover
depicts a patch of the large Tyler quilt!

And you can receive a FABULOUS GIFT, ABSOLUTELY FREE, by collecting
proofs-of-purchase found in each Tyler book, *and* use our Tyler coupons to save
on your next TYLER book purchase.
